SWEPT OFF HER FEET

<u>Sonia</u> was torn by conflicting emotions. Her strong spirit of independence demanded that she bring up her dead sister's son alone as best she could—anything to keep him out of the clutches of his irresponsible playboy father, <u>Guy Farr</u>. But did she have the right to deprive her nephew of the Farr name and the advantages that went with it? In desperation, Sonia turned to <u>Michael Farr</u>, Guy's brother, for help.

What she encountered was a handsome, angry young man who refused to believe that the boy was really a Farr at all . . . a man who then wheeled suddenly on Sonia and demanded curtly, "Will you marry me?"

Books by Emilie Loring

❧ FOR ALL YOUR LIFE
❧ WHAT THEN IS LOVE
❧ I TAKE THIS MAN
❧ MY DEAREST LOVE
❧ LOOK TO THE STARS
❧ BEHIND THE CLOUD
❧ THE SHADOW OF SUSPICION
❧ WITH THIS RING
❧ BEYOND THE SOUND OF GUNS
❧ HOW CAN THE HEART FORGET
❧ TO LOVE AND TO HONOR
❧ LOVE CAME LAUGHING BY
❧ I HEAR ADVENTURE CALLING
❧ THROW WIDE THE DOOR
❧ BECKONING TRAILS
❧ BRIGHT SKIES
❧ THERE IS ALWAYS LOVE
❧ STARS IN YOUR EYES
❧ KEEPERS OF THE FAITH
❧ WHERE BEAUTY DWELLS
❧ FOLLOW YOUR HEART
❧ RAINBOW AT DUSK
❧ WHEN HEARTS ARE LIGHT AGAIN
❧ TODAY IS YOURS
❧ ACROSS THE YEARS
❧ A CANDLE IN HER HEART

❧ Published by Bantam Books, Inc.

EMILIE LORING

WE RIDE
THE GALE!

BANTAM BOOKS · TORONTO · NEW YORK · LONDON

*This low-priced Bantam Book
has been completely reset in a type face
designed for easy reading, and was printed
from new plates. It contains the complete
text of the original hard-cover edition.*
NOT ONE WORD HAS BEEN OMITTED.

WE RIDE THE GALE!
*A Bantam Book / published by arrangement with
Little, Brown and Company, Inc.*

PRINTING HISTORY
William Penn edition published 1934
Grosset & Dunlap edition published April 1949
Bantam edition published April 1967
2nd printing
3rd printing
4th printing
5th printing
6th printing

Published simultaneously in the United States and Canada

*Bantam Books are published by Bantam Books, Inc., a subsidiary
of Grosset & Dunlap, Inc. Its trade-mark, consisting of the words
"Bantam Books" and the portrayal of a bantam, is registered in the
United States Patent Office and in other countries. Marca Registrada.
Bantam Books, Inc., 271 Madison Avenue, New York, N.Y. 10016.*

PRINTED IN THE UNITED STATES OF AMERICA

To

CLARA ENDICOTT SEARS

Whose Stirring Poems and Buoyant Spirit
Have Helped Many a Storm-Tossed Mariner
Ride the Gale!

Chapter I

The door of the outer office opened cautiously. A head appeared.

"Is the going smooth or do I enter at my own risk?" inquired a theatrically hoarse voice.

Two women looked up from their work. The one at the desk settled her bone-rimmed spectacles with a nervous hand, brushed back sparse gray hair above a puckered brow, tightened thin lips and answered acidly:

"Depends on what you call risk, Mr. Guy. He's pulled the feathers out of everyone who's been near him since lunch."

Guy Farr whistled, a contemplative whistle, as he closed the door softly behind him. His eyes, above a suggestion of purple eye-shadow in the wrong place, were blue as ice under a sapphire sky. The slight droop of the left lid gave a devil-may-care touch to a face which had a rakish charm. His smooth hair was almost yellow; his full lips below a wisp of reddish gold mustache were as crimson as if rouged. He glanced at the woman in the covert-gray dress at the desk, then smiled at the Titian-haired girl in the slim frock of navy, with its sheer white collar and cuffs. He adjusted the red carnation in the lapel of his gray coat.

"Safe for me to enter the king's countinghouse, Miss Hale?"

Little flames flickered in the girl's brown eyes.

"Sure, it's safe. Sara Grimm is low in her mind. She's been mixing papers again and got what was coming to her. You don't mind losing a few feathers, do you? A great big explorer like you."

Guy Farr's eyes sharpened. He pulled out a cigarette and snapped a lighter.

"Cut that out! You know that the king—you see, I've picked up your nickname for your brother—doesn't like smoking in the office. If you happen to want a favor of him—of course you don't—you'd better consider his wishes."

"Linda!" protested Sara Grimm in a shocked whisper. "You forget whom you're talking to." She looked apologetically at Guy Farr, but his amused eyes with a hint of appraisal in their depths were on the red-haired girl.

"Don't think much of me, do you?"

Linda Hale shrugged and adjusted a sheet of paper in the typewriter.

"You must be psychic." She glanced at a pad beside the machine. "If you want to talk with your brother you'd better hustle. He has a date in ten minutes. Shall I tell him you are here?"

"Thanks so much, but I prefer to do my own announcing." Hand on the knob of the door to the inner office, he turned. His eyes were cold, still. "During the ten minutes you've allowed me, Hale, I'll take time to suggest that he give his red-headed secretary the air. She's too fresh to his callers. Think it over. This isn't the year I would select for being fired."

Michael Farr looked up from behind his broad desk in the richly paneled office as his brother slammed the door behind him. The brows above his gray eyes contracted, his clean-cut mouth tightened. The early June breeze dancing in through the open window on a ray of reflected sunlight brought in its train the faint far roar of traffic, the whir of a propeller. A petal fell from a rose in a slender crystal vase. It lay like a miniature crimson pool on the green blotter.

"Here I am, Michael, m'lad. All dressed up and somewhere to go. Got my cheque?"

Guy Farr's confident greeting eased the tension. He dropped into a chair opposite his brother who picked up a slip of pink paper from the desk.

"Sure you want this, Guy? Fifty thousand dollars is a whale of a lot of money. Twice as hard to get hold of now as when Father made his will. The estate has taken some terrific losses, it is worth barely half of what it was five years ago. Tenants are demanding reduced rents, mortgagors are defaulting on interest payments—in some cases we have had to take over the property. Can you do as well with investments as the trustees?"

Guy Farr snatched the cheque from his brother's reluctant fingers, glanced at it and with a satisfied nod slipped it into his breast pocket.

"Nothing doing in the investment line of yours truly, Mike, certainly not after the tale of woe you have just spilled. What's the big idea piling up more money for our heirs—your heirs? No woman will ever slip the ball-and-chain on me. When I reach thirty—I've reached it, worse luck—according to Father's will I'm to be paid fifty thousand bucks."

"If you wanted it."

"Of course I want it. I'll always have an income from the trust fund, won't I? Kingscourt, house and land, was left to you. Don't think I'm kicking about that; I don't want a blade of grass on it. Too much care. Too much expense. Why don't you shut it up? I'll answer why—sentiment. And sentiment is the most expensive indulgence in the world. Not any in mine. I'm hopping off in a couple of hours to South America with an exploring party. Haven't told you before. Knew you'd put up a holler."

Michael noted the puffiness under his brother's eyes, the unsteadiness of his hand. Apparently he had spent the night celebrating his departure.

"Is that last crack an apology or an explanation? Sure that it is my holler from which you are gumshoeing? I did considerable mopping up for you after you started on your last safari, remember."

Guy Farr's color deepened, his eyes shifted. It was a look Michael had learned to translate. What mess was he side-stepping now? He didn't like the laugh with which his brother acknowledged the reminder.

"My life's an open book from now on, fella. Don't take the world so seriously. Just because a girl threw you over, you're as hard as an ice-floe and about as warming. Oh, all right! Don't glare. I'll quit. Sorry I mentioned it; my mistake. Should have known better. They told me outside that you had been making the feathers fly since lunch."

"Who told you that?"

"The twitchy Sara. Gosh, I should think that female would drive you wild!"

"She does, but she was Father's loyal secretary for years."

"Allah be praised that she wasn't included as an asset in the trust fund! Trouble with you, Mike, is, you're too soft—in spots. You're an easy mark till you get your teeth set in an idea, then granite is putty in comparison. Your Congressional campaign is an example. With a veteran running against you, what chance have you in the fight? Take your fool idea of making the issue of your campaign the reduction of crime. In this district, too. I ask you, has the crazy stunt ever been tried before?"

"All the more reason to try it now. It is one of the big movements in Washington. I want to hop on the Federal band-wagon. Think back on the atrocious things which have been done in the last year or two, the perpetrators of which never have been found, to say nothing of having been brought to justice. I may get licked, but I'll have the other candidate in a sweat shirt."

"You'll get more than licked, you may get put on the spot."

3

"Cheerful Charlie, aren't you?"

"Someone's got to make you stop, look, listen. What do the sleek, well-fed citizens in this district care about the reduction of crime? They are too secure. You've got to kick a voter on his own shin before he'll take an interest in conditions. 'Let George do it,' is the burden of his cry."

"Where did you get your knowledge of the psychology of the voter?"

"I have friends among the politicians—wait and see. Sara Grimm is another of your soft spots. Pension her and put the skids under her. Neatest trick in the world."

"Quite—if one doesn't feel responsible for the effect on her when she is out of a job. Off in two hours?"

"Yep."

"Been to Kingscourt to say good-bye to Aunt Serena?"

"No. Why the dickens did you take her in?"

"Where could she go with her reduced income? I don't know how I could have helped her falling into the jaws of that investment wolf who ate up a big slice of her fortune, but I feel in a way responsible. It looks as if I might salvage something from the wreck; then she will be off on her travels again—unless Doctor Jim Neville's wife dies. That would stop her globe-trotting. I am glad to have her at Kingscourt. You'd better stay at home and join our happy family."

"And listen to Serena tell me what a bad boy I am and what a noble martyr you—"

"Cut it!"

"You are ready to bite, aren't you? Here's my address in case of emergency—but there ain't going to be no such animal. It will take weeks to reach us after we get into the wilds. I've cleaned up everything. Get me? Everything. For Pete's sake, don't let anyone put anything across on you this time!"

Michael Farr picked up the slip of paper his brother dropped to the desk.

"I'll be a solid chunk of granite. If you have cleaned up, why the fervent rejoicing that you can't be reached? You are the only person who puts things across on me."

Standing behind him, Guy Farr gripped his shoulders.

"You're a prince. No one would believe that you are four years older than I. There is nothing for you to worry about, honest. You have power of attorney. Here's the key to my safety-deposit box. My will is there. If I pass out—bet your life I have no intention of doing it—everything goes to you. No claims on it. No strings. You will dispose of the money better than I could. Besides, you are the only person on God's earth for whom I really care."

4

He cleared his voice. "Chuck this political stuff. You need a change of scene. Get away; then when you come home, start over."

"Get away! Just like that! Even if I gave up the Congressional fight—which I won't—how can I go with such uncertainties in the business world? With this new deal with its codes and its changes? I've got to be here, to stand between some of these panicky, frightened men and the estate trustees. Many of them are desperate, old, tired, ready to give up the struggle. If I can help them hold on, they will get on their feet again and fight, and if I stand by, they won't feel that they are fighting alone. Some days the very air seems thick with tragedy. Get away! That's a joke."

"Joke or not, I say, get out for a time. Why should you carry the burdens of a lot of men who mean nothing to you? Take your ponies across the water, get in some practice with the Englishmen. You're the best bet of your team here. Put the ocean between you and this office, Aunt Serena, and—"

He picked up the brass-framed calender from the desk. He appeared intently interested in the black figures as he asked:

"Have you heard that your late bride-to-be, Phyllis, and husband Bill, the newly-wed D'Arcys, have bought The Cedars?"

"Where did you hear that?"

"Ran into a man who knows them. He said that as The Cedars adjoined our estate, thought of course I would know."

"He did! Why was he in such a hurry to tell you, then?"

Michael Farr crossed to the window. Guy followed him and closed his hand tight about his brother's arm. His debonair voice roughened:

"Don't you mind, m'lad. Don't you mind. There's the buzzer. A hint from the efficient and acid-tongued Hale that my time is up. If I weren't going away, something tells me that that red-headed maedchen might prove interesting; she needs disciplining."

Michael wheeled from the window.

"Don't look so black. I said 'if,' didn't I? There's that buzz again. I'm going. I'll be one load from your shoulders, Mike. I've got your number, even if I'm not your kind. Guess I inherited the first Michael Farr's temperament along with his drooping eyelid. If deponeth saith truly, he was one grand playboy besides being a cursing, fighting old sea-dog."

The diamond sunk in a broad gold ring on his finger caught the light and glistened like a brilliant eye. Michael motioned toward it.

"Going to wear that in the wilds?"

"Wouldn't go without; it's my talisman. Need it all the more now that I am making a break for freedom, for a place where there are no conventions to keep one toeing the mark."

"Where's the mark you've toed to date?"

"One in the eye for me. Bye-bye, old fella." He gripped his brother's hand tight and released it.

"I'll picture you in this cool shaded office, or at the Club unfolding at breakfast your morning paper, when I'm in the midst of hot strange jungles, with a black storm blowing up under a swift tropical wind. I'll picture the king in his countinghouse counting out his money. Watch out that filthy lucre doesn't get you in its grip."

He stopped with his hand on the knob of the door.

"Think you ought to know that I was told also that the fickle Phyllis is boasting that you will forgive her, pronto, that she will have you eating out of her hand again. That's about her size. Watch your step, m'lad. Watch your step. Don't let the protection complex catch you again. So long! I'll be seeing you!"

The door closed. Hands hard in his pockets, Michael Farr turned to the window. He could see far off dots, scows dumping debris, crawling like shark fins on drab water. From among neighboring skyscrapers loomed a mooring mast for airships. When his father had moved into the office in which he stood, it had been in the tallest building in Manhattan. Now it was a pigmy among giants.

Eyes on a plane skimming through a cloud which looked like a scarf of violet malines swathed about the Empire State tower, his thoughts returned to his brother's news about Phyllis D'Arcy. His heart smarted and stung as if it had been scraped raw. It was not because of disappointment in love, but the realization that he had been such an easy mark that rankled. He squared his shoulders. He deserved all that had come to him of humiliation and embarrassment. Ever since prep school days he had had an ideal of the sort of girl he would love and marry, and then, because year after year had passed and he had not found her, he had concluded that he was expecting too much of the modern girl, had compromised with his soul and had taken second best. Phyllis had proved to be not even that. She was boasting that she would have him back! Would she? He would show her what New England granite could be.

What should he do? Get out of the neighborhood for a time? That would mean giving up the Congressional fight. Not for a million dollars. He was in that to the finish. Two fights on his hands. Phyllis and his political opponent. Unless he missed his guess, the latter would keep him from dwelling too much on the former. Donald Brandt, because he was a veteran of the World War, would be hard to beat. What the dickens had prompted the man to buy a place in the county three years ago? Political or social ambition—or did he think it a good background for his real estate operations? For an instant, Guy had made him wonder if he were wasting time and energy trying for election. Guy! Why be influenced by a man for whose philosophy of life he had no respect?

How like him to thrust at Linda Hale. His entrance into any situation had the effect of stirring up antipathy and complication. It had been so since boyhood. A game might be under way peaceably and merrily; let Guy step into it and immediately everyone went haywire.

He hadn't liked the shifting of his brother's eyes when he had declared that his life was an open book. The present leaf might be clean, but the preceding pages would make snappy reading, or he would miss his guess. Neither had he liked his reference to his secretary. Perhaps she was attractive. She had a fine mind, it worked logically. That wouldn't count with Guy. Only the bodies and faces of women interested him, their minds and souls not at all. What was the use spending a moment's thought on him? He would do as he liked, regardless of the result to himself or others, regardless of the fact that sometime for something payment would have to be made —in full. During his father's lifetime he had been cautious, afraid of the consequences if he angered him, but now that he was secure in his inheritance he had blown the lid off what he called "life."

He touched a bell. As promptly as if she had been waiting outside the door, Linda Hale entered. He looked at the pad on his desk.

"You rang. Have I forgotten a date?"

"Usually you ride at this time. I thought you shouldn't miss it today. It must be beautiful in the Park."

A laugh brightened Michael Farr's grave eyes, erased the crease like a cut between his brows, widened his fine mouth.

"Have I been so bad as that? My brother said he was warned."

"You did hurt Sara's feelings."

"Then why in thunder does she touch my correspondence? It's your job."

"I know, but she took care of your father's and—"

"All right, she took care of my father's. Is that any reason why she should take care of mine?"

"I didn't mix your papers," Linda Hale reminded crisply.

"Sorry. You know, don't you, that it's because of your efficiency that Grimm drives me almost out of my mind." He picked up the slip of paper from his desk.

"File this. It is my brother's address. He is off to South America."

"For good?"

Michael Farr's lips tightened. From the buoyancy of her voice apparently Linda Hale was as relieved as he to have Guy out of the city. She had helped in the last cleaning-up process.

"We'll hope it is for his good. Any messages?"

"Yes, Mr. Farr. Donald Brandt, the real estate man, called up to ask if you had decided to sell him that piece of lake front at Kingscourt for development. He said to tell you to think it over, that he would be out of town for a week, and when he returned he would increase his offer ten per cent."

"That man doesn't know the first letter of the word 'No,' does he? They tell me that he has tried almost every job in the world, has jumped from one business experience to another, has landed safe each time, and has grown obtrusively richer with each change. Now he is dipping into politics. When he phones, tell him that I have not the least intention of cutting up the estate. I shall not consider his offer. If I were to sell, I wouldn't sell to him. You needn't tell him that last, though. Any other message?"

"Yes, Mr. Farr. Mrs. D'Arcy phoned."

"Who! Which Mrs. D'Arcy?"

"Mrs. Bill D'Arcy, she said."

Michael Farr felt the blood rush to his hair. It couldn't be Phyllis. Hard-boiled as he knew her now to be, she wouldn't do that. He stared incredulously at Linda Hale.

"Are you sure it was Mrs. Bill D'Arcy?"

She nodded.

Great Scott, his voice was hoarse! Why advertise to his secretary that the married name of the girl who had thrown him over a week before the day set for her marriage to him had sent the nightmare of publicity, pictures, and glaring headlines jangling through his memory? He cleared his voice, stretched his stiff lips in what he hoped was a smile.

"So she's back from her honeymoon! Nice of her to think of me so soon. Why didn't you put her on my line?"

"You were busy with your brother."

"Right, as usual. What did she want?"

"She wanted you to know that she and her husband

were settled at The Cedars, and would you come to a house-warming Thursday evening?"

Michael regarded his secretary unseeingly. Was this invitation the opening gun in Phyl's campaign to regain his interest? It was too fantastic to believe. But it fitted perfectly with Guy's warning. He was aware of Linda Hale's imperturbable regard. He instructed briskly:

"Phone Mrs. D'Arcy that it will be quite impossible for me to—"

A curious look in the eyes watching him gave Michael pause. He would have to meet Phyllis sometime. Why put it off?

"Wait a minute. Thursday, you said, and today is Monday. I can shift an engagement. Phone her that I am delighted to know that we are to have her for a neighbor and that I accept for Thursday. Make it cordial, Miss Hale."

For an instant the girl behind the secretary smiled in face and voice.

"Leave it to me. I'll make it cordial, all right." She turned on the threshold. "Glad you've got a sporting spirit," she said, and left the room.

Michael glowered at the closed door. Sporting spirit! Had anyone questioned his sportsmanship? Because he didn't go in for Guy's dissipations, was his sportsmanship doubted? One couldn't call the trail of affairs Guy left behind him sportsmanship. As for himself, it would be a long time before he fell for a girl again—if ever. There were plenty of charities to which to leave the Farr fortune—if there were a fortune when changing conditions and the tax collectors got through with it. Doubtless some day Guy would appear with a wife, someone who had caught him when he was not quite sober. Perhaps it had happened already. He had not liked the shift in his brother's eyes when he had said that his life was an open book.

"What's the catch?" Michael wondered aloud.

Chapter II

The thought recurred to him the next morning as he glanced at the newspaper on the desk in his office. The South American Expedition was front page news. A picture of Guy Farr at his most debonair smiled up at him. Under it was the caption:

The write-up went on to sketch Guy's family background, even to the reputed wealth, polo reputation, political aspirations, and the matrimonial fiasco of his bachelor brother. It went into lurid details as to the danger of the locality into which the exploring party planned to penetrate, danger from insects, fever, and tribesmen.

Michael Farr read to the end and flung the paper to the desk. Would the papers ever allow his broken engagement to be forgotten? What a chance for one of Guy's gold-diggers to attempt a little blackmail stunt. Hands hard in his pockets, he gazed down into canyons which were streets, off at turrets honeycombed with dots which were windows, that had the effect of innumerable prairie-dog holes. Some of them glittered like sheets of brass where they reflected the sun. The wind crooned about a tower which stabbed at a sky of incomparable blue. His adventurous self flamed rebelliously. Nothing he would like better than to take his chance at hardship and thrills with that expedition. How could he? One of the family must have a sense of responsibility. Responsibility! He had been born with the complex. Even when they were children he had felt an absurd anxiety for Guy's safety and well-being; and now he felt constrained to fight the man who was trying for Congress; to help men, whom he barely knew, to tread water till they could reach the shore of financial security; and as for taking his polo ponies across the water—Guy would fly into the air if he knew that he had cut out the expense of those at the time he had given up his apartment in the city. Some day he would chuck care and—When? he asked himself ironically. He must stand by, he couldn't desert the estate—or Aunt Serena.

"The king was in his countinghouse!" The words recurred with the mockery of his brother's voice and eyes. He shrugged. Where would the "Millionaire Sportsman" be if "the king" didn't stick to his countinghouse? He would be clerking somewhere. The shrunken Farr investments, conservative as they were, needed tender nursing in these days of the unpredictable jockeying of the wheel of fortune. He turned as the office door opened.

Linda Hale stepped into the room and leaned against the closed door. She was trim as a tailored model; her red hair might a moment before have been waved and dressed.

"What is it? Have I forgotten an appointment?"

"No, Mr. Farr. A—a woman—a girl insists upon seeing you."

For the first time in his life Michael knew what the term creeping of the flesh meant. Premonition? Something in his secretary's voice? More mopping up for Guy? That was a crazy idea. Hadn't he been emphatic about the open book stuff? Hadn't he declared that there could be no claims on his estate? No strings to it? Some woman after a contribution for charity, doubtless. Was it? It was rarely that a person, man or woman, couldn't be tactfully handled by Linda Hale.

"Did you tell her I was busy?"

"Yes, Mr. Farr. She said she would wait until you were at liberty."

"Is she in the outer office?

"Yes, sir. She is different from—from the others. She's wearing real clothes."

"Real! What do you mean?"

"Smart—made by a fine tailor. Nothing second class about her."

She colored as his eyes met hers. No doubt but that she suspected that the woman was here because of Guy. Had a vibration from her mind when she entered given him the creeps?

"Send her in."

Hale was right. She was different from those others, Michael Farr told himself, as he looked at the girl who faced him across the expanse of desk. She was slim, almost to attenuation. Perhaps it was the tailored severity of her gray suit which gave the effect. A brilliant green turban was matched by her bag. He agreed with Linda Hale, nothing second class about her. Could a person with a face like hers, sensitive, delicately modeled, with such a firm mouth and chin, be attracted by a philanderer like Guy? He had not known that eyes could be so dark, so brilliant. Her hair was like black satin. A faint pink tinged her pale face as he looked at her without speaking. She moistened parched lips. Had she cut out her lipstick for effect?

"Are you Mr. Farr?"

"Michael Farr. Won't you sit down?" He indicated the chair across the desk from his, the chair into which Guy had flung himself—was it only yesterday? It seemed ages ago.

"Thank you."

He seated himself as she perched on the edge of her chair.

"Can I help you?"

Why had he asked that? He had intended to get rid of

11

her with a cheque, if he couldn't dispose of her any other way, but there was something about her—

She drew a news clipping from her bag and laid it on the desk. It was the write-up about Guy.

"Is that your brother?"

"Yes."

"Stand by to crash!" The words clanged through his mind.

"Guy Farr has a three year old son."

It had come. Blackmail? Always he had expected it. Through the open window stole the peal of the chimes from the Metropolitan Tower clock. Sixteen melodious notes, then the first stroke of the hour. Curiously enough he didn't doubt the truth of her statement—yet—Guy had sworn that he had left no entanglements.

"Of course you have your marriage certificate to back up that statement?" His voice was rough from anger. Why had he allowed her claim to impress him for an instant?

"There is a marriage certificate—but not mine, my sister's." Her voice went his one better in bitterness.

"Your sister! Why didn't she come herself?"

"She died two days after the child was born."

"How unfortunate—for your claim."

Her breath caught as if water had been dashed in her face.

"You think me a common blackmailer, don't you? You won't after you have seen the boy. I don't want anything for myself. I have been in hospital—flu. Because of the present condition of business, I lost my job. The combination terrified me. I am all the child has. Every little while I felt as if I were drifting out to sea. I kept thinking, 'What will happen to him—if—I go? I am the only person who knows who he is. I have no right to keep him from his heritage.' And now the doctor says that Dicky—the boy, Guy Farr's son—must get into the country where he will live out of doors. My chance of work is in the city. I had heard that you were —were different from your brother, that you stood for the—the best in the city, and—and so I came to you. The boy should take his own name." Her hands clenched. Her throat contracted. "You must believe me! You must help him! You must!"

Michael had a fleeting impression that he had seen eyes before with that same tormented look. Where? One of those others with whom he had settled for Guy? On the screen? She knew her line. She was good at it. The dead sister was a new twist to the racket. The girl was reducing his resistance to jellyfish consistency. What Guy had called his "protection complex" was straining at its leash.

"Why wait until my brother is out of the country before making your claim?"

"Don't be so hard. I didn't know they still made wooden Indians." She bit her lips. Color stained her white face. "I had told you that I had been in hospital and didn't know that he was going. Not that he would let me know. He knew that I detested and distrusted him."

So she thought him a wooden Indian! Michael Farr regarded her steadily. Wooden Indians had their uses. They couldn't be moved by appealing dark eyes.

"Where is the certificate? Is it witnessed? Where did the marriage occur?"

She laid a folded paper on the desk. He opened it. It was a marriage certificate. Genuine or faked? It was dated four years ago in a New York town. Four years? Must have been at the time of his father's last illness. That thought gave plausibility to the story. Guy would be very sure that his father did not hear of a secret marriage. Guy Farr and Ruby Carson. Country girl and city man stuff? Nothing provincial about the sister across the desk. She was chic from the top of her head to her smart shoes. He glanced up from the paper.

"Who witnessed the ceremony—yes, I see the names, but who were they?"

"A girl friend of Ruby's and the justice's daughter."

"Why were you not present? Is your name Carson?"

"Yes. I did not know she was to be married. I—I had protested against her seeing your brother—she was so young and—and sweet, but—he won out. I did not know of the marriage until a month later."

"If she deceived you, why are you so passionately concerned now?"

He had not meant to be sarcastic, but the yarn was so evidently a touch for money—nothing easier to fake than a marriage certificate—and for some reason it hurt infernally to think that a girl like the girl across the desk from him would try to put across such a shopworn trick. His voice brought her to her feet.

"I know what you are thinking. That this is blackmail. It isn't. I am here to save the child's life and to inform you who he is in case—anything should happen to me. I swear I am telling the truth. His mother is dead. Do you think I am after money for myself? I wouldn't touch Guy Farr's money if I were starving. I have been living and working for three years—fearing, dreading that he might find us, claim the boy, and bring him up with his own rotten philosophy to get all the fun there is in life without paying for it."

She stopped for breath, but only for an instant. Her words poured on as if a dam which had kept her emotions in check had burst and released them.

"Don't look so contemptuous. I knew when I came that you wouldn't believe me, but I strangled my pride. There is someone who would adopt the boy without knowing who his father is, but that would be unfair to the child. Dicky must have his chance, and for the first time since he came into the world I doubt my ability to give it to him. I'm an architect. I have lost my job. I have a hundred dollars in a bank. What does a bank amount to these days? Not much to stand between that child and the world. You must believe me! You must! Don't be so wooden. It isn't the boy's fault that his father is an unscrupulous playboy and that his mother was too young to recognize a degenerate when she met one. That touched you, didn't it?"

She caught at the desk with her gloved hands. She was shaking as if with a chill.

"You must believe me! You must help Dicky! I may not be able to—"

Michael caught her as she swayed. The face against his arm was colorless, her eyes half closed. He half carried, half led her to a chair near the open window.

"Take it easy, Miss Carson."

He brought a glass of water and held it to her mouth. "Drink this."

She pushed away his hand. "No. I—I'm all right."

She pulled herself half way up, sank back in the chair with a frightened little gasp.

"Drink it!"

She caught the glass eagerly. Drained it. Michael Farr watched her. If this were acting, she was a comédienne of the first rank. She looked up as she returned the glass.

"That did help. I know what you are thinking—that—my faintness was the last—perfect dramatic touch in my program. It wasn't. I told you that I was just out of hospital. Perhaps you would like to confirm that information."

"What hospital?"

"City. Where else can a poor working girl go? My name is Sonia Carson."

She sat erect and gripped the arms of the chair. "I can see that it is useless to appeal to you. You are as hard as your brother is unprincipled, and without his fatal charm."

Seated on the arm of a chair, the glass in his hand,

Michael Farr winced in spirit. In his boyhood he had been achingly aware of Guy's easy conquests. To be sure, he had kept his friends, and his brother was forever off with the old and on with the new, but he had not appreciated the significance of that in his youth—and then, a girl had thrown him over for a gayer, richer man. Sonia Carson's curt appraisal had been a rough touch on a wound over which the scar tissue had not yet formed. He said as he returned to the desk:

"Don't be so sure that I will not help—the boy."

He made notes from the certificate, folded it and brought it to her. She put it into her bag.

"Of course your brother will repudiate that ceremony, will say that the certificate was faked."

"You say that it is genuine, don't you?"

"I do. I do—but money can make people forgetful." Her voice and eyes were contemptuous.

"You mean that Guy might have bribed the registrar. If the ceremony itself were a fake, that would be unnecessary. May I see the child?"

"Of course. Shall I bring him here?"

He looked at her as if considering. "No. I will send a car for you. The Farr home, Kingscourt, is twenty-five miles from the city. I would like to have him come there. Will you be able to make the trip?"

"Able! Of course I am able. I never was ill before a day in my life. I wouldn't have gone to the hospital here had I not been afraid that Dicky might pick up the germ. Are you planning to drive us?"

Michael detected suspicion in her voice, distrust in the depths of her eyes. Did she think that he planned taking them for a ride? For the first time since she had entered the room he smiled.

"No. Should I be a few minutes late in arriving at the house, the butler's wife, who has looked after the Farrs for years, will be there to greet you. Dow, the chauffeur, will call at two-thirty."

She rose.

"We will be ready. Dicky's name is Richard, but it seems too sedate for him. He is such a merry child. Good-morning."

"Just a minute! Where shall I send the car? Come to the desk and write your address."

"That is important, isn't it?"

The lilt in her voice and eyes hinted at a gay spirit submerged in present anxiety. She pulled off her gloves. Her hands were expressive, with long, graceful fingers tipped by palely lacquered nails, fingers which looked as if they had brains in them. Michael's eyes followed the moving pen. Her writing was as firm and full of character as her lovely mouth. What would an expert deduce from it? Certainly not that she was a blackmailer.

"It is a studio apartment. Tell the chauffeur to ring bell three." She crossed the room.

"Wait. I'll call a taxi."

"Taxi! I don't need it. I shan't slump again. I feel as if I could move a mountain or two, to say nothing of designing a skyscraper."

As Michael opened the door, she looked up at him with a hint of mockery in her eyes.

"You'd better call the hospital and confirm my statement. Sonia Carson, the name is. We will be ready at two-thirty. Good-bye."

Back at his desk, hands clasped behind his head, Michael Farr frowned at the beamed ceiling. He was a director in the hospital she had named. He would inquire about her. Guy had said:

"For Pete's sake, don't let anyone put anything across on you this time!"

He wouldn't. He dialed. His name cleared the way to the head interne with miraculous speed. The young physician answered his question promptly.

"Yes. Miss Sonia Carson left the hospital yesterday. Was here a week. Flu. Sharp attack. Left her with a type of nervous exhaustion. She thought it was her heart when things faded out—frightened her like the dickens—it isn't, she's paying for pulling too heavy a load. Had the devil of a time keeping her that long. Evidently worried to death about something. Left too soon. She would go. Ought to quit work for a couple of months. Likely to pick up any kind of germ. . . . Always glad to answer an inquiry of yours, Mr. Farr."

Michael paced the floor. So much of her story had been true. "Sharp attack!" He had been criminally negligent to let that girl go until he had seen her safe in a taxi. How white her face had been! And he had suspected that she was acting. Suppose she were not in her apartment when the chauffeur called? Suppose "things" had "faded out" in the street? How would he find her? Suppose he didn't find her? Perhaps she would change her mind and decide that there were easier, safer ways to get money than by blackmailing.

Not too late to reach Guy by radio somewhere, somehow. He stopped his restless pacing. What good would that do? He would swear there was no truth in the story—if he answered at all—and would keep on merrily with the expedition. It was up to him to sift the matter to the bottom before he communicated with his brother.

Chapter III

Michael Farr telephoned directions to Dow, head chauffeur at Kingscourt; dictated letters; ate a solitary luncheon at his club high up among the clouds; drove his roadster through the roar and rattle and shrieks of the city, with the memory of Sonia Carson and her amazing story rushing like a subterranean torrent deep in his mind.

It boiled to the surface as he came to open country and sent his car along highways winding like black cirè ribbons between trees and shrubs decked out in springtime green. Suppose when he saw the boy he were convinced that he was Guy's son? Would he acknowledge it before he heard from his brother? What a complication! If it were true, how like Guy to wriggle out of the snarl and leave it for someone else to untangle. If Sonia Carson's story proved but a clever attempt at blackmail, it would be easier to handle.

It was fragrant in the country, with a thrush singing its heart out in a red maple, and young green leaves fluttering a greeting. Roadsters passed. Girls driving in floppy hats and amazingly lovely frocks. A bus with the hopes of a ball team hanging from the windows. Spirals of smoke mounting from white chimneys. The scent of coffee drifting from an open chapel. A snatch of song from the radio of a passing automobile. Somewhere high up an engine droning.

The beauty of the world cast its soothing spell on Michael's troubled thoughts. He drove slowly as he entered a small village; one never knew when a child would take it into his head to dash across the road. It was hardly a village, merely a group of white buildings at a cross-roads. Shops there were, three of them, with artistic swinging signs. A stone church. Smart and shining automobiles, a dozen. He remembered now that a daughter of a pre-crash plutocrat had opened an "inexpensive gown shop." It was a Mecca for her friends. Inexpensive gown shops had become epidemic.

"Yo-hoo! Mi—chael!"

A girl was waving to him as she ran down a flagged walk. Phyllis! Phyllis, in a blue frock, the blue she affected which was the color of her eyes.

A rush of memories swept Michael Farr. Should he stop? He glanced at the mirror above the windshield to see what was behind him. The reflection of his own face shocked him. Could a sight of the girl who had thrown him over line it like that? A tinge of white at the temples accentuated the darkness of his hair; there were crinkles at the corners of his gray eyes; his mouth was tight-lipped. He stopped the roadster.

"Why the hold-up, Phyl?" he asked with what he hoped was the light touch.

The girl stepped to the running-board. He looked at her small mouth with its pettish implication. Had it always been like that?

"I wanted you to cross-your-throat-an' hope-to-die promise that you will come to our house-warming, Thursday, Michael."

"Didn't Miss Hale tell you that I was coming?"

"Yes—but—" Long gold-tipped lashes drooped for an instant and swept up disclosing appealing blue eyes with wide irises. Michael Farr knew the trick. It had been used on him times enough. "I wanted to be sure that you understood the invitation and would be friends. Now that it is *de rigueur* for former wives to send a note of congratulation to their successors, it is quite proper for a girl to invite her ex-fiancé to her party, isn't it?"

As she poised on the running-board like a blue butterfly which had lighted for an instant to fan its wings, Michael's hand clenched on the wheel. She was lovely. Lovely as a false-hearted peach was lovely. Subconsciously he had realized that during their engagement. A hot black wave of anger swept him at her insouciance. No love in that, thank goodness! He fought an impulse to push her off. There had been nothing since she had eloped with Bill D'Arcy to compare with it in intensity. It wasn't because she had thrown him over, it was the way she had done it. He resisted an urge to clear his voice of hoarseness, and smiled.

"Of course I understand the invitation to your party, and of course I am coming. Wouldn't miss it. Hop off, will you, Phyl? I'm late for a date."

He waited only for her to step back from the running-board before he sent the roadster ahead. He brushed a hand across his eyes. That was that. Why was she reverting to before-their-engagement tactics? What did she want? Whatever it was, she wouldn't get it, he would set up some sort of impassable barrier.

The roadster shot between dignified stone posts which supported ornate iron gates, and speeded round the curves of a winding drive. At the last turn his house loomed. Stone, rambling, it looked like a miniature English castle against a backdrop of fleece-dotted cerulean sky and crouching purple hills.

Michael regarded it with affectionate eyes. Nice old place, but he realized now how Phyllis had hated it. She had begged for a modern house; had shivered delicately; had said that Kingscourt made her think of dungeons and of bodies being mysteriously dropped into a moat. He had laughed at her and had given her *carte blanche* to have the interior—except for the library and his study—redecorated and furnished to suit herself. She had been wildly enthusiastic—and extravagant—until the work was finished—and then —Why indulge in post mortems? Why dwell on the past? It was gone. He would wipe his mind clear of it. He knew that he had been hurt more in his pride than in his heart.

Nice old place, he thought again, as he stopped at the steps. Guy had suggested closing it. He might have to, but not yet—it would throw too many out of work. Farrs had lived here for generations. Generations! His thoughts snapped back to the girl and the child who were coming. Was there a new shoot on the family tree, or was he being buncoed?

A butler in immaculate blue livery opened the door. His washed-out eyes warmed; dark color stole under a skin which was as brown and tight as a pecan shell. His slightly stooped shoulders straightened.

"You, Mr. Michael! 'Tisn't often we see you here this time of day." His jaw trembled. "No bad news from Mr. Guy, I hope?"

"No, no, Elkins. Come into the library. I want to talk to you. Miss Serena in?"

"No, sir. This is her contract class afternoon."

Elkins followed Michael through the great hall, with its second floor gallery and its railing hung with rich-toned rugs, into a room walled with books set in age-darkened oak, warm with velvet hangings which picked up the color of the blue coat in the painting above the fireplace. A beautifully proportioned room, built in a period when its owners had time and inclination for reflection and gracious living. At one end sunlight poured through glass upon palms, massed Canterbury bells in pots, spikes of anchusa, royally, brilliantly blue. A fountain trickled into a mossy pool, through which darted living streaks of red-gold. Deep cushioned seats lured; ferns waved fronds by the beckoning score in the soft breeze from an open window.

Michael turned his back on the beauty and color of the conservatory. Perched on a corner of a massive table desk, he looked up at the portrait above the carved mantel, which, with doors and window trim, years and years before had been brought from a castle overseas.

Michael Farr, Admiral. He had commenced his sea-going career as shipmaster's apprentice. When war broke out between England and America he had been commissioned captain by the Continental Congress. After he had surprised the garrisons of two forts, spiked their guns and fired the shipping in the harbor, he had been promoted to Commodore, later to Rear Admiral. He had survived terrific engagements and storms at sea.

The story had come down through the generations that once when menaced by the fury of a storm, with his ship tossing like a chip in foaming seas, with wind roaring, spray hissing, the rigging rattling, moaning, creaking, splitting, he had clung to a mast, had shaken his fist at the mountainous waves, had shouted above the tumult:

"Damn you! We ride the gale!"

His defiance had been handed from father to son as the Farr challenge to difficulties and defeat:

"We ride the gale!"

"I'll bet you rode it, no quitting for you," Michael said to the portrait. "And the country has been riding as gallantly these last few years as you rode."

It seemed to him as if the Admiral nodded agreement. He had been one grand playboy, beside being a fighting, cursing old sea-dog, Guy had said. He looked it, but there was an underlying strength in this face which the descendant who had so classified him had not inherited. White peruke, high stock, frills and a blue coat with brass buttons could not detract from the resemblance of the painted face to that of the man looking intently up at him. They had the same resolute mouth, the same acquiline nose, the same compelling gray eyes—except that the lid above the left eye of the living did not droop. The painted hand holding a painted map was the same strong, sensitive hand which now held a lighter to a cigarette. Michael Farr turned to Elkins.

"Is Libby at home?"

"Yes, Mr. Michael."

"I am expecting guests. Dow is bringing them from town. A lady and a little boy. I want Libby to be at the door when they arrive, not you. She is to ask them to wait in the morning room, then come to me here. Understand?"

"Yes, Mr. Michael. Shall I serve tea, sir?"

"Don't 'sir' me when we are alone, Elkins, and don't look so infernally gloomy. This visit isn't a tragedy."

"Isn't it, Mr. Michael? I had a queer feeling it might be more trouble for you."

"Forget it. Be sure that there are things to eat a boy of

three would like. You ought to know what. Guy and I robbed the pantry times enough."

The butler chuckled. "I'll eat my hat if they raise such appetites these days as you two had. And now you don't eat enough to keep a bird alive."

"Depends on the bird. Slim pickings for a vulture perhaps, but a gorge for anything smaller. Hustle now and get Libby on the job. The car may be here any minute."

He crossed to the French window and stepped out on a terrace which extended the length of the house. In all the years he had lived at Kingscourt the beauty of the place never failed to quicken his blood. From the steps a flagstone walk, bordered by giant larkspur, foxglove, Canterbury bells and tall, late pink tulips, crossed the wide stretch of lawn to a delicately wrought iron gateway. Beyond that was the blue-tiled swimming pool, and further on the sporthouse, built of stone and set at present in a mass of rhododendrons and azaleas. Over its roof he could see green fields which sloped to the shore of a lake, a lake so still that the boathouse on its bank seemed to be standing on its roof in the water. Near it was a crimson streak where a man was painting a canoe. The reflection of a spring board was as clear as if cut out of wood.

Michael's brow contracted as he looked at the distant greenhouses. Two of them had been closed last winter. It had hurt like the dickens to throw the men out of work—he had kept them on a reduced payroll—but it was bad for them to be idle. That stretch of lake shore glinting with silver birches was the land Donald Brandt was after. A new highway had made it desirable for a residential development. People were moving out of town, away from apartments, the realtor had argued. The price offered had been startling, and now it had been raised ten per cent.

Conditions had changed since he had snootily told Linda Hale to refuse the offer. Had that been yesterday? It seemed days ago. Ought he to take it? The money Brandt paid for the land could be put away for this boy of Guy's—if he were Guy's. His father—if he were his father—would have nothing left for him.

He would hate looking across the lake at a messy lot of houses, and any houses the massive and white-haired Brandt would put there would be designed as money-makers. Did the man think the owner was holding out on him because they were political opponents? No matter how much he balked at the idea of selling, he couldn't afford to be high-hat about the sale. He would think it over after he had made up his mind about the boy.

21

He filled his lungs with the fragrant air. It was life-giving after the soot of the city. Life-giving! That was an idea. What a place for a boy who needed the out-of-doors! What a strength-restorer for a girl just out of hospital! Acres of spicy forest, a chattering stream, the lake for paddling and swimming, plenty of neighbors to keep her from being lonely—

Neighbors! There would be neighbors all right. Phyllis D'Arcy for one. Neighbors who would whisper behind their hands, raise carefully groomed eyebrows. Suppose they did? Would he let a lot of women stop his bringing the child here? Not if he were honestly convinced that he was Guy's—whether by benefit of clergy or not. Kingscourt would be a solution of the problem of the boy's health—but —what would it mean to the girl? He couldn't bring one here without the other. Women could be brutal to another woman.

He returned to the library and glanced at the tall clock in the corner. Time for them! Suppose—suppose Sonia Carson had collapsed in the street, suppose she had not returned to the apartment? He should have told Dow to phone Kingscourt before he started back.

Voices in the hall! Libby! Libby would know the truth the moment she saw the boy; that was why he had had her open the door. She had taken care of Guy and himself from the days they were born until they went away to Prep. School. She would see the resemblance if there were one.

"Have they come?"

He took a quick step toward the dove-eyed woman who entered. Her pink-cheeked face was framed in little soft silver curls a shade lighter than her gray silk gown. She was plump without giving an impression of bulk. One tear rolled down her cheek. She smoothed the frill of her incredibly fine organdie collar. Her lips trembled.

"They've come, Mr. Michael. Who is the child? He's the image of you at his age, except he's got the old Admiral's drooping eyelid." She nodded toward the portrait. "It's faint, but it's there. That would stamp him as a Farr if nothing else did. Is he your boy and you never told your old Libby?"

"No! No! Pull yourself together. Have you forgotten that two months ago I was planning to be married? Do you think if I had a three year old son he would not have been in this house from the moment he was born?"

"Then you know how old he is?" the woman cross-examined shrewdly.

"Bring them here. After Elkins has served tea, show the

child your parrot and cat. Look here, Lib, if Aunt Serena should come in, steer her off from the library, will you?"

"Sakes, Mr. Michael, this is her contract lesson day. She won't come to this part of the house, she has her own entrance. Besides, she'll have her beauty hour the minute she comes in."

"I will ring when I want the boy."

"I hope you'll keep him here forever; 'twould make us all young again. I can see him running round the place at the gardener's heels, the way you used to. I'm going! I'm going!"

She brushed plump fingers across her wet eyes as she hurried from the room in response to an impatient motion of his hand. That was the dickens and all when it came to old servants, Michael told himself, they had vested rights in the family and never hesitated to express their opinions.

They were coming! His heart seemed to stop as Sonia Carson and the boy entered the room. What had the next moment in store for him? For an instant he evaded looking at the child and kept his eyes on the girl. She was dressed as she had been in the morning, was as straight and slim. Ridiculous conclusion—had he expected her to put on flesh in a few hours? Her cheeks, which had been white then, burned with spots of color; her dark eyes were brilliant; her lips—accented but not smeared—trembled.

Her apparent nervousness steadied Michael. He pulled forward a chair.

"Won't you sit down?"

She sank into it as if her knees had turned traitor. She flung her arm about the boy and drew him near. He looked up at Michael gravely, almost appraisingly, with eyes as blue, though not icy, as Guy's.

Libby was right. There was a faint droop to the left lid. He felt an immeasurable sense of relief. He had been afraid, afraid to the depths of his soul, that the child would prove a fake. That would have meant that the girl in the chair was lying. He had been through humiliation unbearable because of one lying woman.

The boy leaned, a graceful little figure, in blue shorts and blouse, against her knees. His bare legs above his striped socks were like thin white sticks. Michael thought of the chronic state of black and blueness, the smears of mercurochrome which had illuminated his legs and Guy's when they were the boy's age. This one was in tragic need of being turned loose in the country. Soft rings of silky red-gold hair lay close to his finely shaped head. Noble. An old-fashioned word—but it expressed him. He was too pale. That could be remedied speedily.

Michael sat down and held out his hand. "Shake hands, old man. I'm your—friend."

He felt the blood mount to his hair. He had caught himself in time. He had almost said: "I'm your Uncle Michael." He didn't intend to make that acknowledgment so soon, perhaps never. He heard the quick uneven breath of the girl. Did she know what he had been about to say? He resisted the temptation to glance at her. The boy looked up questioningly.

"Go to him, Dicky."

For an instant Michael struggled with embarrassment. What did one say to a possible nephew, a nephew who, until a moment before, one did not admit one possessed? The child was untrammeled by self-consciousness. He laid his hand in Michael's and leaned confidingly against his knee as he inquired:

"Any boys in this house?"

"Sorry. Not a boy."

"A dog? Got a dog?" He pounded the supporting knee with a small fist. "Saw one this mornin'. White an' fuzzy. Sonia said he looked like shwedded coconut."

His laugh was like the tinkle of silver bells. His eyes were blue stars. His white even teeth gleamed with the soft lustre of pearls between his red lips. What a boy! Michael caught the contagion of his laughter, and smiled.

"I don't own a dog like that, but there are some big ones down at the stables. Perhaps I can find a fuzzy white one, though."

"This one was lame. We took him home an' fed him. Sonia cawied him. She cwied a big tear. She can't bear to see anything hurt." His chin quivered.

Michael laid his hand on the boy's shoulder.

"How about cake and sandwiches and tea? Here comes Elkins."

The equipment on the huge silver tray jiggled as the heavily veined hands which held it shook. Elkins' cheeks blanched—as much as brown skin could whiten—his jaw sagged. He stared at the radiant, eager little face; then his eyes rested on the portrait above the mantel. They brimmed with slow tears as he set the tray on a low table.

"Libby never told me, Mr. Michael, that there was another Farr."

"We will serve, Elkins. Will you pour the tea, Miss Carson?"

Almost any girl or woman he knew would have settled in the chair behind the tea-table with a little air of importance, Michael told himself, as without a hint of self-consciousness she deftly handled the massive silver pot. He answered absently her inquiries as to lemon and cream. The child hovered near like a bee about a pot of honey.

"Pass the tea to Mr. Farr, Dicky."

The boy took the saucer in his two small white hands. Eyes intent on the liquid contents of the cup, he crossed the rug slowly. He drew a quick little sigh as Michael relieved him of his charge. That responsibility behind him, he offered a plate of sandwiches and indicated with a slim finger:

"That one looks gwand."

"You take it, or shall we give it to your——"

"Sonia wouldn't take it. She says, alwus give the gwandest to our guests. I like you. You our guest?"

"We are Mr. Farr's guests, Dick. Come and get your cambric tea."

The boy selected an array of sandwiches, and carefully steered himself and his refreshments toward the conservatory. Seated on the rim of the pool, he nibbled as he watched the darting fish. He gave no evidence of a boyish appetite. The girl behind the tea-table ate nothing. Was she still terrified about the uncertainty of the child's future?

Michael pulled the old-fashioned bell-rope, which in its time had served four generations of Farrs. Libby appeared with the instantaneousness of a rabbit shaken from a prestidigitator's hat.

"I'm sure that Dicky would like to see to your parrot, Libby."

The boy darted from the pool and caught the woman's plump, smooth hand.

"A parwot! Does he talk? Is he all wed and gween, Mrs.——Mrs.——"

"Call me Libby, my lamb. He talks like a house a-fire. He likes little boys. Come with me and you'll see."

Dicky turned questioning eyes on the girl. She nodded. Holding tight to the housekeeper's hand, he hopped and skipped along beside her. His high childish voice, his musical laugh drifted back from the hall. The sound diminished gradually till a closing door shut it off.

Elkins appeared and removed the tea things. Michael regarded him impatiently as he left the room. What a doddering old chap he was. Did he always putter like that?

The butler reappeared.

"Anything more, Mr. Michael?"

"Nothing. Tell Libby to keep the boy until I ring."

Elkins stopped to readjust a rug. He lowered a Venetian blind to shut out a vagrant ray of sunlight which was setting innumerable prisms of color from a huge glass bowl full of red roses flickering on the dark ceiling. With a last appraising look about the room, he departed.

Michael drew a breath of relief and held out a silver box of cigarettes to the girl, whose eyes were on the portrait. "Smoke?"

She shook her head. With his back to the fireplace he looked across the room at her. What should he say? How approach the subject of the child's paternity?

She spoke before he could. Hands gripping the arms of the old brocade chair, she demanded:

"Don't you believe now that Dicky is your brother's son?"

Michael looked up at the painted eyes above him.

"If I did not, the Admiral would step from his frame and beat me up. That drooping eyelid is not to be ignored. Besides—you won't like this—Libby says that the boy looks as I did at his age."

"And you believe in the marriage?"

Michael felt his color deepen. He didn't believe in that, knowing his brother as he did, he couldn't. Hadn't Guy said that no woman would slip a ball-and-chain on him?

"From your hesitation it is evident that you don't. The rights of a wife to name and fortune no longer matter—my sister is gone. But the boy should bear the name legally his. I am prepared to go to any length to get it for him."

Her voice, her cool, brilliant, slightly contemptuous eyes set Michael Farr's cheek-bones burning.

"Is that a threat? If it is, you are wasting ammunition. The boy will have his chance. Of course you have his birth certificate?"

"Birth certificate! I haven't. Where—where would I get it?"

"From the registry in the town where the child was born. Don't worry, I'll look it up. Won't you tell me something about yourself and your life before you and your sister met my brother?"

"Not much to tell, except that like young Lochinvar we came out of the West to New York State."

"Have you no family?"

"No relations except a distant cousin, Tom Nash. He is a Croesus in a small way. He canned something which never before had been soldered into captivity and made a fortune. He is the person who wanted to adopt Dicky without knowing who his father was. But, even while hating your brother as I do, I had sense enough to know I had no right to give his son away. There is no danger of a hungry horde of relatives fattening on your nephew's fortune."

Her tone fired Michael with an urge to shake her till her teeth chattered; instead he said thoughtfully:

"That, of course, helps. I had been worrying about the relatives."

Why had he said that? The thought had not once occurred to him.

"And you are an architect?"

"Yes. I have made a specialty of small houses—but—well, you know that architects have been badly hit. I was to have had the planning of a land development, but it has been so uncertain that I did not dare depend on it."

"You are a courageous person, aren't you?"

"What do you mean?"

"Daring for an instant to try to keep a child out of his inheritance."

"In our anger and disillusion, my sister and I would have dared anything to keep Dicky out of his father's hands. We were wrong. When we found that Guy Farr meant never to come back, we should have insisted upon a divorce and the mother's legal custody of the child that was coming. Endurance of the sort of treatment your brother put across is out-dated. We should have met the situation with resolution and good sense. We had no one to advise us—and then—Ruby died and the divorce did not matter. To disappear seemed the easiest solution, but this slight illness shattered my belief in my reasoning. It is a risk to let Guy Farr know that he has a son, he may ruin him, but I had to take it. You will love Dicky, you can't help it. He is adorable. Will you write to your brother? Make him understand that he is not asked to take the responsibility of the boy. He won't be permitted to."

Was there a hint of fear in the depths of her eyes? If her story were true, why should she be afraid? Of course it was true. She would not lie. She was everything a woman should be. He knew it. She was his ideal girl come to life.

"I can't be in love with her! I can't!" he told himself with a touch of panic. "But I am," he added doggedly.

"Why are you so silent? You will write?" Sonia Carson demanded tersely.

"I will. Tonight. Did Guy know that the baby was coming?"

"Yes. He came to see Ruby but once after he knew."

"And he did nothing to help? I can't believe it."

"I wrote him that the child had died at birth."

"You wrote that?" Her color deepened as she met his

eyes. "It helps a little to know that my brother is ignorant of the existence of his son. I will see that the child is adequately provided for until I hear from Guy. Meanwhile I want the boy here this summer."

"Here! Why? Why should he come here? If you believe that Dicky is your brother's son, acknowledge him, make him an allowance and I will take him to the country."

"What better place could you find than this? I want him here."

"Shylock! Demanding your pound of flesh! I can't do it! I won't!"

"A little afraid of the validity of that marriage certificate?"

Why had he said that when he knew in his heart that she was the soul of honor?

If eyes could kill, hers would have slain him where he stood.

"I am not afraid of anything. Certainly not of you. I have no choice but to accept your ultimatum, have I? Safety first. Not for me; if it were only myself, I wouldn't be submerged and smothered in it—but for Dicky—I am clutching at it for him. If we came, how would you explain us to your neighbors and guests? Are you ready so soon to acknowledge Richard as your brother's son?"

"I had thought of that. Convinced as I am that the boy is Guy's, I have no right until I hear from him to broadcast the fact that he has a child. I—"

The telephone rang. Rang twice. Michael sat on the corner of the flat desk and picked up the instrument.

"Michael Farr speaking."

He waited for an instant. Then he heard the little laugh which always preceded Phyl's phone conversations.

"It's Phyl, Michael."

"What is it? I'm busy."

"You would be. Michael, the Rusts want us to dine with them before the house-warming."

"Who do you mean, 'us'?"

"You and me and Bill."

"Why lug me in?"

"I asked them. I'm not very happy, Michael. I want people to know we are friends—we are, aren't we—dear?"

The low "dear" sent the dark color to Michael Farr's hair, a wave of fury surging through him.

"Cut that out, Phyl. Tell the Rusts that it will be impossible for me to dine with them."

"Why?" It was more a wail than a word.

Michael Farr heard a voice answer:

"Because—I am dining with my—fiancée."

Had that been his voice?

"Your what? I didn't get the last word, Michael."

He banged down the instrument. Lucky she hadn't caught the last word. What imp had put it into his head? His eyes flashed to the girl watching him. Had his subconscious juggled Sonia Carson to the surface of his mind?

Color burned high in his cheeks. Why not? He loved her. Of course she didn't love him—yet. She would serve as a barrier against Phyl. The problem of her living at Kingscourt would be solved. He took a quick step toward her.

"Will you marry me?" he demanded curtly.

Chapter IV

Sonia Carson regarded Michael Farr as if she suspected he had gone mad. She retreated with her hands out-thrust to ward him off as he approached.

"Don't run. I'm not crazy." He twisted his stiff lips into the semblance of a smile. If his expression as he had turned from the phone had reflected his fury at Phyl's tactics, no wonder he had frightened her.

"Are you sure?"

"Quite sure. Sit down—please—and let me explain."

She shook her head and commenced to pull on her gloves.

"There can be but one explanation. Brainstorm. I'll go, before you have another. And I had thought you different from your brother! You have the same line when it comes to girls, haven't you? I can manage quite well without your help with Dicky. I—I thought of something while you were at the phone. Will you call the child, please?"

"You can't go until you hear what I have to say."

"But I don't care to hear. I'm going."

"Then you will leave the boy—here."

"That is the funniest thing I ever heard."

"All right, it's the funniest thing you ever heard. I suppose that a father has more authority than an aunt. I will have Guy appoint me his son's guardian."

There was battle in her eyes as she looked back at him, but a quiver about her lips.

"You—you wouldn't do that?"

Michael felt like a brute, but there was enough of the poison of anger coursing in his veins to steel his determination. Better not let her suspect that he loved her or she would be convinced that he was a lunatic at large.

"Not unless you force me to it and refuse to listen to my explanation. I can't let you go thinking that I ask every woman I meet to marry me."

"Don't you? I thought it might be a Farr trait."

"I'll let that ride—for the present. When the phone rang, we were considering how to explain Dicky's presence here without acknowledging his parentage, weren't we?"

"You were."

"All right. I was. I wonder if my subconscious had been at work on the problem and flung that question I asked you to the surface as the solution?"

"If it did, your subconscious must be suffering from arrested development."

"Who is being hard now? The girl who phoned me was the girl I was to have married. Who—"

"Who jilted you a week before the date set."

"How do you know?"

"I read the papers. I have expected to see an announcement of Guy Farr's marriage. In consequence, I am posted on all the lurid details of your broken romance."

He looked at her steadily. His voice was uneven as he observed:

"And Dicky said: 'Sonia can't bear to see anything hurt.' He doesn't know this side of you, does he?"

She bit her lips to steady them. "I'm sorry. I was brutal, but I couldn't tell from your face as you listened to that call whether you were being unbearably hurt or were white with anger. I saw my sister's heart pulled up by the roots by your brother, and when you hurled that question at me, I knew that you were being as casual as he about something which I hold sacred."

"I wasn't being casual. I was a drowning man grasping at a raft. Mrs. D'Arcy—"

"I was the raft? Thanks."

He ignored the crisp interruption. "Mrs. D'Arcy has boasted that 'she will have me eating out of her hand again' —that's her phrase, not mine. Already she had arranged a dinner invitation for me."

"Was that when you grabbed for the raft?"

"It was. Apparently she is not satisfied with a husband, she wants two men at her heels. Cheap sharing is not in my line."

"It's being done."

"Not by me." He approached so close that she stepped

back. "Look at me. Answer honestly. Do I look like a man who would go in for that sort of thing?"

"I'm not a character reader."

"And you won't be my raft?" He smiled.

"Of course I won't. You are laughing about it already. Do you think I would so degrade myself as to enter into a marriage which I knew to be a farce? Marriage means too much to me. It means love. Love which is a flame, which burns and hurts. Which makes one radiantly happy and unbearably miserable. Which carries one over a sea of trouble as if one were riding a surf-board through breakers. It means companionship and sharing joy and sorrow and responsibilities and—and having children and growing old together. Husband and wife against the world. And you—you propose it as if it were the missing piece of a picture puzzle!" She stopped for breath.

As Michael regarded her steadily, it seemed to him that he could hear gates closing on his old life and opening softly again on the new. Uncanny feeling. He conceded gravely:

"You are the missing piece of a picture puzzle, a long missing piece, I realize that now. Forget my touch of madness. Even the most conservative go blooey at times. You will bring Dicky here, won't you? Libby, who has no children, will spoil him—and that will be the one danger you have to fear. As to gossip—my aunt, Serena Farr, lives at Kingscourt. You and the child could be relatives come to spend the summer—let it go at that until we hear from Guy. Will you?"

A faint line of concentration appeared between her arched brows. Was she considering money? He suggested quickly:

"Leaving the city for months would mean that you could not take a position. I shall make you an allowance—until I hear from Guy."

"No. Are you proposing that I be paid for looking after the boy? I will come. Dicky must have his chance at health and strength. That slight illness terrified me, shattered my assurance that I was sufficient in his life, made me realize the injustice to him of keeping you in ignorance of his birth. How long before you will receive an answer to your letter to your brother?"

"Months perhaps."

Michael regarded her speculatively. How she detested him! Was he out of his mind to bring her into this house? Why didn't he give her an allowance and let her take the boy to the country? An easy solution—but—he wanted to know the boy, and—why not be honest—he wanted her here. He said lightly:

"I am always practical. I'm prosaic. As you reminded me this morning in the office, I lack my brother's fatal charm."

He hadn't intended that hurt note to creep into his voice. He said hurriedly:

"What has the boy been called?"

"Richard Carson. That has told the world nothing."

"How you hate the name of Farr! There is no excuse for Guy's desertion of your sister, but he was a terribly spoiled boy in fear of his father. He would lie like a trooper to escape the consequences of his escapades. Will you be ready at eleven tomorrow morning? Better get Dicky out of the city as soon as possible. I will send Dow for you and a truck for your luggage."

For the first time in their brief acquaintance she smiled. Her eyes warmed; pink tinged her cheeks; even the color of her lips deepened as parted in charming curves they revealed perfect teeth.

"Will you give us until afternoon? Collecting a vacation wardrobe for a child takes time."

Her unexpected friendliness went to his head. She was adorable.

"Call it three, then." He put his hand in his pocket. "Do you need money—for Richard?" he added hurriedly, as anger stirred in the depths of her eyes.

"No. I have enough now that I know that he will be provided for. Will you send for him, please?"

The atmosphere seemed to throb with things left unsaid as Michael waited in silence for the answer to his ring. He was relieved when the child entered holding tight to the hand of the buxom housekeeper. The white curls which framed her rosy face bobbed in her effort to keep pace with him. He dashed across the room and flung his arms about the slim figure in gray.

"Sonia! Mrs. Libby has a funny parwot! I gave him a cwacker. He winked an' said, 'Attaboy.'" Laughter bubbled through his excited voice.

"What fun, Dicky. Say good-bye to Mr. Farr, Most Dear."

The child looked up at her; his lip quivered.

"Won't I ever see that funny parwot again, Sonia?"

Michael stooped and laid his hands on the child's shoulders.

"Sure, you'll see him again, old man. You are coming here tomorrow to spend the summer."

The boy looked back at him gravely.

"Not wifout Sonia?" There was a hint of panic in the question.

"Certainly not without Sonia. She—she is all excited about coming with you."

There was more than a hint of disdain in the eyes which flashed to his, but Sonia Carson ignored his sarcasm.

"Come, Dicky."

At the door of the limousine, Michael Farr held out his hand.

"My aunt will be here to welcome you when you arrive, Miss Carson."

The clouds of disillusion and anger in which he had been smothered so long lifted. He laughed.

"You will like Serena. She never has brainstorms and she wouldn't clutch at a raft on a bet."

He waited until the musical fanfare of a French horn warned approaching automobiles that the car was passing between the stone gate-posts into the highway. As he entered the house and crossed the hall he seemed to emerge from a dream, a dream in which one event had followed another so fast that he had not had a chance to waken between them. It was beginning to break up into episodes now. Sonia Carson's appearance in his office: her arrival at Kingscourt with the boy: his decision that he wanted the two at Kingscourt for the summer: his own amazing realization that she was his ideal girl in the flesh: his more amazing request that she marry him.

He had been desperately in earnest at the moment. Suppose she had said, "Yes." He stopped on the broad stairs, one hand on the balustrade. He could see her glowing dark eyes, hear her low passionate voice demanding:

"Do you think I would so degrade myself as to enter into a marriage which I knew to be a farce? Marriage means too much to me. It means love. Love which is a flame, which burns and hurts."—"Husband and wife against the world," she had said.

That last was a thought. Had she loved that she knew so well what it meant? What did he know about her. Nothing but the little she had told him, and what had she told him except that she had come out of the West and that she had a cousin who was a Croesus in a small way? She was right. He had had a brainstorm when he had whirled on her and asked her to marry him. No wonder her eyes had gone big with fright. He would never forget them. Had love prompted him, or had it seemed a heaven-sent way of escape from

Phyl? Hot color burned to his hair. He certainly had gone a deep and murky yellow when he had grabbed for that raft. Trying to set a girl between himself and a woman for whom he no longer cared. A touch of madness was right. Had he been quite as mad when he had insisted that Sonia Carson and the child come to Kingscourt for the summer? Too late to question the wisdom of his decision now. He had burned his bridges. He could smell their smoke behind him.

He knocked at the door of his aunt's suite. Had she returned from the contract class? If so, he was intruding upon what was awesomely respected in the household as Miss Serena's beauty hour. It took a brave person to crash that. He must dare it. He had a dinner engagement in the city. He must talk with her before he returned to his club to dress. He needed her help.

How much should he tell her? Should he make a clean breast of the matter? Of course. Half truths always were dangerous. They would prove especially so with Serena Farr.

The door opened. The slatey eyes in the thin face the color of old parchment of the angular woman in the black silk uniform warmed a trifle as they met his. Her heavily veined hand tightened on the knob.

"You, Mr. Michael? Miss Serena is—"

"I know, Bates, that she shouldn't be disturbed. But I must see her. I have a dinner engagement in town. Tell her that I want to talk over a family matter about which I can't decide until I have consulted her."

That wasn't quite true, Michael admitted to himself, as the maid stood aside for him to enter. Already he had decided.

"I'll tell her. Just wait until I get her into her tie-up and perhaps she'll see you."

Hands in his pockets, Michael stood in the middle of the living room and looked about him. White Venetian blinds and off-white walls—silver and white curtains and yellow roses in dull golden bowls—ivory sheen on the beige and white rug—chairs and couch in white velvet—golden and ivory cushions—a cabinet of rare gold coins—tables of old red lacquer—the portrait of a man in a white suit, a man with a drooping eyelid—his grandfather when he had been ambassador to Spain. Sunlight weaving thin patterns on the tiled floor of an enclosed porch, casting green shadows as it shot through the plant life in a row of aquariums which were like miniature moving pictures of deep sea life. At the other end of the room, beyond the openwork red lacquer doors to the game alcove, stood an antique backgammon table with ancient horn dice-cups.

Good effect, he approved. The decorator had done over these rooms under Phyllis' direction. He hadn't looked into the suite she had selected for herself since—but—why not use it for—

"Miss Serena says will you please come in, Mr. Michael."

Bates' grating voice broke in upon his thoughts. He followed the grenadier-like woman into a boudoir all violet and pink and silver. In the middle of the room was a white figure in a wheel chair which faced a mirrored wall beneath which stood a glass and chromium dressing table crowded with silver-topped jars and crystal jugs. The white band which covered the forehead to the eyebrows accentuated the lines of the finely modeled nose; the head was swathed so tightly that Michael wondered if the red lips could open. The eyes which looked back at him, ordinarily blue, had a charming violet tinge superinduced no doubt by the color of the walls. Bates gave a few deft touches to the mummied head before she closed the door behind her.

"Well, Michael," Serena Farr's voice was surprisingly crisp considering the tightness of the band under her chin, "you are the only person on earth I would allow to see me like this. What has happened? Another cut in dividends or —is it Guy again?"

It was evident from her tone that Serena Farr was post-ed at her guns. He must proceed with care.

"Mind if I smoke?"

"No. Wish I could, but Bates has this chin-strap so tight that I can hardly mumble."

"Why torment yourself? You don't need it. You look like a million."

"A million years! Sometimes I think I do, but I still keep my self-respect. I don't mean to give an imitation of a crumbling ruin so long as I have a brain cell left. You didn't break into my beauty hour to tell me how young and fair I am, did you?"

"No, but you are a wonderful looking woman, Serena." He tossed his cigarette into the fireplace; then, realizing that it was an electrically equipped imitation of coals, painstakingly fished it forth and laid it on a tray.

"Not a cut in dividends, but it is Guy. I have just seen his son."

"His what?" The back of the chair snapped up as the white figure sat erect.

"His son. His child."

"Any more announcements up your sleeve, Michael? If so, get them over with. No play-by-play broadcast for me. How do you know? Can you be taken in by a blackmailer?

Not that I'd put it past Guy. He's a philanderer. Where is he? What does he say about it?"

"He is on his way to South America where there are hot strange jungles and black storms blowing up under swift tropical winds."

"Stop talking like Kipling and tell me when he went."

"He left—is it possible it was yesterday, it seems years ago."

"Isn't it just his luck to have stepped out before this story broke? But he can't have the breaks with him always. Bret Harte said that the only sure thing about luck is that it will change. Remember that? Of course you don't. Who reads Bret Harte now? Why don't you stop him? Make him come back and face this—this woman—I suppose a woman bobbed up, or is a fake attorney appearing for her? Why take it on your shoulders? Of course she will settle for money. She—"

"That's just the point, Serena. The mother died. It is her sister who is pressing the child's claim. She wants nothing for herself, only for the boy."

"That's been said before, too. What started her after you?"

He told her of Sonia Carson's call at the office—he couldn't believe that it was this very morning; of his skepticism of her story at first; of the marriage certificate; of his strengthening suspicion that there might be a sub-strata of truth in the claim; of his plan for the child to come to Kingscourt; of Libby's tearful recognition of the boy's likeness to himself when he was young; of the drooping eyelid; of Elkins' shaken surprise.

"When I looked at him, my doubts vanished. I was sure that he is Guy's son."

"What's the woman's line? Brazen or simple?"

"Neither. To use a pre-war term, she is a lady."

"A lady! Has the creature bewitched you, Michael? Has she any people?"

"Apparently only a cousin, Tom Nash. I think I know of the man in a business way. Rich. He tries to make up for lack of education by lavish spending."

"Why didn't she appeal to him?"

"Why should she if the child is Guy's?"

"What will you do? Buy her off?"

"She isn't after money. She wants the boy to have a name. She has lost her job. The doctor has ordered the child to the country."

"The doctor! What doctor? Could it be Jim Neville?"

Michael's eyes were tender as he smiled.

"Jim Neville isn't the only child specialist in the big

city, Serena. Besides, apparently she hasn't the money to pay his fees. I thought that this place couldn't be bettered for country so they are coming here."

"Here!" Only the white swathing kept Serena Farr's lower jaw from permanent dislocation. "What do you mean by 'here'? Not Kingscourt?"

"Yes."

"Have you gone stark, staring mad, Michael? Do you intend to recognize the child's claim before you have given Guy a hearing? Goodness knows I'd believe anything of him —that wasn't good—but he should be consulted before he has a son shackled to his ankles."

"That's where you come in, Serena. It may take months to hear from Guy. While we are waiting the child might die. Of course, I could give them money and let them go to the country—but I had a curious hunch that they should come to Kingscourt."

"Money! More expense for you, and Guy beating it to foreign parts. Always carrying him on your shoulders, aren't you, Michael? What does he care that you've closed the greenhouses, given up your town apartment, sold your polo ponies—"

"Serena! Who told you that?"

"Think I don't know what all the servants know? You say the child looks like the Farrs. What does the aunt call herself?"

"Sonia Carson."

"What was the alleged wife's name?"

"Ruby."

"Movie names. It never has been supposed in the family that my mental brilliance would set a muddy creek—to say nothing of a river—afire, but I wouldn't fall for those. Do you believe that Guy really married the girl?"

Michael Farr became absorbed in the examination of an exquisitely carved ivory tiger which he lifted from its red teakwood stand on the mantel.

"I think Miss Carson is honest in her belief that the marriage was legal."

"But you doubt it. So do I. But I suppose for the honor of the family we must give the child a chance. Let me see— you remember, don't you, that your father and I had a sister who ran away with a man named Carson?"

"A man named Carson! I know that there was a sister who died away from home, but—"

"'But' who can prove that she wasn't married? Don't stand there mumbling, Michael! You want a background for these relatives who are arriving, don't you? Now that I am improvising one, you go balky."

"Not balky. Dazed at your quick uptake, Serena."

"Oh, I'm good when I let myself go. Contract is supposed to sharpen the mental processes."

"Then yours ought to be keen as a fine steel blade."

"Don't be saucy. Let me see, the Carsons were swept off in the flu epidemic—*the* flu epidemic—that sets them far enough back so there will not be embarrassing questions—leaving two daughters. One of them married, and she and her husband died soon after a child was born—"

"Boy, what wholesale slaughter!"

"We've got to account for the child, haven't we? My late sister had brought her daughters up in detestation of the family who cast off their mother, but when the daughter who was left, the independent Sonia, lost her job, afraid of what might happen to her parentless nephew, she wrote to me. She and the child, who has the drooping lid of the Farrs, arrive—when?"

"Tomorrow."

"Tomorrow! You are a quick worker. Suppose I had refused to play your game, Michael?"

"I know you, Serena."

"You know that I'm a jellyfish where you are concerned, that's what you know. Is the girl good-looking?"

"Yes. My secretary, Linda Hale, says that she wears real clothes—if you know what that means."

"Of course I know. Real clothes mean real money. Where'd she get 'em, I wonder. Hope you are not being fooled."

"Wait till you see her."

"I'll wait. Now that I am getting used to the idea of a niece I am all excited. I was becoming bored with contract. I'll give a big garden party to introduce her to the neighbors. I can afford it, can't I, even if my finances are, to put it conservatively, like the Federal machinery, temporarily out of order? What rooms will you give our visitors?"

"The west wing."

"The rooms you had done over for—"

"Phyllis. Don't be afraid of the name. That's through. Done with."

"It was 'done with' before the break, wasn't it? For a long while you had had your doubts, hadn't you, Michael?"

"I had. It was trying to get to the facts behind those doubts that infuriated Phyl and sent her flying off at a tangent with Bill D'Arcy."

"Thank heaven, she flew the track! I never liked her.

I saw her grow up in the neighborhood, and could have scratched out her blue eyes when I realized that she had determined to marry you, that she was appealing to that protective side of you which filled Kingscourt with a menagerie of lame, halt, and mangy animals when you were a boy. But you'll have to admit that I behaved like a perfect lady to your fiancée, Michael, in spite of the fact that the probability that she might one day wear my pearls and emeralds gave me a nervous chill whenever I thought of it. She's not bad, she is not vicious, but she can't bear to have a man look at another girl when she is among those present. She's a sleek pussy. I always hated cats. Have you seen her?"

"Yes. She held me up in the village when I came through."

"What did she want?"

"She and Bill have bought The Cedars. She wanted me to promise that I would come to their house-warming Thursday evening."

"You won't go, will you?"

From the threshold Michael Farr looked back at the swathed figure.

"Go! Of course I'll go. Do you think I will pass up the opportunity of springing the news of my newly acquired cousin on the county—and Phyllis?"

Chapter V

The sun hung above a hilltop clear as a shining plaque, like a mammoth red-gold medal. The eastern sky was sapphire; in the west a few clouds were turning pink and silver at the edges. Garden borders were no more colorful than the frocks of the women which made a decorative pattern on the stretches of emerald green lawns. A scented breeze stirred the leaves of giant oaks and elms, fanned the turquoise surface of the swimming pool into lazy ripples, fluttered the canvas of the pastel pink and blue and green and yellow umbrellas which matched the painted tables beneath them and brought in its train the faint music of piccolos, drums and strings, the sound of laughter, of voices calling the score in the tennis courts beside the sportshouse, the tinkle of silver on china. Serena Farr was entertaining.

"Would the guests never stop arriving?" Sonia Carson wondered, as in a chartreuse green frock and droopy matching hat she stood beside her hostess whose gown, hat, and cape were all fashioned from the same lovely print, many toned pink roses on a black ground. Her face would stiffen into a permanent smile if she didn't watch out, she warned herself. At first she had attempted to reply to all introductions, but gave it up. The women's eyes knifed her with suspicion; their voices drenched her with honey; there were a few who seemed sincere. Almost invariably they stopped to exclaim:

"A niece, Serena! Where have you kept her all these years? How do Michael and Guy like the idea of another heir popping out of the everywhere into the here?"

They never waited for an answer, but passed on to give place to someone else who expressed the same thought, perhaps in other words. The men were different. Their greetings warmed her heart.

Behind Sonia's smile and courteous attention, the chatter was cutting into her nerves like thongs bound tight about raw flesh. What a fast worker life was! A month ago she would have been furiously indignant at the suggestion that she would enter the Farr home; here she was—a long lost niece—smiling and murmuring inanities. It was unbelievable. It was fantastic. She was an entirely different person from the girl who had gloried in her independence, who had been so sure that she could snap her fingers at the world and keep Dicky from his father. Michael Farr had confessed to a touch of madness when he had asked her to marry him; hadn't she been slightly mad when she had rushed to him in frenzied fear of leaving Dicky?

Which was the real person? The person who had been valiant and unafraid, or the person who had demanded help? Perhaps she had other personalities which this hazardous deception to which she had agreed would bring to the surface. More than all else the deception troubled her. She felt as if the distant purple hills she was facing were sinister, crouching shapes ready to spring and denounce her.

"You're a fraud! A fraud!" they would rumble from hilltop to hilltop.

Why had she consented to the deception? Of one thing she was sure, no thought of the Farrs' social position or wealth had influenced her. Safety and his rightful place in the world for Dicky was the answer. Why should she help the Farrs protect their adored Guy? When on the afternoon of her arrival at Kingscourt with Dicky Miss Serena had explained the plan she and her nephew had worked out, why hadn't she protested? Because nothing had seemed of importance except getting that frail little body where it would gain in health and weight—and the boy was gaining, even in a week his color had improved, he was blithe and gay.

If that were so, why was she regretting, she demanded of herself, and turned to the woman beside her. She was beautiful. Her short, silvery hair curled close at the back of her neck; her skin was flawless; her eyes were brilliantly blue, as blue as Guy Farr's, but, where his were cruel, hers seemed gaily amused at the human comedy as the pageant passed. A woman with a keen sense of values, a woman who in her conversation was pungent and distinctly modern. She was in love with life, that was evident. Her pearls were exquisite.

"Why, Jim! Jim!"

The shaken incredulity of Serena Farr's voice brought a rush of tears to Sonia's eyes. For an instant she saw the man, whose hand her hostess was clutching, through a mist. He was tall with iron gray hair, a thin, strongly lined face and quizzical dark eyes set deep beneath shaggy brows. His clothing was up to the minute for a garden party except for a battered felt hat which was tucked under one arm. Sonia never had seen its equal for shabbiness off the screen. His voice was gruffly tender as he replied to Serena Farr's greeting.

"You sent me an invitation, didn't you? Don't tell me that you didn't expect me to come, Serena. It would be a blow after Bigges got me into this rig. He held off patients at the office while the tailor took the measures. My secretary assured me that I would knock the eyes out of the assembled party. Like it?"

"Jim! Jim, it's wonderful! I—I'm surprised, that's all."

Serena Farr's voice broke. The man stepped between her and Sonia, as if to shield her, and held out his hand.

"The rest of my name is Neville, Miss Carson, in case you are interested. I used to know your mother and I wanted to meet her daughter."

Sonia felt the blood burn to her hair. Her mother! He believed that she was really Serena's niece! His bushy eyebrows met, his eyes seemed to bore into her heart.

"Hmp! Perhaps it's my mistake. Perhaps I didn't know her after all."

"Doctor Jim! Doctor Jim!"

He turned at the chorus of voices calling his name. Billows of color surged toward him. Blue gowns. Green gowns. Yellow gowns. Pink gowns. Red gowns and flowered gowns. On they came until Neville was surrounded by a laughing bunch of girls. They clung to his arms. They patted his sleeves. They chattered:

"Doctor Jim! You at a garden party! Is the world coming to an end?"

"You old lamb!"

"Looking like a million, aren't you?"

"Why didn't you come to my wedding? I don't believe you know who I am," an auburn haired girl questioned and accused in one breath.

Jim Neville chuckled. "You are Babs Byron. Think I'll ever forget the time your nurse called me out in the middle of the night because you were screaming with anguish? When I arrived I discovered a pin sticking into you. Been married about two years, haven't you? Any babies?"

"Not—yet." There was a lovely light in the girl's eyes as they met his.

"Hmp. Well, when he comes bring him to me. We'll see that he gets the right start in life. Now what do you want, Bigges? Can't I have a minute without being reminded that a patient is waiting?"

He frowned at the chauffeur who was pulling at his sleeve. The worried lines in the short man's face deepened as he thrust a faultless Panama hat into the doctor's hand. At the same moment he extracted the battered felt from under his employer's arm. He turned to Serena Farr and touched his cap. His voice was the voice of a man carrying the burdens of the world as he apologized:

"I don't know how he found that old hat, Madam. I thought I had hidden it."

Jim Neville chuckled. "Don't cry about it, Bigges. Run along. I'll be with you in a minute."

The girls closed in about him.

"You can't go until you have had some eats, Doctor Jim."

He looked back over his shoulder and laughed as he was swept along in a cloud of color.

"Who are the girls and why do they take possession of him like that?" Sonia asked Serena Farr.

"They were all 'his babies'; that is what his patients call themselves when they grow up. He is a child specialist. Their mothers consulted him about them, probably until they were ten or twelve years old. They never forget him. Who does?"

Sonia looked away quickly. It hurt to see the unsteadiness of Serena Farr's lips. She said lightly:

"His chauffeur apparently is bent double under his responsibility toward his employer. Isn't the doctor married?"

"Yes—but he is so busy that he wouldn't take time to

eat if Bigges and his servants didn't look after him. Here come some late arrivals."

"Do you know all the people in the world, Miss Serena?"

Serena Farr blinked the moisture from her eyes, shifted from one high-heeled foot to another, and straightened.

"My family—your family too—" she corrected herself hastily, "have lived here for generations. We know everyone worth knowing for miles around, and some that are not worth knowing now that the country club membership list reads like a list of the tax payers. It was death or democracy this year, and the club governors chose democracy. At last! Here come the D'Arcys. I have been waiting for Phyl to see you. Who is the man with them?"

Sonia looked curiously at the trio approaching. A small girl, in a filmy rose beige lace frock and big hat, had slipped a hand through the arm of a slight, black mustached youth with lacquered hair—for such a young man he had an uncommon number of fine lines radiating from the corners of his eyes; the other hand was on the arm of—Sonia shut her eyes and opened them. Was that man in clothes almost as white as his hair, with the fresh youthful face, really—

"How curious that you should know Donald Brandt, Miss Serena!"

"Who?"

"Donald Brandt. He is a realtor who makes a specialty of land development."

"So that's Brandt! The man who bought the old Pastor place! I have refused to meet him since my return to Kingscourt. Until last winter I have been away for months every year. What colossal impertinence of Phyllis to bring—Phyl dear—so good of you to come, and your husband, too. I know how men hate garden parties," Serena Farr crooned. She looked inquiringly at the white-haired man who was staring at the girl beside her.

"We brought our neighbor, Donald Brandt, to meet you, Miss Serena. Mahomet and the Mountain stuff. He is a coin collector. I thought that you—"

"Phyllis, stop chattering and meet my niece, Sonia Carson."

"I'm mad to meet her. Why didn't you come to my house-warming with your cousin Michael?" The woman's voice was that of a spoiled child; her red lips pouted.

Sonia met her eyes with their curiously wide irises—had suspicion or dislike narrowed their lids—murmured an answer, before she looked up at Brandt.

"You are the last person I expected to meet here."

"Then you will acknowledge our acquaintance? I held my breath for an instant."

His booming voice attracted the attention of guests passing. Sonia's face was warm with embarrassment.

"Why shouldn't I acknowledge your acquaintance?" She kept her voice low in the hope that it might suggest that he modulate his. "You aren't a Big Shot in disguise, or any little thing like that, are you?"

His laugh was loud and indulgent. "I am eminently respectable. Why didn't you tell me long ago that you were related to the Farrs?"

"Do you mean that you have not heard the romantic details of the return of the prodigal—or words to that effect? The story shook the countryside for a day or two. I was bitter against them"—that's the truth at least, Sonia comforted herself—"then I lost my job, was ill, and became panicky about my nephew Dicky. I looked up the family, presented my credentials—and here I am."

"I have been out of town for a week. That's why I missed the news. I—How are you, Farr?"

Sonia hoped that Michael had not seen her start of surprise. As she looked up at him, his curt, "Will you marry me?" flared through her mind. Where had he come from? She had not seen him since her arrival at Kingscourt. His aunt had given the indefinite information that he was out of town, but Mrs. D'Arcy had said that he had been at her party. Was he keeping away from his home because she was there? Perhaps he had been investigating her claim that Dicky was his brother's son. What a contrast his lean brown face, his smooth dark hair was to the ruddy skin and the white hair of Donald Brandt which the sunlight turned to spun silver.

A tense pause. A pause full of wireless feelers reaching out, of dramatic possibilities and latent animosities.

"Welcome to our city," she said flippantly, and then hated herself for the outworn cliché.

"Thank you—Sonia. It is good to get here. Serena, it would be tactless to suggest that you are tired, but have you two had anything to eat or drink?"

"I was about to suggest to Miss Carson that she come over to that empty table and let me get her something," Donald Brandt cut in smoothly. "Will you?"

Sonia looked at Serena Farr. She encouraged.

"Go, dear. Michael, bring me a chair, please. My shoes are tired."

Sonia lingered. "Can't I loosen the straps, Miss Serena?"

"Run along! Run along! Don't treat me as if I were

44

an old woman to be waited on." Sonia heard her add in a low voice to her nephew:

"Jim came. I suppose the ubiquitous Bigges—I'd like to wring his neck—rushed him off again to keep an appointment."

As Sonia and Donald Brandt strolled away, his eyes met hers with disturbing intentness. He stopped at a sun dial and followed the words on the bronze with a meticulously manicured finger:

" 'I ONLY MARK THE HOURS THAT SHINE' This is a shining hour for me, Miss Carson."

He drew a pastel pink chair from a pastel pink table.

"Sit here. I hope you appreciate the care I have shown in selecting settings which will complement your stunning frock. One can't associate with artistic architects without becoming color conscious. I'll be back in a minute with something to eat and drink."

"Your stunning frock." Sonia repeated the words as she watched him cross to the marquée. Evidently he knew smart clothes when he saw them. Her gown was lovely. What a piece of luck that Tom's wife, Jane, should have turned over her summer wardrobe to her. She had written:

> "Tom's brother has died. Tom insists that I go into black. Can you beat it? I am sending my colored clothes to you. They'll become you. You've worn my things before—Tom is ready to bite because you won't let him help you with money—don't be stuffy because there are so many. Rejoice and be glad."

She had rejoiced as she had peeped into the boxes which had arrived by her cousin's truck while she was at Michael Farr's office that epoch-making morning wearing a gray suit Jane had sent her not long before. The clothes were like manna dropping from heaven. Tom Nash wasn't really her cousin; her mother and father had brought him up when his parents died. She had stubbornly refused to take money from him. Clothes which his wife could not use were different. She adored clothes—and a long lost niece of the Farr family needed them here.

Elbows on the table, chin in her clasped hands, she looked up at the stone house with its colorful, crowded window boxes, at the terrace with its inviting white wicker chairs with their white cushions bound with green. The Farr home! Guy had said little about it in those distant days, but he had told enough to give an impression of its importance. He had talked of the time when he would take Ruby there.

How credulous her sister had been. If Ruby had been credulous, she, herself, had been incredibly blind. Guy had pursued her in a whirlwind courtship first. When she had turned him down with a contemptuous expression of her opinion of him, why hadn't she suspected from his sullen silence that he was planning a reprisal? Behind her back he had won Ruby. Perhaps had she been more politic, had she disguised her feelings and kept him devoted, she could have saved Ruby, could have made her realize that the man was vain and shallow. But she had detested him too passionately to think of diplomacy. Luckily Michael Farr had no suspicion that she had at one time attracted his brother.

She looked across the lawn. Serena Farr was seated and surrounded by men. She was laughing and talking gaily now, there was no trace of her late emotion on her animated face. Sonia's eyes traveled beyond her to the lake, a rumpled mass of blue-green water flecked with white. Luminous clouds, faintly pink, piled like puff balls on the horizon beyond it, disintegrated and piled again. A sliver of silver moon was riding high in the clear sky. How little she had suspected when, in desperation, she had gone to Michael Farr's office, that she would be sitting here, the guest of honor at a garden fête at Kingscourt, the very button on the cap of county society. When she thought of the deception which was being carried on to shield Guy Farr, she was tempted to cry out:

"It's a lie!"

She had burned with embarrassment when Doctor Neville had said that he had known her mother. How quickly the expression of his eyes had changed. Had he concluded that she was an impostor? She thought of Dicky and of the change in him. The smart of her conscience eased. One week in this lovely country had wrought magic. The child's flesh was hardening; his skin was browning; his legs were liberally dotted with bruises, old and new, and he was developing a talent for mischief which amazed and frightened her. Were his father's traits cropping up in him already, or was it—

A quarter dropped into her lap. She looked up at Donald Brandt smiling down at her with questioning eyes. He waited until a servant had placed cups, glasses, and plates of sandwiches and cakes on the table. As the man left, he seated himself opposite.

"I brought a little of everything not knowing your tastes —you have stonily refused to dine or lunch with me, remember. That filthy lucre is for your thoughts. I never carry pennies. They wear out my pockets, so I had to substitute the quarter. You looked as if you were a thousand miles away."

With one finger on the piece of silver, Sonia outlined a design on the pastel pink surface of the table.

"I was not far. I was thinking of my young nephew and wondering whether the doctrine of original sin was to be credited with his outbreak of mischief, some remote primordial tree, or if it were the six year old daughter of the superintendent of Kingscourt who was leading him astray; she has taken him on as a playmate. I discovered them in the highway the other day throwing stones at passing automobiles. I can't believe that Dicky thought that thrilling pastime up for himself."

"Doubtless as usual the woman tempted him." Brandt lightly disposed of the child problem. "Does all this—" the wave of his hand included lake and house and gardens— "mean that you have given up your profession, that you no longer feel the yen to plan houses?"

Sonia hastily set down the teacup she had lifted.

"Give up my profession! Of course not. What put that fantastic idea into your head?"

"Is it so fantastic? As one of the heirs to this luxury—"

"But I'm not . . ." Sonia caught back the denial and went on somewhat breathlessly: "I'm not happy unless I'm—I'm terribly busy." Her heart skipped a beat as she met his eyes which seemed to have sharpened to steel points. "Of course you have heard the story going the rounds that—that—the run-away Farr daughter and her heirs were cut off from the inheritance."

"That and a lot more—a whole lot more." Brandt's eyes were on a glass he was twirling. "I'm glad to know that you intend to go on with your work. I have a grand development plan up my sleeve."

"I hope that it won't be prestidigitated into thin air as the last one was. Do try one of these toasted mushroom sandwiches; they are luscious."

"No, thanks, I prefer a cigarette. Have one?"

He opened a gold case and offered it.

"Now I will say, 'No, thanks.' "

He looked at her above the flame of his lighter.

"You are an enigma to me, Miss Carson. You don't smoke, you 'hate cocktails,' try as I would I couldn't lure you to one of my penthouse parties, and yet you are as modern in your outlook as any girl I have met. What's the answer?"

"Perhaps it is my line to be enigmatic. Perhaps that's what makes me so nice."

He leaned across the table. "Then you realize that you seem extremely 'nice' to me?"

Sonia's heart did its queer trick of stopping and galloping on again. "What the dickens is it about that man's eyes which seems to take my breath?" she thought, before she answered gaily:

"Don't mind my foolishness. The let-up for a while from earning daily bread—with marmalade on the side—for Dicky and me has gone straight to my head. My mind has thrown off ballast until it is lighter than air. I neither smoke nor drink because I can't afford to acquire expensive habits, and a working girl has no time for wild parties." Those were not the only reasons, but all that he would understand, she assured herself. "I could die eating those sandwiches, but I won't. Tell me about the new development," she urged eagerly.

"Nature should provide eyes as brilliant as yours with blinkers." There was a hint of exultation in his voice. "I am planning to start with five houses—much larger than the last ones we talked about. The land I have just contracted for is top-notch and will stand for a more expensive type. Immediately I thought of you. I know that I can make a tremendous success of the experiment."

"You might say, 'We.' What I do will count, won't it?"

"Of course, though the whole enterprise is my conception. Now that you are in the social swim will you have time for work?"

"Time! Nothing else but. What is there to do here? Miss—Aunt Serena, who has gone quite mad about Dicky, superintends Libby, the housekeeper, who superintends the little nursemaid I brought to help with the boy. I hardly see him until after his supper when I read to him and tuck him in. This arrangement is only for the summer. Of course I want work. You don't think I intend to live on the Farrs forever, do you?"

"The Farrs hope that you will live with them—forever," a voice said behind her.

Sonia twisted round in her chair. Why hadn't Donald Brandt warned her that Michael Farr was approaching? He must have seen him. She had said nothing she would not have said to his face, but the family had tried to be kind and she didn't want to appear to be discussing its affairs with a comparative stranger. She remembered a point of strategy— put the other fellow in the wrong before he has a chance to put you in—and said with a trace of indignation in her voice:

"I didn't hear you stealing up behind me."

"Do you expect to hear the clatter of footsteps on the

lawn? Aunt Serena wants you to assist at speeding the departing guests. Sorry to break up this tête-a-tête."

At the moment Sonia cordially hated Michael Farr, hated him because as she met his eyes that absurd "will you marry me?" danced through her mind.

"It wasn't a tête-a-tête. It was a business conference. I—"

"I was trying to persuade Miss Carson to take on a piece of work for me," Donald Brandt cut in suavely.

"Miss Carson doesn't need work."

"Of course I need work—Cousin Michael. I am simply mad to get to work. There is nothing to do here. Nothing. I have been thinking of advertising for a job—it pays to advertise," she concluded flippantly in an effort to lighten the tension she felt in the atmosphere.

"And I have one waiting for you—near home, if you call this your home. Farr, I wanted that piece of land across the lake we signed up for yesterday for several reasons, one of them to give Miss—your cousin a chance to work out some of the corking ideas she has."

"Why should she take a job?"

"But—" Sonia began stormily. Somewhere a village clock sonorously chimed six.

"Aunt Serena is waiting for you."

Sonia angrily resented the compelling power of Michael Farr's steady eyes. She started toward the waiting hostess. As he picked up her gloves and fell into step beside her, she looked over her shoulder.

"I accept your offer, Mr. Brandt."

"Both of them?" he asked, and laughed.

"Now what did he mean by that?" Sonia wondered, as, chin slightly raised,—to express disdain, she hoped—she walked beside Michael across the lawn which was as vivid and soft as emerald green velvet.

"So—Brandt has made you two offers?" Farr mused aloud. "Was one of them by any chance matrimonial?"

"Suppose it were? Suppose I accepted it? Just because you dictated that I should come here doesn't mean that I cannot accept an offer of marriage, does it?"

"Depends upon who makes it. I asked you first, remember. You turned mine down, pronto."

Sonia stopped and looked up at him in exasperation.

"Don't remind me of your fantastic request. Every time I think of it I rage."

"Don't think of it."

"I can't help it. It flashes in my mind like one of those

49

Neon signs—whenever I see—" She broke off abruptly. How dumb of her to let him know that she remembered.

"I take back that, 'Don't think of it.' "

His low, amused voice tinged Sonia's face with pink, her angry eyes met his. She opened her lips. Before she could speak, he added:

"Because the request still stands."

Chapter VI

Sonia could not decide whether it were her conscience, her mind, or her heart which burned and smarted as if recently in contact with a clump of nettles as an hour later in her mirror-walled dressing-room she stepped out of the filmy chartreuse frock and slipped into a crêpe house-coat the exact shade of an American Beauty rose.

She frowned at the girl looking back at her as she smoothed the shining waves of her dark hair. She had been abominably rude to Michael Farr, but hadn't he brought it on himself? How dared he remind her that his offer of marriage stood while all the time he made her feel that he didn't trust her? Did he think her so provincial that she did not recognize a sardonic, sophisticated man when she met one? He brought out the worst in her—she hadn't realized before her capacity for being disagreeable—had, since the day she had entered his office in terror and despair. That miserable flu, that curious physical sense of drifting out to sea on a mysterious tide, conscious only that she was leaving Dicky alone, had been responsible for sending her to him, had made her break a part of her promise to Ruby, a promise she never should have made, she knew that now. The other part, to write to Guy Farr that both his wife and child had died, she had carried out. Even as she had written the words she had hated doing it. A lie was so cowardly. But, in her shock and grief, in the knowledge that her sister could not live, nothing had seemed too hard to do for her. Ruby had begged her to take the boy and keep him where his father never would find him, to bring him up so that when he reached manhood he would have been trained to a sense of duty and honor which would hold him fast against temptations which would warp his character. How lightly she had promised. She realized now that a growing boy needed the sympathetic understanding of a man as well as of a woman.

And then, as if she had not made mistakes enough, she had come to Kingscourt as a long lost relative. She was plunged in a sea of deceit to her neck. All she could do at present was to tread water and hope against hope that someone would fling her a life preserver before she went down for the third time—or a raft. Rafts seemed to be Michael Farr's idea of rescue.

After all, one got nothing for nothing, she thought, as Dicky's happy laugh came from her boudoir where the nurse was giving him his supper. The surety that the child was gaining in health and strength should make up amply for her uneasy conscience—but it didn't—quite.

"Why should your conscience be uneasy?" she demanded of herself. "Why can't you take life as it comes? Why dramatize it? One would think that you were foisting a pretender on the house of Farr, that Dicky was not Guy's child."

From the long window she could see men busy on the stretch of emerald green lawn. All signs of Miss Serena's late party were being removed. Eyes on the still lake, streaked with crimson reflections of the afterglow, Sonia tried to visualize a few of the persons she had met. Doctor Jim Neville had been etched on her memory indelibly; the couple called "the D'Arcys" and Donald Brandt were clear-cut. They stood out like figures on a screen. Mrs. D'Arcy was the girl who had thrown Michael over. She had recognized her at once from her pictures which had been front-page news until a new sensation had driven them off. How could a man so intelligent as he—she would grant him intelligence—trust a girl like that, to say nothing of loving her? One had but to look at her to know that she was false-hearted. Men certainly were easy marks—some of them—no one could impose on Guy Farr. He reserved that pastime for his philandering self. Why think of him? She must keep the past out of her mind. It was sheer waste of strength and emotion which she needed today—not yesterday or even tomorrow—today.

Donald Brandt was today. She liked him. He was sophisticated of course, but not sardonic. She had liked him from the moment the head of the firm for which she was working had introduced him to her and had recommended her as being the person to work out the houses for his development scheme. She had been tremendously thrilled and excited by the chance to show what she could do—and then, almost over night, the project had collapsed. It had not been Donald Brandt's fault, it was just one of the happenings of this unpredictable decade. Curious that he should have bought a house in this neighborhood. She had turned down his numerous suggestions that they dine or lunch together to talk over plans. There was no place for a man in her life—the one who had touched Ruby's had wrought havoc enough—she intended to fill it with Dicky and her work. She didn't even know whether Brandt was married. Would he buy a country place if he were not? What difference did it make to her? What she wanted was work, and it looked as if he might give it to her.

Work. She had been working since she was twenty without a rest—until now. Five years was too long to keep in harness without a vacation. She had not dared stop. It would have been different if her mother and father had lived, she would have had much of luxury and culture, he had been on the road to fortune. Guy Farr would not have come into her life. If only Ruby had never seen him and had lived. It was a strange and lonely feeling to be the last grown-up of one's family.

Had she been right in her decision to go to Michael Farr? Decision! Nothing so sane. It hadn't been a decision, it had been unadulterated panic. He had not been the only one to clutch at a raft. Hadn't she done the same thing when she had appealed to him? There she was again, back in the past. Nothing was more futile than to get panicky over what had been done. She would much better get ready for what was coming. Donald Brandt's eyes had set her pulses quick-stepping. Michael Farr's had started chills tobogganing down her spine and creeping up.

The nursemaid appeared at the door. Her slanting black eyes and her clipped black hair made Sonia think of a Chinese doll which had been a prized though not a loved possession. She never had been able to imagine expression into its wax face. This girl's was as inscrutable.

"Dicky is ready for you to read to him, Miss Carson."

"I will come at once, Nanette."

The modernity of the boudoir which had been assigned to her surprised Sonia afresh every time she entered it. One didn't expect to find such ultra-fashionable furnishings in a house so old as Kingscourt. The green brocatelle which covered the walls was reflected in two Chippendale mirrors; a Chippendale secretary housed a radio. There was a fire place and long recessed windows. Pale beige silk sacking covered the furniture. The pillows on the broad lounge were in pastel pinks and blues and amber. She had added her Lares and Penates. Silver boxes: bits of choice brocades and embroideries: family photographs in frames which she had picked up in the memorable months she had spent across the sea: a few of her favorite books. They made her feel at home.

Dicky, in blue and white striped pajamas, flung himself at her and encircled her with his arms.

"I like you, Sonia," he said with a little catch in his breath. "I haven't seen you all day."

She drew a low chair to the window and lifted him into her lap. His head snuggled to her shoulder as a chicken nestles under its mother's wing. She pressed her lips against the silky red-gold curls.

"I have missed you, Most Dear." She picked up Edward Lear's Nonsense Verses from a low stand. "What shall it be tonight, Dicky?" She knew his answer even as she asked the question.

"T'Owl an' the Pussy-Cat first, an' then—"

"Come in!" Sonia called in answer to a knock.

The door to the hall opened a trifle. A shaggy white head with a square black nose, one black ear, and two bright beadlike eyes poked into the room. Short white legs followed. The Sealyham looked at the boy. The boy looked at the dog for a startled instant. With a joyous whoop he dashed forward.

"It's the dog who looks like shwedded coconut, Sonia! See the ticket on him. What does it say?"

Legs akimbo, Dicky sat on the floor. His eyes were like sparkling blue jewels. The dog wagged his short white upright tail as if not quite sure what his next move should be.

Sonia dropped to her knees. With one arm tight about the child that she might snatch him out of harm's way should the visitor prove unfriendly, she lifted the tag and read aloud:

"My name is Shredded Coconut. I'm called Shreddy for short. I've come to live with a boy named Richard, Dicky for short. Know where I'll find him?"

With another whoop the boy flung himself on the dog.

"I'm Dicky! I'm Dicky!" he shouted. Together they rolled on the rug.

"Be careful, Most Dear. Remember that Shreddy doesn't know you very well. His coat does look like shredded coconut, doesn't it?

The boy sat up and looked at the dog who, with mouth open and tongue dangling, blinked beady eyes at him.

"He knows me now, don't you, Shweddy? See, he's laughin'."

Sonia smiled in sympathy. The dog certainly was grinning.

"Is he my vewy own, Sonia? Just like I'm your vewy own boy?"

"He said he had come to live with you, Most Dear.

Suppose we let him lie on the rug until he gets acquainted while I read The Owl and the Pussy-Cat?"

"All wighty. G'wan!"

Sonia settled his head more comfortably against her shoulder and picked up the book.

"The Owl and the Pussy-Cat went to sea,
    In a beautiful pea-green boat;
    They took some honey—"

"Shweddy's gone to sleep!" The hoarse whisper snapped open one of the dog's beady eyes.

Sonia closed the book. "He is tired probably. Perhaps he came from the city today and wants to go to bed."

"May I have him in my woom? Nanette, look! See my dog? He's a pwesent!"

Not a muscle of the little nursmaid's face moved as she stood in the doorway. The arrival of a strange dog was all in the day's work to her.

"That Filipino Johnny brought up what he called a dog couch to keep the pup out of drafts on the floor—in case Dicky wanted him to sleep in his room, Mr. Farr said, Miss Sonia. Can you beat it?"

No matter what he thought of her, Michael Farr did like Dicky, Sonia assured herself, as later in a white lace frock, her long jade earrings swinging, she ran down the stairs. Michael Farr stepped out of the living room as she reached the hall. He looked even taller and leaner in his dinner clothes. His white mess jacket accentuated the brown of his skin.

"I'm sorry to be late." She was indignantly conscious of her breathlessness. "I always tuck Dicky in and hear his prayers, but he was so excited tonight over his new possession that I thought he never would settle down. It was wonderful of you to remember about the dog."

"A boy without a dog and a dog without a boy aren't getting the fun out of life to which young things are entitled. My man Johnny is unpacking a truck full of toys in the garage. Among other things there is a wading pool to be set up, with a seat in the corner, and an engine—a gorgeous fire-department red—which runs by electricity with a bell which clangs and an honest-to-goodness siren."

"Please! Please don't do so much for him."

"I had the time of my life selecting the stuff. You need not be troubled because you are late. Serena is dining in her apartment, and I told Elkins we would have dinner on the terrace."

"Alone!"

Sonia could have cheerfully bitten through her tongue for having been party to that exclamation.

"Why not? You are not afraid of me, are you?"

"Don't be foolish. I thought possibly some of the guests might have remained."

The great windows in the glass-enclosed end of the terrace had been dropped. The world was so still that the flames of the two tall yellow candles—the exact shade of the freesia between them on the small table—burned straight and clear.

"How quiet! I can almost hear the earth spinning. The extra hour daylight saving provides is a gift straight from the gods, isn't it? See how light it is outside," Sonia said, in a nervous desire to break the silence between them as he drew out her chair.

"This is the best hour of the twenty-four to me," Michael Farr confided, as he seated himself opposite.

"Twilight does things to me too. It seems to wrap my spirit in something soft and magically soothing after a hard, bustling day. It is as uplifting as music, as spiritually satisfying as color, as warming as my belief in God."

How could she have turned her soul inside out like that? Sonia demanded of herself, as the eyes opposite, disconcertingly cool, looked straight and deep into hers. She felt her color come stealing up. She said flippantly:

"I must have read that somewhere. Ideas stick to my memory. Do all the men who were here this afternoon commute to the gay metropolis?"

"Most of them. Man must work."

"I have never seen so many at an afternoon affair."

"Men like Serena. She is such a real person."

Conversation went smoothly after that. With the huge strawberries to be dipped by their hulls in miniature pyramids of sugar, they discussed the spring plays; with the boned squabs, guava jelly, and melting green peas, they ripped up a novel or two; with the cool, crisp tomato salad, they switched to national politics—a certain dispute over a code always would be connected in Sonia's memory with the most delectable puffed cheese balls she ever had tasted.

"Serena—I feel terribly familiar but she won't permit me to call her aunt—told me that you are a candidate for Congress. She—"

Michael Farr laughed as Sonia hesitated. "You were about to say, weren't you, that she told you also that I hadn't a look-in? Time and the voters will tell. I don't expect to prove a miracle-man and make over the world, but I do expect to take a crack at crime prevention and make a dent at least. However, diligent politicians, a negligent public or voting list—and—I'm licked."

In spite of the doubt expressed, there was a note in his voice which made it the voice of a man whom no discouragement could daunt.

"Haven't you chosen the most dangerous and unpopular issue that you could possibly find?"

"I hope that it will prove dangerous to the crooks. Are these ices cold party, Elkins?" he inquired, as the butler set a peach with hectic cheeks before him.

"Yes, Mr. Michael. The caterer left them."

"That pink looks poisonous. Serve the coffee on the terrace."

Did Michael Farr intend to spend the evening with her, Sonia wondered, as a few moments later she sank into a low chair with a silver and porcelain cup of black hot coffee on the stand beside her.

A violet and opal dusk was stealing forward from the purple hills. The silver crescent moon, with one lonely, lovely star as lady-in-waiting, was slipping into the rose and lemon and jade tinted west. Beyond the lace-like iron gates which led to the sports center, the swimming pool was stippled with the reflections of low-hung golden stars as they blossomed slowly in a purple black sky. Across the expanse of velvety lake, lights were flickering in distant houses. The regular dip of a paddle stirred the fragrant air. The sound ceased, then came the twang of a ukulele.

Michael Farr leaned forward.

"Listen! Johnny, my Filipino boy, doubtless has the gardener's daughter on the lake in a canoe. He does the troubadour thing rather well."

A man's voice floated across the water:

> " 'I've told every little star
> Just how sweet I think you are
> Why haven't I told you?' "

The song died away. A paddle dipped. Sonia threw off the spell of the music and the twilight and said lightly:

"An old song, which by this time has slipped into the limbo from which odd overshoes, loaned books, lost faith, return no more forever, but I love it."

"Do you believe that lost faith never returns? Once I believed that too, but now, I wonder." Michael Farr cleared his voice. "At least, Johnny gives old Debil Disillusion no chance to get his claws on him. He drops one girl and picks up another before they so much as dent his heart. But that isn't what I lured you here to talk about."

Dusk had reached the terrace, but Sonia could see Michael Farr's grave eyes as he hesitated. A shiver quivered through her. Why, she wondered. She had nothing to fear. She bit her unsteady lips before she encouraged:

"Then you had a reason. I suspected it. When I see the firing line ahead, I prefer to walk straight up to it. Tell me at once, please."

"There will be no firing line. I have been to the town where Richard was born. I found the record of his birth—"

"Well?"

"His mother's name is recorded as Ruby Carson."

"I told you that was her name."

"I know. But the father's name—"

Sonia leaned forward. "Why hesitate? What did the record say?"

Even in the dusk she was aware of Michael Farr's keen eyes as he answered:

"Father unknown."

Chapter VII

"Father unknown."

The words reverberated in Sonia's mind. Ruby, even in her weakness, had insisted upon giving the physician who had attended her *accouchement* the data for record. She had not told her sister that she had refused to name the father of her child. Poor little girl. How she must have hated Guy Farr; how determined she had been to protect her boy from him. She had been willing to slip out of life trusting her sister, and her sister had gone panicky. Sonia said abruptly:

"Now more than ever you will think us adventurers."

"I still believe that Richard is Guy's son, but I can't understand why the name of the father was not given."

Sonia looked unseeingly into the purple dusk. The swimming pool and the lake beyond were mere glimmers. A little breeze had sprung up. She watched a meteor hiss across the sky leaving no trail.

"Must I go all over that again? I have told you that we had intended never to let your brother know he had a son, and then—my conscience, my sense of justice, inflamed doubtless by that touch of flu, sent me pell-mell to you. Have you written to Guy?"

"Yes."

"How long before you will hear from him?"

"It may be weeks, perhaps months."

"Suppose he swears there is no truth in my story?"

"Time enough to consider that when we hear. Meanwhile Dicky is getting some flesh on his bones. I hope that you are not too bored?"

"Bored! I never was bored in my life. I may be if I have nothing to do. But I shall have. Donald Brandt—"

Sonia broke off the sentence to listen. Was that the smooth purr of a motor she heard? Was a boat banging against the float on the shore of the lake beyond the sportshouse? How clearly one could hear voices and laughter. The boat party was approaching the house! Friends coming to call? She would disappear.

Michael Farr caught her arm as she moved.

"Don't go!"

"But they are not coming to see me!"

"How do you know? I hear Brandt's booming voice. He certainly is not calling upon me."

"But I don't want to see him tonight."

"Neither do I. Come here."

He drew her quickly into the enclosed end of the terrace in the black shadow made by tall shrubs outside.

"Yoo-hoo! Yoo-hoo!"

At the gay call from the steps the hand on Sonia's arm tightened.

A man's petulant, not too steady voice just outside said:

"I told you that you wouldn't find anyone at home—to callers, Phyl. Farr told me that he was staying in town—"

"Don't lurch against me, Billy! If you would take that last drink you should have stayed at home. Don wanted to see the new niece—who are you and I to stand in the way of love's young dream."

Sonia shut her teeth hard in her lips to keep back a furious retort. Apparently the woman's implication roused no such reaction in Brandt. He laughed.

"Not so young, Phyllis. As I explained to you at length, I want Miss Carson to do some work for me. She not only is a competent draughtsman but her ideas are up to the minute."

"So are her clothes. That was a Chanel model she wore today if ever I saw one. Where did the money come from for it? Do you suppose Michael provided it that she might make a proper impression on the county?"

"Miss Carson dressed smartly long before she came to Kingscourt."

"I forgot that you and she were old friends, Donald.

Wonder how she likes the rooms which were done over for me. I hear that she and the child—whose child?—the county has its composite eyebrows raised as it buzzes with the question—are occupying my suite. I hope the adorable green boudoir I planned is becoming—Oh, come on, boys! This place has all the glitter and merry prattle of a mausoleum after the mourners have departed. My idea was to give Michael a whirl. But if he is in town—the chance of bringing the long lost niece down on us leaves me cold. Let's go!"

"Okay with me. I'm hot. B-boilin' hot. The King of France and twenty thousand men marched up the hill and then marched down. . . ."

Bill D'Arcy's voice thinned into a silly laugh and died away. An occasional word floated back from the garden path. As Sonia walked out on the open terrace she said to Michael Farr who followed:

"Never have I felt quite so foolish as when hiding in that corner. Why did we do it?"

"You said that you did not want to see Brandt, didn't you?"

"I did. I like him immensely—when I am not with him —but he is a sort of—of smothering person. He has one enmeshed in his plans, all signed, sealed, and delivered before one knows where one is. Hear that motor boat engine sputter."

"Billy D'Arcy is trying to start it, and from his voice when he was on the terrace I judged that his mind is a bit hazy. Then you are not keen to take the job Brandt offers?"

"I must do something. Dicky does not need me, except when I tuck him in at night. I have been accustomed to having every moment of my life full, I can't seem to adjust myself to gilded leisure."

"Other women manage."

"Because they grew up in it. If there were anything to do about the house—I adore home-making—but Kingscourt runs like a perfectly oiled, perfectly synchronized machine. I haven't a card mind, otherwise I might join Miss Serena—"

"Serena."

"My mistake. I forgot my new relations,—Cousin Michael. I must keep busy while I am waiting to hear from your brother. I even have thought of leasing that little white shop in the village and starting a bookbar. I adore books. I am sure I could sell them."

"You are restless, aren't you?"

"I'm not restless. I am looking toward the future. Suppose—just suppose that Guy Farr repudiates Dicky? I shall have the boy to bring up and educate. I must have money."

Leaning against the parapet, Michael held a lighter to his cigarette. As it flamed, Sonia could see the crease between his brows, two sparks which were his dark, unsmiling eyes. Evidently he did not intend to reply to that last supposition of hers. What had she expected? What could he say? He abandoned thin ice.

"It is evident that Brandt admires your—work. He has been hot on my trail for a piece of the lake shore, and yesterday I agreed to sell to him. I presume that this is the development for which he plans to engage you. He has the reputation in the business world of being a champion picker. As he has set his seal of approval on you—I am sure that you won't stand for architectural atrocities on our lake front."

"Then you won't mind if I take the contract? Not that it will make any difference whether you do or not; I shall take it."

"Then asking my consent so prettily was mere form?"

"I try to be a perfect lady."

"As it will make no difference what I say, I solemnly give my consent. You will need a workroom, won't you?"

"Nothing more than that adorable boudoir." She remembered Phyllis D'Arcy's flippant comment on the rooms which had been planned for her. "I'm—I'm sorry that it is I —in them and not—"

Michael Farr was but a dark blur against faint starlight as he stood by the parapet. Sonia could not see his face, only the lighted end of his cigarette which alternately glowed and smoldered.

"Don't be sorry about—anything. I told you the first day that you came to Kingscourt what had happened. You ought to be glad that the lady found out her mistake before it was too late. I hope that green is your color."

"Don't be bitter. I am sorry. I'm terribly sorry."

"Why? Phyllis had been lying to me for months. If she would do that before marriage, what chance of enduring happiness would there be after? Don't waste sympathy on me. Only my pride hurts now."

"A woman who would do that to you is not worth even hurt pride. Good-night."

"Must you go in? It is but the edge of the evening."

"I want to look in on Serena, if it is not too late. She has been wonderful to me."

"I'll go up with you. Half the fun of a party is talking it over."

Neither of them spoke as they mounted the broad stairs in the hall side by side, as they walked along the gallery.

"She had been lying to me for months."

The sentence echoed over and over in Sonia's mind with the monotony of a merry-go-round. What did Michael Farr really think of the deception to which she was party, posing as a long lost relative? Why worry? It had been his own suggestion. She could understand now his coldness and bitterness. If only she had not called him a wooden Indian. How unfair it was to judge a person. How little one knew what thoughts were going on behind the mask of a face.

Serena Farr looked up from a card-laden table as the angular Bates admitted them to her living room. Her orchid evening gown was a lovely bit of color against the ivory background. Sonia hesitated.

"Are you going out?"

"Out? No. Why?"

"Serena dresses for dinner even when she dines alone," Michael Farr explained lightly.

His aunt looked up at the portrait of the stern-faced man in white clothes.

"I was not dining alone. I dined with my father. Sit down, both of you."

"I hope you are not tired, Serena."

"Tired! Why should I be? I eat up parties. They make me positively skittish. It was amusing meeting some of the girls with whom I grew up. Sonia, did you notice the woman in the old-ladyish print whose skin was drab, whose eyes were set in sunbursts of wrinkles, whose thin mouth seemed a mere slit in her face? She hadn't even the saving grace of rebuilt teeth. She said to me:

" 'Serena, what are women my age wearing in Paris?'

"I looked at her for a minute—a woman who is letting herself go to seed; she is six years younger than I—before I said:

" 'Darling, there are no women your age in Paris.' "

Michael chuckled. "Ever hear the derivation of the word sarcasm, Serena? It comes from a Greek word which means—to bite."

"A woman who lets herself go like that deserves to be bitten. It isn't that she can't afford the upkeep, she has permitted the age complex to coil tight about her spirit and squeeze out every vestige of youth. I heard voices outside. Who came up through the garden, Michael?"

"The D'Arcys and Brandt."

"Did you see them?"

"No. Cousin—Sonia and I remained in the shadow. Welcoming callers after your party struck us as being anti-climax."

"The D'Arcys! Phyllis is putting on the clinging vine

61

act, I noticed; she is beginning to twine about that Brandt man. Why not? Clinging vines still smother oaks and will to the end of time. And the maddening thing about it is that oaks eat it up. Talk about a changed world. Men haven't changed. They still preen their feathers when a girl looks up at them with worshiping eyes and murmurs,

" 'You're so big and strong!' "

Sonia laughed. "Don't you believe in romance, Serena?"

"Thank heaven I do. I belong to a generation which believed in it, which shivered a little when a man's eyes looked deep into ours, when a man's lips set hard, when his face whitened—it really happened—when he asked a girl to marry him. But now I understand that a proposal is to be presented with the light touch:

" 'What do you say to trying a three room and kitchenette apartment with me, gal?' "

"So that's the way it is being done now! I thought there was something wrong with my technique," Michael declared.

The laughter in his voice, in his eyes as they met hers stirred Sonia's resentment. Evidently his mad proposal to her had become a joke to him.

Serena Farr dropped her cards. "Michael, I haven't seen you so light-hearted, so like your young self, since Destiny, or whatever was in the saddle, took a shot at the world's iridescent glass ball of prosperity and blew it to smithereens. You have carried such a load of responsibility and have shouldered the burdens of so many during these last years."

"Forget it, Serena. You make me feel like a stuffed shirt. Can't you see that I'm on the crest of the wave now?" He laughed as he raised his arm in theatrical defiance.

" 'We ride the gale!' You had a grand party."

"It was a good party, wasn't it? I think we put our deception across successfully."

Sonia flushed at the word "deception." She said hurriedly:

"Across and then some. 'One would know you were a Farr, my dear, if one met you in the Arctic wilds, or Timbuctoo, or any other old place.' If that was said to me once it was said fifty times."

"That must be what is meant by crowd psychology. You don't look in the least like the family. So Brandt came again. It is plain enough what he is after. Sit down, Michael, don't prowl."

At the mantel Michael Farr picked up the ivory tiger. "Did you talk with him, Serena?"

"For a few moments just before Phyl D'Arcy dragged him away."

"Did he speak of the land?"

"Land! What land?"

"Evidently he didn't. I have agreed to sell him a strip between the projected highway and the lake, the tract with the grove of silver birches."

"Michael! Are things so bad as that?"

"Things are not bad at all. He made a fantastically extravagant offer. With financial conditions as they are, I decided that it was flying in the face of Providence to turn it down. His plan is to develop fifty acres, dividing it into ten-acre places. What is the use of paying steadily rising taxes on vacant land? Besides, the development will provide work for any number of men—"

"And, don't forget, for a struggling architect as well. Mr. Brandt has engaged me to plan the houses, Serena."

"He has! What do you think of that, Michael?"

"What difference does it make what I think? Criticizing a girl because she wants to go into business is as out of date as thinking a woman fast because she uses a lipstick."

"What effect will selling part of the estate have on your candidacy, Michael?"

"It ought to help, though that is not why I am doing it. My political opponents are eternally haranguing about the narrowness of my viewpoint, that I am of the special privilege class—I wonder if they really know what they are talking about, or if they have picked up a catch-phrase. That I know nothing of the revolutionary ideas which are epidemic, that I know only high finance, that I am ignorant of the point of view of the laboring man. With building going on across the lake, I will make it my business to get his point of view. I have been doing a tall amount of thinking this last week."

This last week! It was little more than a week since she had gone to Michael Farr's office, Sonia remembered. Had he decided to sell the land because of Dicky? He had said that the child's future would be provided for. Was he making sure of money in these tricky times by selling to Donald Brandt? Had his income been slashed like every other income? Miss Serena had exclaimed: "Are things so bad as that?" Had his reason for having Dicky and herself come to Kingscourt been to save expense? If so, she was thankful that she had come, but the idea that Michael Farr would have to economize was fantastic.

"If you are going to sleep, Sonia, you'd better go to bed."

Sonia laughed and rose.

"Did I look in a somnolent state? I wasn't. I was

visualizing the type of house I would design for a ten-acre place on that beautiful lake front. Good-night, Miss Serena, and thanks heaps for that gorgeous party."

"I have told you before to stop 'Mr.' and 'Missing' the family, Sonia, or the neighbors will start a whispering campaign. They are beginning to whet their tongues now; I felt it this afternoon. Who is knocking at this time of the evening?"

Michael Farr opened the door. Elkins took a step into the room, whispered hoarsely:

"They've just phoned from The Cedars, Mr. Michael. Mr. D'Arcy has had a horrible accident—fallen into the lake—they can't find him. Mrs. D'Arcy wants you to come at once."

"Good God! Bill was on the terrace a few minutes ago. Come on, Elkins, we'll go by boat. You may be able to help."

Michael Farr charged into the hall without a backward glance. His aunt tapped her fingers on the table, smoothed her slightly sagging chin with the back of her hand.

"So—Phyllis will be free! She will weep and weep— 'wet weather is good for transplanting'—and promptly marry again."

Sonia shivered. "Elkins didn't say that Mr. D'Arcy was drowned, Miss Serena. People have been resuscitated after they have been in the water a long time. I can't believe he has gone. To be here laughing and singing under the stars one minute and then—"

"He was lucky to go while he was still laughing. Phyllis would take the joy out of life for any man. Oh, dear—oh, dear!"

"What is it, Serena? Were you so fond of Bill D'Arcy?"

Serena Farr's eyes opened wide. "Fond of Bill D'Arcy! I never met the man before today. I am thinking of the effect this will have on Michael. He and Phyllis have been neighbors since they were children. Her father lost everything in the crash. She and her mother flung their problems on Michael—everybody sooner or later flings his or her problems on Michael's shoulders—look at me. When I'm in trouble I feel that if I can put my head on Michael's shoulder and feel his arms about me, things will straighten out. Phyllis parked her head on his shoulder, all right. I saw the engagement coming, but what could I do? Michael is a man grown. That girl may wear my pearls and emeralds after all. She will be after him again—and—and—"

"Get him probably," Sonia finished quickly.

Chapter VIII

"Her husband goes abroad with her every spring, the other man trails along on the next ship, and the husband returns to this country—and there you are. An outwardly respectable triangle which doesn't fool anybody. Your play, Sonia."

"Why doesn't she get a quiet, dignified divorce and marry her lover?"

"Lovers of married women are usually not keen to enter the holy bonds of matrimony. A sequence means cards of the same suit, my dear."

"I'm sorry, Serena."

Sonia hastily retrieved the three cards she had triumphantly laid down. She glanced surreptitiously at the clock. Had she been playing only an hour? It seemed a million since Elkins had brought that tragic summons for Michael Farr. She laid down three kings.

"But doesn't the husband know, Serena?"

"Of course he knows, so does everyone else, but they turn glass eyes on the situation. Here's another king! That's the sort of mess Michael will land in if he marries Phyllis. Draw."

"Perhaps he won't care. Who was it said the biggest men are made in the hardest schools? Wouldn't that apply to marriage? Surely a marriage which weathers prosperity and adversity, storm and stress, which comes through with flags of honest love flying—if somewhat tattered—is big. You see, I still believe passionately in what are now called the old-fashioned ideas of morals and manners."

"So does Michael. That is why my depression touches a new low when I think that Phyllis may attract him again."

For an instant the exquisite room, with its off-white walls, silver and white curtains, and yellow roses in dull golden bowls, faded from Sonia's consciousness like a picture on a silver screen. She saw again the age-darkened panels of the library, the portrait of the man in the blue coat above the carved mantel, and Michael Farr seated on the corner of the desk, his hand on the French phone; again she met his burning eyes, heard him say:

"Will you marry me?"

Then the color had rushed to his hair. She could feel hers coming up now as she remembered. Should she have said, "Yes" and saved him from Phyllis D'Arcy?

"Don't be an absolute idiot. If he hasn't sense to see what she is, he isn't worth saving," she told herself, and flung down three cards.

"You didn't mean to play those, Sonia. My dear, don't think me ungrateful if I say that I hope you are a better architect than you are card player. I'm afraid I have distracted your thoughts from the game by my chatter. It has been a treat to have someone with whom to gossip. Bates is as responsive as one of the stone gateposts. I have talked about everyone else; tell me something about yourself."

"There is so little to tell."

"Have you no people? Draw, girl, draw!"

Sonia picked up a card. "I must have some drifting about the world, I suppose, but the only relative with whom I keep in touch is an adopted cousin, Tom Nash."

"Adopted! Is he married?"

"Very much married. Jane, his wife, is a dear, but her eyes are as green as emeralds. If Tom so much as looks at another woman, she is set to tear out the siren's hair—not Tom's."

"Has he a roving eye?"

"Not in the way you mean. He is a great overgrown boy, who is still wondering how he made so much money; he would adore Kingscourt. He likes youth and gayety and pretty women—but he stops at liking."

"How does the jealous Jane feel about you?"

"Me?"

"You're a pretty woman, aren't you?"

Sonia laughed. "Thanks for those kind words. Jane knows me. She is wonderful to me and she adores Dicky. She longs for children. She and Tom have been married eight years and none have come. I think that is one reason she is so jealous of Tom. She thinks that she has failed him. She gives me all my clothes, that is, my on-parade clothes; I buy my business gowns. I am telling you this, Miss Serena, because on the terrace tonight Mrs. D'Arcy wondered audibly where I got the Chanel frock I wore at the party and if Michael provided it that I might make a proper impression on the county."

"Did Michael hear?"

"He must have heard."

"I wonder—we will invite Tom and Jane for a weekend. They sound different, refreshing, and I am bored stiff with people who are all run in the same mold as they are in this community. They go abroad for their clothes, read the best-sellers, go to the talked-of plays, but they have no inner maturity. Answer the phone, Sonia. Quick! It must be—"

Serena Farr leaned forward as Sonia lifted the instrument.

"Miss Carson speaking.—I will take the message for Miss Farr, Elkins.—Yes.—Yes, I understand."

She replaced the receiver. "They have found—the body."

Serena Farr swept up the cards. "So that is that! Don't wait any longer, Sonia. Thank you for staying with me."

"Shall I call Bates?"

"She will come when the door closes."

On the threshold Sonia lingered. "Good-night, Serena. Don't worry."

Serena Farr sat erect. One hand smoothing her chin, the other twisting her pearls.

"You're a sweet thing, Sonia. When I look at you— I wonder why Guy passed you by for your sister."

Sonia felt the color burn in her cheeks, saw Serena Farr's eyes narrow in response.

"Perhaps he didn't, my dear, perhaps he didn't. Good-night."

Seated before the dresser in her bedroom, Sonia, still in her white lace dinner frock, absentmindedly removed her jade earrings. What had made Miss Serena suspect that Guy Farr had made hectic love to her before he had turned to Ruby? Anything that she herself had said? What difference did it make? The man was thousands of miles away. Why should she fear that he would return when he heard that he had a son? The fact wouldn't make a dent in his selfishness. Why think of him? She hated the very sound of his name.

She must learn to play cards. She could repay some of Miss Serena's kindness in that way.

Could she? Sonia laughed as she thought of Serena's fervent hope that she was a better architect than card player, and the mirror girl laughed in response. She wasn't too good, she acknowledged. Life had offered so many absorbing interests that she had given little time to cards.

Life. What did it mean? To her it had meant a challenge to make it thrillingly worth while. She hadn't known the first letter of the word fear. She had looked for adventure, opportunities; had pushed the thought of accompanying dangers and vicissitudes to the back of her mind; then in one terrifying moment she had capitulated to conscience and apprehension. The fact that it was one of the nightmare brood of bogies generated by the flu didn't excuse her; she should have had more faith in herself.

"Everybody sooner or later flings his or her problems on Michael's shoulders," Miss Serena had said. That was what she had done when she had gone to his office. Did he respond always as quickly and generously as he had responded to her?

What a change in Phyllis D'Arcy's life since she had run up the steps of the terrace a few hours ago. One moment her husband had been with her, laughing, singing, babbling that he was "b-boilin' hot," and in a second he had flashed out of life with the speed of the meteor she had watched. That had left no trail. Had his life left a mark on the world? What had happened? Where had he gone? What was death? Were spirit and personality the same? Did they burn on forever like the light before the Cenotaph, or did they go out like a spark when there was no breath of wind to blow it into living flame?

What would Bill D'Arcy's passing mean to Michael Farr? Was he at this moment thanking whatever gods there be that he was free, that Sonia Carson had not accepted his mad proposal? Curious how Miss Serena's room had faded from her mind and the close-up of the library had flashed on. Uncanny. Had his proposal been any more mad than the speed with which she had flung herself into his arms—figuratively speaking—when she had felt herself and Dicky being drawn under? Would Phyllis attract him again, or had she cauterized his heart when she had thrown him over? Did he still feel the smart of it? He certainly had not given the impression this afternoon or evening that his spirit was permanently maimed. Would Miss Serena's prophecy prove true? Would Phyllis lure him back? Having once thrown him over—curious, one couldn't think of Michael Farr as defeated—why should she want him? Couldn't he see what she was now that his eyes had been torn wide open? Why were men such easy marks? A woman would get her number in five minutes. Perhaps she would occupy these charming rooms after all.

Sonia's dark brows met in a thoughtful frown as she regarded the reflections in the mirror. The bed's frame was white with mirrored panels set in the ends; the columns were crystal surmounted by crystal balls. It stood high from the floor on a circular dais lighted indirectly by a dome-shaped cupola. The white satin bedspread which usually covered it almost to the rug was now folded over a chair. Soft satin hangings the color of sunshine-plated gold framed open windows; the material was repeated in the coverings of the chairs.

All this loveliness had been prepared for a bride, a bride

who had run away with another man. Why had Dicky and she been put here? Now that she knew for whom the rooms had been made ready, she disliked them intensely. Every time she entered them she would be reminded of Michael Farr's wrecked happiness.

She rose impatiently. Perhaps the memory would obliterate that "Will you marry me?", which burned red in her mind whenever she thought of it. Why let it trouble her? She wouldn't be here long. In the fall she and Dicky would return to the city—but how could they if she were at work on the houses on the lake front for Donald Brandt? She would want to watch construction. Her reputation as an architect would stand or fall with the houses. She could lease a cottage in the village. That was an idea.

The phone! Who would ring at this hour? Elkins again? He must be back at Kingscourt by this time. She lifted the French instrument from its stand beside the bed.

"Sonia Carson speaking."

Her brows met in a little crease as she recognized Donald Brandt's voice. She answered:

"No, I was not asleep. How could I sleep after the news of the accident? It seems so unnecessarily tragic."

"Tragic! Don't talk about it. I was with him. Left The Cedars only a few moments ago. I must get the horror out of my mind by thinking of something else. Promise that you won't turn my business proposition down because Farr put on the dictator act. What is he to you, anyway? I was your friend long before you heard of him."

"Well, saw him, then. I liked his nerve saying that you were needed at Kingscourt."

"I am. Isn't Dicky here? But—I have his permission to work for you."

"Permission! Where do you get that permission stuff? I'll call for you tomorrow morning and we'll drive over to see the land."

"But—"

"I won't listen to a refusal. Ten o'clock. Be ready."

The phone at the other end of the wire clicked on its hook.

Sonia shrugged as she replaced the instrument.

"All the dictators are not named Farr," she said aloud.

Donald Brandt's voice had revealed his excitement, it had been hoarse and shaken. What a day this had been! She had been presented to the county; she had secured a chance to make good in her profession; a man's life had gone out in the flash of a meteor; the course of a woman's life had been changed. Had Michael Farr's future been juggled into another pattern? Days and weeks might have passed without so much happening.

She ought to go to bed, but her brain was wide awake, it seemed to have developed enormous creative activity. It swarmed with ideas. She might pull out her plans and go over them—Was Dicky stirring?

Softly she crossed to the threshold of the adjoining room and listened. Instead of blurring the color scheme, the dim light enhanced the blues that ran the gamut of tints from gray-blue to purple-blue, accented by a few notes of vivid green. The decorator had gone modern in furniture, a sane modern, no metal tubing, but charming wood in simple lines. A restful room. A man's room. Had it been intended for Michael Farr?

A scented breeze fluttered silken curtains. Vague shadows flitted on the ceiling. Night sounds drifted in, the movement of unseen life and the murmur of stirring leaves; the tinkle of a ukulele; a man's voice faint and sweet. Memory supplied the words to the music:

> " 'I've told every little star
> Just how sweet I think you are.
> Why haven't I told you?' "

The amorous Johnny still doing the troubadour act. Did he keep it up all night? Hadn't he heard of the tragedy?

Sonia stopped half way across the room as a shaggy white head with a square black nose, one black ear, and two bright beadlike eyes rose from the bed.

"Shreddy! Naughty boy! Why didn't you stay on your couch?" she whispered. "You—"

Was that a knock? She opened the door to the hall. She stared in speechless surprise at Michael Farr. His white face was smudged with shadows of weariness; his eyes were black with intensity; his hair was plastered to his head as if recently it had been drenched; a dark blue silk lounge coat was tied by a heavy cord about his waist; a negligé shirt was open at the neck.

"What is it? Has anything happened to Serena?" Sonia whispered breathlessly.

Chapter IX

Color swept back to Michael Farr's face as Sonia stepped into the hall and softly closed the door behind her.

"No! No! Nothing has happened here. I thought I heard you moving as I passed the door. Must talk to someone. Couldn't resist the impulse to stop and tell you what happened to Bill. Interested?"

"Of course. Tell me."

"He had had too much to drink. Near The Cedars' float he announced that he would swim in to cool off. Before they could stop him he dove. He didn't come up. Brandt doesn't swim—said he didn't. By the time I got there they had all lost their heads. Finally Bill's body was brought to the surface."

"What a terrible shock for Mrs. D'Arcy! Is she prostrated?"

"I really don't know. I didn't stop to find out. Her people arrived and I was not needed." His voice was curt. "Is the dog making himself at home?"

"At home! He owns the place. Come in and see?" she invited in the hope of taking his mind from the tragedy for a few moments at least.

They stole across the room to the bed. In the middle of it lay the boy in spread-eagle abandon. His red-gold hair curled moistly upon his forehead, his cheeks were softly flushed, the corners of his lips curved as if he were smiling in his dreams. One arm in its blue and white striped sleeve was flung across the rough white back of the dog who snuggled close and kept a beadlike eye on the two faces bending over him.

"Shreddy ought not to be there," Sonia whispered.

"Shall I take him up?"

At Michael Farr's low question the boy stirred and opened drowsy eyes. He smiled enchantingly.

"H'loa!"

He raised himself on one elbow and blinked heavy lids. The dog stood up and stretched.

"W'y don't you snuggle your face in my neck an' say, 'God bless you, good-night, Mos' Dear,' way you alwus do, So-ni-a?"

The last word was a drowsy murmur. Sonia turned him gently until his head rested on the pillow. She nodded toward the dog, and as Michael lifted him, she drew the sheet over the boy. Already he was asleep.

"Put Shreddy on his couch."

She stood looking down at the child. Whispered:

"Isn't Dicky adorable?"

"He is. Come out to the hall. I want to ask you something."

"What is it? It's late."

"Nonsense. It isn't twelve yet. If you were in town you would be beginning to go places. Let's raid the pantry." As she hesitated, he added: "I'd like to get certain things out of my mind."

Sonia remembered his face when she had opened the door. He had been in the storm center of tragedy, tragedy the more terrible because it had been so swift, so unnecessary.

"I'll come."

At the top of the stairs, Michael said aloud:

"We needn't whisper like conspirators. We are not breaking and entering, remember."

A few moments later, in the glistening white pantry, Sonia reminded:

"The cook will think someone has been breaking and entering if you don't stop taking things from that icebox. Do you dare cut that roast chicken?"

"Quote: 'I dare do all that may become a man.' Unquote. What shall we do with it?"

His gayety was a revelation. He seemed so lighthearted. Was it because Phyllis D'Arcy was free? The thought was like a stab.

"Well? What shall we do with it? Action, woman, action."

Sonia forced herself out of the cloud of depression which had suddenly engulfed her.

"Sandwiches. We'll use some crisp lettuce, a paper thin slice of that luscious pink ham, some mayonnaise, and the chicken. You carve the bird and I will do the rest."

"What will you have to drink? Ginger ale? Beer? Sparkling grape juice? That's service, what?"

"Iced coffee. It sounds wild, doesn't it? But a tall thin glass, full of ice cubes,—can't you hear them tinkle?—and black coffee and thick cream—"

"Don't say any more or I shall perish of thirst before I get it. Know how to make it?"

"Of course. I'll borrow this." She slipped an apron over her white lace frock.

Later, perched on high stools, they ate sandwiches and

drank iced coffee and talked. It seemed to Sonia, at moments, as if she were living in another world, a world in which she was being swept along, with no choice given her as to the direction in which she would go. Swept along with an utterly strange person as a traveling companion.

Suddenly and irrelevantly Michael Farr inquired:

"Have you decided to work for Brandt?"

A note in his voice put her on the defensive.

"I have. I've signed on the dotted line—figuratively speaking. I had to. This is my chance. The chance for which I have been waiting for years. I couldn't turn it down. I've got to try out my ideas. If I don't, I may lose the urge and someone else will pick them out of the air. My sense of rhythm and color drives me. Don't you see? Don't you understand that this is my chance? Besides, I must keep busy."

"Trying to forget some—thing?"

"If you mean by something, some man, I am not. I have seen too much to trust one—and after hearing tonight Miss Serena's stories of some of our neighbors—nothing doing, thank you."

"You must take her yarns with a dash of salt. She is lonely and her own love affair seems hopeless."

"Her love affair! She is fascinating, so modern, so gay. I had wondered why she is unmarried."

"You saw Jim Neville this afternoon?"

"Yes, and Serena's expression as she looked up at him twisted my heart unbearably. Is he the man?"

"Yes. It's the old story. Years ago her father, my grandfather, put his wrecking-crew on her romance. Jim Neville was a nice enough fellow, just starting practise, but the family dictator had other views for her. The boy—they were very young—was caught on the rebound and married. His wife has been a hopeless invalid for years, mentally gone. Now he is one of the biggest men in his line, is sent for in consultation from all over the country. Serena might have been a countess, a marchesa, the wife of an American plutocrat, but she turned the offers down. Whenever she is near New York she and Neville lunch together—once. I was amazed to see him here this afternoon. They still love one another. She told me a short time ago that he seemed no older to her now than when they were engaged. I imagine that real love is like that. When did you sign on the dotted line?"

His change of subject was so abrupt that it took Sonia an instant to orient herself.

"A few moments before you knocked at Dicky's door

Donald Brandt phoned. He said he wanted to talk business to get the accident out of his mind. Did he—did he find the—"

"Forget it. As we can do nothing more to help, let's not talk about it, let's talk about you and the assignment to plan those houses. Your boudoir is no place for work, real work. There is a room in the sportshouse which would make a perfect studio—it has north light and a big window. When will you begin on plans?"

"Mr. Brandt has asked me to drive over to the land tomorrow. After I have seen it I shall know whether a house I have in mind will be suitable."

"Tomorrow! Brandt is a fast worker."

"One must be, these days, to get anywhere."

"This building enterprise will put him in strong with the county. His election may go over with a bang."

Plate in hand, Sonia stopped on her way to the icebox.

"What election?"

"Don't you know that he is trying for Congress from this district?"

"But I thought you were the candidate."

"I am one of two. Don't bother with the dishes. Leave them."

Sonia proceeded to rinse and pile plates and cups and saucers.

"I was trained never to leave a pantry or a room in confusion. 'Suppose you were brought home after an accident to a messy house. Think of your sense of mortification,' Mother would say—she was a New Englander. It seemed to me that if I were sufficiently collapsed to be brought home, my mortification complex would slack on the job. However, believe it or not, early training does tell—behold, the result!" She pulled off the apron and glanced at a clock on the wall. "Two! Do you realize how long we have been here?"

"It hasn't seemed more than a minute to me."

Michael Farr reached over her shoulder and pushed open the door which led to the dining room. The charm of its walls, Chinese in design, painted in natural colors, combined with silver on a beige field, set the theme for the coloring. Bits of blue cloisonné repeated the tone of the brocade in chair coverings and hangings.

"Lib! What are you doing here at this time of night?" Michael demanded of the woman who hurried into the room. Her dovelike eyes were full of tears, the plump hand with which she clutched a scant beflowered kimono across her ample breast was shaky, her lips trembled.

"Michael dear, I had to know that you were all right. I—"

"Of course I'm all right, Lib. Toddle along to bed now, hustle."

"Sure you haven't a chill, honey? Elkins said you dove and dove and dove until you found Mr. D'Arcy and—him who made your heartache."

"Libby!" The word was a cross between a command and growl.

"I'm going. I'm going. Only, only that man's taking off does seem the hand of God, don't it? He checks up on us at the end of every day. If we sin we're put down to pay for it in sorrow. Sure you don't need an electric pad to get you warm?"

Michael seized her by the shoulders.

"Going, Lib, or shall I have to carry you?"

"You carry me! I'm going, dear, I'm going. I'll send Elkins—"

"You'll send nothing. Go."

The plump woman turned on the threshold.

"Make him drink something hot, Miss Sonia. He may take it for you when he won't for his old Libby."

Sonia looked up at Michael Farr.

"So—that is why your hair resembles the wet back of a seal and you are prowling about in a lounge coat! And I made you drink iced coffee. Why didn't you tell me you had been in the water? Why didn't you tell me that it was you who—" She shivered.

"Don't let Libby hear your teeth chatter, or she will be back to prescribe hot drinks and electric pads for you. Go on. I'll snap out this light."

At the foot of the stairs he caught her hand.

"You couldn't say, 'Good-night, Mos' Dear,' to me, could you?"

As she looked at him Sonia had a sudden impulse to draw his head to her shoulder and smooth his hair. It was so compelling that it caught at her breath. She refused crisply:

"I certainly could not." Half way up she turned. He was watching her.

"Good-night," she whispered.

Why had he asked that absurd question? Absurd questions seemed to be his line. Hadn't she discovered that the first time she had come to this house? Why hadn't he told her what he had done? Why had he let her think that someone else had brought that body to the surface?

Not to be wondered at that he wanted to forget the gruesome experience, she assured herself later, as she snuggled into the luxurious bed and snapped out the light on the stand beside it.

A fragrant breeze stole in through the open windows. She could see stars in the dark sky, stars so near together that they looked like golden coins strung on a chain. How they blinked! Had a beam just started from one of them which would be filtered through a photo-electric cell to set in motion an Exposition forty years from now? What a day this had been! Libby believed that God checked up on one at the end of every day. The old housekeeper's words had brought back faith in her own spiritual power; it had been submerged since her illness. Miss Serena was a darling too. How wonderful they both were to her!

"Am I really I," she questioned drowsily, "or am I dreaming that I have a chance to make good with a development scheme, that Michael Farr and I have just had supper in that glistening pantry? Will I wake and find myself back in the apartment with Dicky, with the sea ahead rough with breakers?"

That was a thought! Was she asleep? She snapped on the light. She was not dreaming. The soft yellow hangings stirred in the light breeze which brought the faint, far sound of a motor horn.

"I'm awake," she assured herself softly. "It is not a dream that I am here at Kingscourt and that Dicky's future is secure. Something tells me, though, that there are still breakers ahead, big, white, smothering breakers. What of it?"

She raised herself on one elbow, flung up her other arm in theatrical imitation of Michael Farr.

"We ride the gale!"

With a laugh she put out the light and snuggled back among the pillows.

Chapter X

There was no breeze that July noon, no sound save the soft chatter of the colorful groups about the swimming pool at Kingscourt. In the drive beyond the sportshouse glittered an array of automobiles, large cars and small cars, all smart, all shining. A faint haze, like a breath on a window pane, lay on the surface of the still lake. The translucent pool, in its frame of heavenly-blue tiles, reflected a limpid turquoise sky, a puff of snowy cloud, a branch of emerald green shrub; reflected also a slim figure in tangerine swim suit on the high diving board, its arms poised above its head.

Sonia! Michael Farr paused between the lacy iron gates. In the instant before she dived, he compared her radiant, laughing face with the face of the troubled, desperate girl who had come to his office that June day. That face had been thin, white; the skin of this one was a beautiful golden tan, with a tinge of natural, rich color at the cheek bones. Superb health. The two words summed up the change. Life at Kingscourt, reluctant as she had been to come, had wrought magic.

Perfect dive. He waited until the capped head rose to the surface before he glanced about the pool. Serena's "a few friends to meet Mr. and Mrs. Tom Nash" had expanded into quite a party. It would. His aunt had a party complex. He knew the dozen men and girls whose bare backs still glistened with water, who sprawled or played at backgammon on the flagging. The woman in a white water frock, who had slipped like an eel into the pool to join Sonia, must be Mrs. Tom. They were swimming toward the shallow end where Dicky, in an abbreviated green sun suit, was struggling with an enormous blue medicine ball. The Sealyham stretched on the flagging watched his every move.

The woman in white caught the child in her arms.

"Whose boy are you, darling? Janey's boy?"

Dicky struggled free. "I'm Sonia's boy," Michael heard him protest.

The short, slightly bald, more than slightly overweight man, whose flesh rolled over the confines of his bathing suit, must be Nash himself. He was sitting cross-legged like a tailor gazing up at a woman in filmy white. Her drooping hat hid her face. Except for Serena in a simple mauve frock and hat, she was the only woman present not dressed for swimming. Who was she?

Nash moved. It was Phyllis! Phyllis D'Arcy had been the object of Nash's attention. Was she coming out of her mourning retirement so soon? She didn't belong in that bronzed colorful group, she belonged in a delicately colored illustration. He stepped forward. Dicky saw him.

"Cousin Michael! Cousin Mike! Give me a wide! Give me a wide on your sho'ders!"

The child tossed the ball to the flagging and climbed out of the pool. He flung himself at Michael, who caught him by the arms.

"Hold on! You're too wet for a ride. Think I want you dripping over my gray coat and white trousers? Don't you see that I'm dressed for Aunt Serena's party?"

"Did you bwing me a pwesent, Cousin Mike?"

"Dicky! I have told you that you must not ask for

presents, and that you must not call Mr. Farr 'Mike,' " Sonia reminded sternly.

"Don't scold the lamb, Sonia," protested the woman in the white swim-suit. "Come and give Janey a hug, Dicky darling."

But Dicky darling had caught Michael's hand. He held it tight as Michael parleyed.

"We'll see about the present later. Come on while I speak to Aunt Serena, old man."

With the boy hopping and skipping on bare feet beside him, and the dog dashing ahead, he waved in response to a chorus of variegated greetings:

"Ah there, Mike!"

"Hulloa, Michael!"

"Did your boss give you a day off?"

He stopped beside his aunt.

"Sorry, Serena, to be late to your party." He held out his hand to the man who had struggled to his plump pink feet. Regardless of Dicky's wet body, Serena Farr caught the child close to her.

"Glad to see you here, Nash."

The drab eyes in the man's round face glowed.

"Mighty glad to be here. It was corking of your aunt to ask us. This place goes over big with me. We're crazy about Sonia and the kid. Met the wife?"

He shouted through cupped hands:

"Hi, Jane!"

Michael ignored Phyllis D'Arcy's low, meaning laugh. He said evenly:

"How are you, Phyl?"

Without waiting for a response to his conventional inquiry, he followed Nash, who reminded him of a squat harbor tug propelled by its own power, to the edge of the pool where Sonia and his companion sat like dripping, suntanned mermaids.

"Stand up, Jane, like a little lady and curtsey to your host, the King of Kingscourt," her husband commanded.

Michael liked the brown eyes flecked with green which swept him appraisingly, liked the woman's interesting face with its wide mouth, liked her firm handclasp as she said:

"So you are Michael Farr. Sonia, why didn't you tell me he was the best-looking creature in the country?"

Michael laughed. "I'm willing to bet Sonia's standards of masculine perfection are different from yours." It took all his self-control to refrain from pointing his remarks by a glance at Brandt who was sitting on the edge of the pool. His hair was almost as white as the puff of cloud above, the flesh of his arms and legs was pink in contrast to his trim waisted bathing suit.

Soft chimes drifted down from the terrace. Instead of answering him, Sonia called:

"The dressing bell, everybody!"

One after another, the colorful figures plunged into the pool. Serena Farr, with Dicky's hand tight in hers, strolled toward the lacy gates where Nanette was waiting with Shreddy squatted beside her. With a shout, the boy kicked at the medicine ball, and the dog pushed and rolled it almost to the sportshouse door, before he dashed back to rejoin his young master. Sonia linked her arm in that of Jane Nash. Together the girls' slim bodies bent in obeisance; together two voices supplicated:

"With your permission, your Majesty."

With incredible quickness they did a back flip into the pool. Tom Nash chuckled.

"Those two are the limit when they get together. Just of a size and both full of the devil." He started toward the solitary white figure in the low chair.

"Tom! Get dressed!" There was a hint of irritation in Jane Nash's call from the pool and more than a hint of warning.

"Oh, all right! I'm coming—not swimming—walking. See?" He turned to Michael.

"Have you seen Sonia's model for the house Brandt is to build? It's a corker. Wouldn't mind having it myself. Spent an hour in her studio before the party arrived. Ought to see it."

"I will. Now," Michael announced.

As he passed back of Phyllis D'Arcy's chair, he ignored her soft call. Tom Nash lingered.

"He's a good-hearted little number," Michael thought, as he entered the main room of the sportshouse. Its arched rafters and heavy cross-beams were the silvery gray of weathered timber. The walls and floor were of warm-toned stone. The furnishings were brown, gold, green, cream, and red; the rug a huge Yucatan.

"Nash must have oodles of money," his thoughts ran on. "Doubt if his business income has suffered much in these last years. People still ply can-openers. Is Phyllis making a play for him? Who would have suspected that Bill D'Arcy was bankrupt?"

He pushed back unpleasant memories and smiled as he pictured Sonia's brilliant, laughing eyes. She was like the friendly girl who had had supper with him in the pantry. He had seen her but twice since. Business had taken him to

Washington, business was taking almost everyone to Washington to watch, if not to take a hand in, the framing of codes. He had not had a chance to ask her about her house, but he had gone out of his way this morning to look at the land he had sold Brandt.

Brandt. He mounted the stairs to the accompaniment of voices and laughter which drifted from the dressing rooms in the wings of the house. The night of Bill D'Arcy's accident Brandt had said that he did not swim. Not five minutes ago he had slid into the pool with the slick speed of an alligator. Apparently he could swim when he wanted to.

The door of the workroom was open. He paused on the threshold and looked about. Gray wood walls. Gray rafters sloped to the ridge pole. Straight orange silk hangings were pushed back from one great window which framed an exquisite picture of the pool, the gates, the ascending garden, and finally the stone perfection of the house.

Response to the charm of it swept Michael like a buoyant tide. "Boy, I had forgotten how beautiful this place is!" he admitted to himself, before he brought his attention back to the contents of the room in which he was standing.

A blueprint was spread on a large drafting table; a rack held long rolls of paper and tracing cloth, another was filled with sheets of cardboard; a shelf was stacked with large books which looked as if they might be full of illustrations; a framed set of rendered drawings hung on one wall, beside it were sketches of details of windows; on another wall hung a water color of a small house which had been framed with a colored reproduction of it, and a letter announcing that it had been the prize winner in a contest. On a desk was an array of pens and bottles of ink, triangles and rulers, a paint box with brushes.

On a large high table was a model of the layout of a small country estate. The house was early American. From a green terrace steps descended into a garden. On one side of the hedge which surrounded it was a swimming pool. A pergola separated that from a tennis court. On the other side of the garden was a paddock and beyond that a small stable. Miniature trees cast real shadows; hedges, flowers, and shrubs had been meticulously imitated. The pools were mirrors.

Michael straddled the draftsman stool in front of it and with hands in his pockets marveled at the perfection of detail.

"Will it do?"

Sonia stood on the threshold. She had changed to a white crêpe frock and soft yellow coat, which accentuated the sun tan of her skin and the brilliance of her dark eyes.

"Sure, it will do. It's a knockout. Hope you don't mind my coming up?"

"Of course not. This is a business office."

"I've never seen one in such immaculate order."

"I told you that Mother was a New Englander."

"What's this stuff?"

He touched the stretch of green which simulated a lawn. She crossed the room to his side.

"That is fine sponge colored, and the drives are glue sprinkled with sand. This elevation faces the lake. Good effect, isn't it?"

"Perfect. I drove round by the place when I came from town. Notice that the house is boarded in. Quick work."

"Mr. Brandt is pushing construction. We want to get the house finished by the last of October. That doesn't include the pools and stables. We figured that the purchaser could add those as inclination, to say nothing of finances, permitted."

She answered a ring on the telephone. Her brows met in an annoyed frown as she listened. Her voice was crisp.

"No, Carlos. You've held up the heating plant man, the plasterers, the electricians. You'll not get a cent till your job is finished and finished right."

She snapped the instrument down on its stand.

"Do you have much of that?" Michael inquired. "Are you superintending the building of the house as well as planning it?"

"Yes. If I watch the construction I shall be sure my plan is carried out. I can't afford to have it bungled."

"I hope you are getting paid for it?"

"Of course I am."

"I am properly snubbed. How many acres in this layout?"

"Ten. My boss believes that the present trend is away from suburbs to small country estates far enough from the highways to be free from dust and gas. This is a demonstration of what can be done with a few acres."

"Spend much time there?"

"Every moment that I can spare from work here and tennis."

"I hope you use the yellow roadster in the garage. It needs exercise."

"Thanks lots, but I have a bicycle. Lucky for me they are on the crest of the fashion wave."

"You won't let me do anything for you, will you?" Michael realized that his voice was not as impersonal as he wished.

"I'm here."

"Sure, you're here."

"That is accepting a lot, isn't it?"

"You are here because of Dicky. Think I don't realize that you'd be off in a minute if it were not for him? We'll let that ride for the present. Does Brandt come up here to talk things over?"

There was a suggestion of defiance in her eyes.

"Why not? As I reminded you before, this is a business office. Look! Your guests are beginning to stroll toward the house and luncheon. We had better go down."

"Just a minute. Happy, Sonia?"

"Gorgeously. If only—"

"If only—what?"

"We could hear from your brother."

"What difference would that make—really? I believe that Dicky is Guy's child. His future has been provided for."

"But you don't believe in the marriage, do you? You don't really believe in me?"

"Believe in you! Don't be foolish. Don't tell me that that Neon sign which flashes in your mind has laid down on its job."

Michael felt his color rise and saw hers come stealing up in response.

"You have the most outrageous memory of any person I ever met."

"For some things. I see that the sign is still going strong. That helps. It is maddening that I have to be away from Kingscourt just now when I want—"

As he met her startled eyes he cleared his voice.

"Perfect picture from this window, isn't it? Grand place from which to observe the passing show. Serena's lilac frock makes an effective background for Phyl D'Arcy's filmy white. I was amazed to see her here so—soon."

"She phoned Miss Serena and asked if she might come and 'sit in a corner,' that she must get away from her thoughts."

"She seems to be making a fairly good stab at forgetfulness. There goes Nash to join her. Didn't take him long to get into his clothes. I like your cousin."

"He is a dear. I can't begin to tell you how much I appreciate Serena's invitation to Jane and Tom. The visit will make his summer—if—if someone doesn't spoil it."

Michael looked thoughtfully at the man and woman standing near the edge of the pool.

"You mean that Phyl might spoil it?"

"I mean that Jane might. She is frightfully jealous. There

is a vulnerable spot in all men. Tom's is his pride in the fortune he made. If Mrs. D'Arcy is clever enough to discover that—it doesn't take much intuition—she will have him at her heels. I don't mean that Tom would be more than foolish, but it's apparent she is making an out and out play for him. Oh, let's not stand here talking, let's do something."

"Don't worry about Nash. He looks to me as if he were capable of shaking off sirens as easily as a duck shakes water."

"Then you admit the glamorous lady's charm." Soft color stole under Sonia's tan. Her eyes were apologetic. "I'm sorry —I never can realize that you—I shouldn't have asked that question. I'm not worried about her effect on Tom, it's the effect of that on his wife."

She nodded toward the couple standing on the edge of the pool. Mrs. D'Arcy with much tilting of her head to observe the effect, was arranging a bunch of bachelor buttons in the lapel of Nash's coat.

"I can imagine the fatuous expression of Tom's eyes. He's like that with a pretty woman. Let's go. I will break up that twosome before Jane sees it. Don't think that I am silly enough to pose as my cousin's keeper, but I would like to have this visit perfect, and Jane is unpredictable."

"I repeat, don't worry. Phyl isn't a real menace. Would you be jealous if you loved a man?" Michael asked, as he followed her down the winding stairs.

She stopped and looked over her shoulder.

"But I don't mean to love a man. 'Dicky and my career!' is my battle-cry. I'm coming, Jane," she called, and took the last two stairs in one.

As he left the sportshouse with her and Mrs. Nash, Michael wondered if Sonia were as heart-free as her voice had sounded. She must spend hours with Donald Brandt, and Brandt was notoriously adept in making a woman believe that he was all shot to pieces over her. If only he, himself, could stay at Kingscourt and get in a little intensive devotion. He couldn't at present, so that was that. Tomorrow he was to start for the West. In between business trips he was tied up with conferences regarding his Congressional campaign, and with speaking in different towns. After the first week in November he would be free to devote himself to Sonia. Would she be free? At least she had not forgotten that he had asked her to marry him; he had known that from her eyes and heightened color when he had referred to the Neon sign.

A stifled exclamation startled him out of his absorption.

Jane Nash had stopped. She was frowning angrily at her husband and Phyllis D'Arcy.

"That woman gives me a pain in the neck!" she fumed.

It looked to Michael as if the two had not moved since he had observed them from the studio window. Phyl, and the stocky man in gray coat with black banded sleeve and white trousers, were reflected in the pool as in a shining mirror; the clear water also faithfully gave back the quick linking of arms.

Michael glanced at Jane Nash. If only she knew how little it meant, she wouldn't get steamed up about it. The shuttle of Life. Had it begun to weave Phyllis into the pattern of Nash's life? He glanced at the eyes of the woman beside him and disciplined a smile. He answered his own question. Not if his wife could snap the thread of his interest, and he would bet on her to do it.

Never before had he realized what a telltale a human face could be, nor how incredibly eyes could blaze, nor how swiftly an arm could move, until Jane swooped on Dicky's huge medicine ball. Caught it. Flung it.

"Catch!" she called, and laughed.

It struck the heads of the absorbed couple with a resounding smack. Startled, they lost balance. Arms waving like windmills gone mad, they splashed backward into the pool.

Michael choked with laughter as he rushed to the rescue. He was hotly ashamed of himself, but they were not in the least danger and it was the funniest thing he ever had seen off the screen. He didn't dare look at Sonia, who, keeping pace with him, was making queer little sounds in her throat.

Phyllis D'Arcy was clinging to the rod around the inside of the pool when he reached her. Nash dripping with coolness was climbing out. The glance he shot at his wife before he helped Michael pull Phyllis to her feet would have been screamingly funny had it not bordered on the murderous.

Jane Nash, in an immaculate tailored white crêpe, with not a wave of her smart hair-cut disarranged, with her string of lustrous pearls gleaming softly, regarded the woman's soaked figure, the stringy hat, with horrified, apologetic eyes.

"I'm frightfully sorry! That's what comes from having a playful complex."

Her voice was suspiciously unsteady. Michael had a hunch that it was laughter, not remorse, which was shaking it as a breeze shakes the leaves of a tree.

"Tommy, you muffer, didn't you hear me yell, 'Catch!'?"

"Oh yeah?" Nash was white about the lips; he swelled

like a pouter pigeon as he turned his back upon his wife. "Say, Mrs. D'Arcy—"

"Don't talk to me!" Phyllis D'Arcy's voice was low with fury. "I don't know why I wasted a moment on you, you and your bourgeois wife. I might have known that relatives of Sonia Carson—"

"Cut it, Phyl!" The situation had lost every shred of humor for Michael. "Don't make a tragedy of what was an uncomfortable accident. Better hustle to the house and change. Here comes Aunt Serena; she will find something for you to put on."

"Do you think I'll face that crowd on the terrace like this? My roadster is back of the sportshouse. You'll have to drive me to The Cedars, Michael."

"Michael can't, Phyllis. Michael must stay with his guests." Serena Farr was breathless. "I saw your plunge, told Elkins to phone the garage for a closed car to meet you at the sportshouse, take you home, wait for you to change and bring you back."

"You are a quick thinker, Miss Serena. One might almost suspect that you and the playful ball thrower had planned this slap-stick comedy."

The effect of Phyllis D'Arcy's wrathful blue eyes and scathing voice was somewhat dimmed by the thin streams riveting from the pasty thing on her head which once had been a hat.

"Those chimes mean luncheon, don't they? Don't keep your guests of honor waiting here, Michael. I will drive myself."

"Mrs. D'Arcy, if you will allow me—" Tom Nash's eyes and voice were abject.

"I will allow you to do nothing!"

The stamp of her white shoe made up in spatter what it had lost in sound. She turned and ran, her wet skirts impeding her progress. Tom Nash looked after her miserably. His wife's expression suggested that of a cat who had lapped her fill of luscious cream. Michael started after Phyllis.

"Michael! Don't go! If she wishes to be a martyr, let her."

Michael Farr paused long enough to protest. For the first time in his life he was thoroughly angry with his aunt.

"Martyr, Serena! Hasn't a woman a right to be aggrieved when she falls into a pool?"

"Falls in!" In spite of his indignation, Michael laughed in sympathy with Serena Farr's spontaneous chuckle. She looked toward dripping Tom Nash and his wife and Sonia who were passing between the lacy iron gates, before she confided:

"Take it from me, if more homes were equipped with pools there would be fewer sirens on the loose."

Chapter XI

Moonlight and fragrance and purple shadows on the terrace—stars like distant golden worlds hung against the velvet sky—a swirl of silver tissue on the lake—enchantment working to cast a magic spell over the garden. Deep stillness. Not the flicker of a leaf. Not a ripple on the pool.

Michael Farr drew a long, unsteady breath. What a night! What a night for lovers! If he could lure Sonia here by sheer, passionate desire! If he could tell her that he loved her, not wait until he had tried to win her, not tomorrow even, but now, here tonight; could sweep her along in this swift, tumultuous certainty of their destiny; husband and wife against the world, she had said. He would hold her so close and safe in his heart that the world could not touch her. He—

"Say, Farr, while dummy, I've slid out to say that I hope Mrs. D'Arcy wasn't too sore at Jane."

Like a crystal sphere of incredible delicacy shattered by a rough touch, so Michael's dream fell into fragments at Tom Nash's rueful whisper. He had the curious impression that he could feel the beauty of the world about him wavering into retreat, carrying with it the glowing sense of Sonia's nearness. All things became different, everything became real. Mysterious purple shadows became trees; the pool was a simple pool, no longer a magic mirror divinely designed to reflect and interpret distant planets. A little wind sprang up and set the leaves whispering. Phyllis D'Arcy's anger and reproaches for his indifference as he had driven her home echoed discordantly through the corridors of his memory. He answered:

"Depends upon what you call too sore. She was furious."

"Jane didn't mean to hit us really. She's all broken up about it."

Michael remembered Mrs. Nash's expression and doubted. Tom Nash, perched on the parapet, lighter to cigarette, continued:

"When we get back to New York, Jane will select a stunning dress and hat and we'll send it to Mrs. D'Arcy with our regrets."

"Don't. She wouldn't accept it."

"Oh yeah?" Nash's eyes were the keen, boring eyes of the man who had made a fortune, not those of the boyish, ingenuous person Michael had met for the first time that day at the pool.

"I hadn't talked with her ten minutes before I was sure that I could give her anything I chose—in a fraternal spirit of course. Say, this is a corking place. It's what I've dreamed of owning. It's like fairyland. Ever think of selling it?"

Michael looked out over the garden and pool to the shimmering lake.

"Never. I wouldn't sell—" He laughed. "I won't say it. A year ago, had anyone told me that I would part with any of the land, I would have told him he was crazy. But a few weeks ago I sold fifty acres for development."

"Fifty acres! Is that the strip across the lake Sonia is planning the house for?"

"Yes. Donald Brandt bought it."

"Met him today for the first time, though I've heard a lot about him. He's a wonder boy. He's one of those I men: 'I did this,' 'I did that,' isn't he? I'll bet some personality expert tipped him off that he had personality-plus. When he towered above me at the pool and boomed in his big voice: 'How are you, Nash?' I wanted to sock him, he was so confoundedly patronizing. But I'll hand him one on the snappy game of contract he plays. He and Jane have been piling up points in there. Evident he's that way about Sonia."

"Is it? I've been away from Kingscourt so much that I don't know."

"Hope you got your money for the land."

"I did. Why?"

"There's a rumor in the city that Brandt is hard pushed for cash; but, who isn't these days? I hope Sonia is getting paid as she goes along. You've no idea, Farr, of the independence of that girl. She's got grit without being one of those know-it-all dames who drive a man crazy. She has stuck at her job all these years. She wouldn't let me help her. I thought she worked because she'd picked up the career bug, had no idea that the little people her people had left her was lapped up in the late crash, that she was living on what she earned. Some responsibility she took on to support Ruby's child. Jane and I wanted to adopt him, but nothing doing."

"He will be taken care of. The child is my brother's. We are not telling the world until we hear from him, so keep what I've told you under your hat, will you, Nash? As Sonia's nearest relative, I think you ought to know."

"Gosh sakes, that makes me feel like the big chief of a tribe!" His round eyes twinkled. "Haven't anything else you want to tell me as Sonia's nearest relative, have you?"

Michael laughed. "Not yet—not until I have told Sonia herself.

"Talking of angels—" he said in a louder voice, as the girl stepped from the open French window. Dots of silver on the white net of her frock and the rose net of her little shoulder cape glimmered in the faint light. Laughter heightened the brilliance of her eyes as she asked gaily:

"Were you talking of me?"

Tom Nash flung away his cigarette. "You're not crazy about yourself, are you, gal? You an angel! I guess you've forgotten how you used to go savage and yank my hair when we were young."

"That will be about all from you, Thomas." Sonia slipped her arm in his. "I admit I was a vixen when you teased me. I used to fly into bits like a bunch of fire-crackers. But, alas, the world has tamed this once tem-pestuous spirit." Her voice lost its mocking lightness. "Some-times I have seen a flash in Dicky which made me wonder if he were like his temperamental aunt. Serena sent me out to remind you that you are making a fourth at contract, Tom."

"I forgot. I'm toddling." He turned at the threshold. "If ever you decide to sell or lease Kingscourt, give me first chance, will you, Farr?" He went in without waiting for an answer.

Sonia took a step nearer Michael. Her eyes seemed enormous in the dim light.

"Would you?" she asked in a low voice.

"Would I what? Come over to this chair."

She perched on the parapet. The buckles on her rose-color slippers glinted against the gray stone.

"Can't stay but a moment. I like it up here where I can see the lake. Would you sell or lease Kingscourt?"

"I'm through making statements. How can I tell what I would do if I needed money. And speaking of money—when do you get your architect's commission on this first house?"

"When it is sold."

"That may not be for months and months."

"I know, but as this is a speculative proposition and I was thrilled by the chance to do it, I said I would wait."

"You are bossing the building job, aren't you? Haven't

you a contract which specifies dates of payment? A certain percentage of each bill rendered by the contractor?"

"No. That is the usual method, but I trusted to Donald Brandt and I am sure he will be perfectly fair."

"Like him, don't you?"

"Immensely."

"While you are waiting for a payment on account, what are you doing for cash?"

"I'm doing very well, thank you."

"Let me advance you some, will you?"

"That's a positively world-saving idea—but not for a moment. If worst came to worst, I could ask Mr. Brandt."

"I don't want you to ask him for money."

"Not ask for money I have earned! Dictator! I don't wonder you are called the King of Kingscourt. Now that you have suggested it, I will ask for some tonight. He is winning at contract, he will be so pleased with himself that he will dash off a cheque without pain."

Michael leaned against a pillar facing her. Her face was alight with friendly mockery, her red lips curved in a little derisive smile. She was so ardent, so unspoiled. He looked straight into her eyes until the lids fluttered.

"Do you know, Sonia, there are times when I feel an irresistible urge to seize you by the hair—short as it is— and drag you off to my cave, so watch your step, woman."

" 'Who's afraid of the big, bad wolf?' "

Laughter flashed in his eyes. "Are you a Walt Disney fan too?"

"I adore the Silly Symphonies."

"They are the funniest things on the screen. How come that Brandt is here for dinner and cards?" he demanded with a quick change of tone. "I thought Serena wouldn't stand for him."

"He is a collector of coins. That is one answer. Also, love of contract maketh the whole world kin, or words to that effect. She discovered that Donald Brandt plays a perfect game and she invites him here often."

"She does! Do you play when he comes?"

"I! It is evident that you never have played cards with me. In an effort to please Serena, whom I adore, I spent hours studying contract rules. I knew my stuff, but the first time I used my knowledge I applied it at the wrong time. I played from page 17 when my partner was playing from page 24 of the text book. Result, disaster. I was rattled. I am sure that with practice I could play a good game—I am fairly intelligent—but since then I haven't been invited."

"Do you have to adore a person before you try to please him?"

"You have your pronouns mixed. I was talking about Serena. Is she annoyed with Jane? She was such a dear to invite Tom and his wife here that I want her to like them. They really are wonderful people."

"Annoyed with Mrs. Nash? Why should she be?"

"Don't pretend to be dense. It doesn't suit you. You know what I mean—Jane deliberately threw that ball at Mrs. D'Arcy and Tom."

Michael chuckled as he remembered his aunt's curt comment as she had watched Phyllis drip toward the sports-house.

"No-o, I wouldn't say that her reaction was anger at Mrs. Nash. She supposed, of course, that it was an accident."

"You drove Mrs. D'Arcy home, didn't you?"

"Yes."

"Was she furiously angry?"

"Imagine yourself in her place and answer your own question."

"I can't imagine myself in her place because I can't imagine myself clinging to a married man's arm on the edge of the pool. But you would defend her."

Her tone roused the demon of opposition which lurks in every human.

"Sure I would, poor little girl!"

"Poor little girl! You can say that in that tone about her? Love moves in a mysterious way its wonders to perform."

"Does it necessarily follow that a man is in love with a woman because he is sorry she was dumped into a pool and her clothes ruined?"

"Don't beat me."

Michael's eyes met Sonia's alight with laughter, held them while he responded theatrically:

"You do me wrong. I wasn't thinking of beating you. I was wondring if I kissed you and kissed you hard—"

Sonia slid down from the parapet. Little flames lighted in her dark eyes.

"Don't say any more. I've never before met a man with a line like yours. The second time I met you, you—you—"

"Asked you to marry me," Michael finished steadily.

"Because you were afraid that the girl who had thrown you over would get you back."

Michael felt as if all color had drained from his face,

as if he were fighting with his back against a wall. In spite of that, he smiled.

"I realize now that that was not the sole reason."

"It was reason enough to make me realize that you were still mad about her. I realized it again when you were all jittery this noon when you had a chance to drive her home. Phyllis D'Arcy deserved dumping. Weren't there enough single men to cling to without picking on Tom? She was hateful when she called Jane bourgeois. She isn't. She belongs to a fine family, but when anyone makes a grand play for Tom, she goes primitive. She loves him."

"To look at Nash one would hardly expect him to inspire a grand passion. You have a lot to say about love. What is it?"

Sonia looked thoughtfully across the garden to the lake streaked now with a rippling golden path of moonlight. A soft, scented breeze stirred a little curl of her dark hair as if caressing it.

Michael clasped his hands hard behind his back to keep them from touching it. Not yet. He would have to live down the blunder he had made when he had asked her to marry him. Apparently she thought of him as still trying to resist the lure of Phyllis. He said lightly:

"Well? What is love?"

"Love?" She hesitated as if formulating her answer. "I suppose it is a different thing to different individuals. Biological chemistry to some; a flame which burns high and hot and out to others—what happens to them is anybody's guess; instantaneous attraction for many, which mounts into passion, steadies into enduring love, settles—if love can be thought of as a settled emotion—into a spiritual and physical partnership which the winds of the world cannot shake, which goes marching along as to martial music."

Her earnest voice broke on the last word. Michael caught her shoulders.

"Instantaneous attraction! You've said it! How do you know all that, Beautiful? Do you love—"

"Sonia!"

Tom Nash spoke from the threshold. Had he seen his quick release of Sonia, Michael wondered, in the instant that he hesitated. He crossed the terrace.

"Sonia, your boss, Brandt, and Jane have cleaned me out. You'll never invite me to play contract again, will you, Miss Serena?" he asked, as his hostess with his wife and Donald Brandt, who looked gigantic in white dinner clothes, came out upon the terrace.

"Not tonight, Thomas, perhaps sometime when you can

keep your mind on the game. You played like a demon, Mr. Brandt, so rapidly and expertly that you impressed me as a man who was anxious to get through that he might catch the last car of an express train."

"Miss Serena, my hat's off to you. Your understanding is uncanny. I liked the game but—I wanted to get through in time to take Sonia to get a moonlit glimpse of my property from the water."

"She can't go. The canoes are locked up. The wind has changed and the water is likely to be rough," Michael Farr protested.

"Besides, canoeing at this time of night is dangerous, Sonia," Jane Nash warned.

Brandt's smile fired Michael with an almost uncontrollable urge to wipe it off with his bare hand.

"I rowed over, my boat is at the pier. There really is no danger, Mrs. Nash. There is no one enough interested in me to push Miss Carson into the water."

"Say!" Tom Nash took a quick step forward. Sonia slid between the two men.

"Of course I'll go, Mr. Brandt. To hear my relatives and friends protest—" for a second her eyes met Michael's —"one would think I was not yet free and twenty-one. Let's go."

She paused on the top step of the terrace.

"I have been hoping ever since I came out that someone would feel the urge to invite me out on the lake in the moonlight. And now it has happened. If hope were not stronger than despair, we women would turn into sob-sisters. Having made which contribution to contemporary thought —I'm ready. Good-night, Cousin Michael."

Michael held a lighter to his cigarette. "Not good-night, Cousin Sonia. I'll be waiting on the pier for you. Don't keep her out too late, Brandt."

Chapter XII

The oars dipped, turned, and dripped molten silver as they rose. The surface of the lake stirred into ever widening circles. Reflected stars dotted it as if a giant striding over the water had scattered a trail of golden coins from a leaky money bag. From somewhere in the distance rose the music of a song. The caressing voice sent Sonia's heart winging to her throat, set Michael Farr's warning echoing in her mind.

"There are times when I feel an irresistible urge to

seize you by the hair—short as it is—and drag you off to my cave, so watch your step, woman."

She looked back. The white mess jackets of Tom and Michael on the pier were mere blurs of light. She snuggled deeper into the crimson cushions in the stern of the boat. She must watch her step or she might like Michael Farr too much. And never, never, never would she allow herself to care for a brother of Guy Farr.

"What's the matter? Cold?" Donald Brandt inquired.

"Cold! It's heavenly warm."

"You shivered. Better put that sweater over your shoulders. It's a pity to cover your stunning gown, but I can't have my architect laid up."

The singer had changed his song to something gay and martial. The oars rose and fell to march time. Brandt leaned forward.

"Glad you defied the authorities and came?"

"I don't know whom you mean by 'authorities' but I am glad I came."

He rested on his oars. The light was faint, but Sonia detected the glint of suspicion in his eyes. She lowered hers quickly to the single lustrous pearl in his shirt front.

"I meant Michael Farr—Nash doesn't count—it struck me that this recently acknowledged cousin of yours is getting a little high-handed. What is he to you—really? Why are you at Kingscourt?"

Darn! Why had she come in the boat? Sonia answered herself. To defy Michael Farr. It seemed a silly reason now. Just what reply could she make to Donald Brandt's question? Something Miss Serena had said flashed into her mind. She laughed.

"What's the joke?" The usual suave note in Brandt's voice was conspicuous by its absence.

"It's not a joke, it is a fact. I am thinking of what Serena said the other day, that sooner or later every female in the family, or near it, flung her problems on Cousin Michael's shoulders. That's why I am at Kingscourt. I went panicky, started on a sort of emotional jamboree, and sobbed out my troubles—figuratively speaking—on his shoulder."

"I'll make a guess that Mrs. D'Arcy has the habit, too. Why didn't you go to Nash?"

"To Tom?" Sonia fenced for time. "To Tom! Tom isn't a real honest-to-goodness relative."

"Is Farr?"

Sonia pretended not to have heard the imperious question. The boat skirted a fern covered point. It swished through tall grasses into a cove.

"Perfect, isn't it?" she whispered, as if she feared by speaking aloud she would disturb the enchanted stillness. "Those silver birches make me think of ghostly sentinels guarding the property."

"Shall we go ashore?"

"No, oh no!"

"Why so horrified? Afraid?"

Sonia leaned elbow on knee, rested her chin on her fingers curled into her palm, and smiled into his aggressive eyes.

"After that taunt, if I were absolutely modern, I suppose I would jeer, 'Afraid!' and insist upon landing. But I confess that I don't like prowling through the woods after dark,—certainly not in this gown—and the trees are still thick although we have done some clearing. Turn back, please. It is getting late. I must be up early in the morning. I want to be at the house before the men begin to plaster. I mean to earn the extra money for superintending the entire building job. Yours being my one and only commission, I can give it my undivided attention. That was what you intended, wasn't it? And, while we are on the subject, do you think you—you could conveniently make me a payment on account? I am financially embarrassed."

She had said it! She had been framing the request in her mind while she had been talking so fast. The last sentence had been theatrically wistful. Not too bad. Michael Farr didn't dislike having her ask Brandt for money half so much as she disliked doing it.

"Do you really need it?"

Sonia regarded him incredulously. This wasn't the suave, eager-to-please person with whom she had dealt before. It was as if the man frowning at her had taken on a protective coloring. Were men like that when a woman asked for money? If they were, she didn't wonder that wives left homes for jobs. The wonder was that more of them didn't. She had been made to feel hotly uncomfortable when asking for a payment to which she was entitled. Michael Farr was right, she should have had a written contract.

"Do you really need it?"

Brandt's repetition brought her thoughts out of the little whirlwind of indignation in which they had been caught.

"Need it! Of course not. I asked only to make conversation. What would a girl want with money?"

"Don't be sarcastic. I hate sarcasm in a woman. That was one of the reasons why I separated from my wife."

94

His announcement was no more surprising to Sonia than the petulance in his voice.

"Your wife! I didn't know you had a wife."

"I haven't, really. I married when I was young. I forged ahead. She stayed as she was. As I prospered she grew unsympathetic, wasn't interested in what interested me. We haven't lived together for years."

As Sonia listened with apparent attention while he enlarged upon his grievance, her thoughts were poking into cracks and corners of her memory. Little things he had said came back to her now, bits like the clues a mystery-yarn writer sows through his story, clues which are dull and meaningless to the absorbed reader until the spotlight of the denouement sets them glinting. She should have known. She said aloud:

"I see. You are one of those misunderstood husbands one hears about. Keep on rowing, please. I really must get back."

"You won't let the fact that I'm married make any difference in our friendship, will you, Sonia?"

"Don't you think business relations better describes the situation?"

"I'm sorry, dear, to think I have hurt you. I shall start proceedings for a divorce at once, and then—"

His hesitation was more expressive than words could have been. Did he think that she was interested in his future plans? She frowned as if puzzled.

"Still talking about the wife? I'm sorry. My thoughts were back on that payment on account. I would like it."

The tenderness vanished from his eyes so quickly that with difficulty she camouflaged a nervous chuckle by a cough. Paying out cash evidently was the man's Achilles heel. He gripped the oars which had been trailing. His jaw tightened.

"If you are suffering for money I can come across, but I'm pretty well tied up. Can't you get along until the trim is on? I'll let you have some—"

"Don't speak as if you were giving me money! Haven't I earned it?"

"You're adorable when you are angry, Sonia." There was an amused man-of-the-world tolerance in his voice. "Of course you have earned the money. The trouble is, I haven't it. I'm rather neglecting business for this Congressional fight. I intend to leave Farr at the post. I can do it."

Sonia forgot money, forgot his evasion. She leaned forward.

"But—can you? I don't know much of the practical

working of politics, but the Farrs have lived in this Congressional district for generations and you are comparatively a new-comer. Won't the voters stand back of the man they have known for years? I suppose that even in politics there is such a thing as loyalty."

"That's gone by. It is the man who counts. There's a new deal all round."

"Michael Farr has enthusiastic backers here."

"How do you know?"

"I have talked with some of them. They realize that he is a man used to great responsibilities which he has handled with skill and courage during these last tricky years. If he can inspire admiration and loyalty among a few, why won't his personality be felt outside his local community?"

"Because his platform, suppression of crime, is a joke. It might have had a pull when he launched his candidacy, but now that the Federal authorities have started to combat organized crime, he isn't needed."

"I haven't noticed that the country has been swept so sweet and clean of criminals that one more worker couldn't help. You don't like Michael Farr, do you?"

"I don't. That man has had everything he wanted handed him on a silver platter from the time he was born. I've had to sweat blood for everything I wanted, and look where I am! Look where I'm going! To Congress. I have the voters pretty well tied up now and—a bomb in my pocket to drop at the strategic moment which will blow what little there is of Farr's chance of winning to smithereens."

"A bomb! What sort of a bomb?"

"He and his family are putting up a grand bluff, you know that. Remember the saying, 'Truth will out'? It's old but still going strong."

"Bombs have been known to go off in pockets."

"This one won't. Why are you staring at me?"

"Was I staring? I was thinking how true it is that a human has several personalities. You, sitting opposite me now, are quite different from the man with whom I thought I was starting out. It is as if a magician had waved his wand, had chanted, 'Abracadabra!' and changed you into someone else. Why accept the hospitality of Kingscourt feeling as you do about Michael Farr?"

"You are here, aren't you?"

"I shan't be here long if you don't bend to those oars," she parried lightly. "This boat is doing the Dancing Dervish act. Let's get back quickly. How dark it is! Michael warned us that the wind had changed."

The moon and stars had disappeared as completely as

if a dirty, wet sponge had been smooched across the sky. From north to south, from east to west there was not a freckle of light. The shrubs and trees along the shore writhed like sinister beasts about to spring. The wind had broken the water into a choppy sea. High overhead a night-hawk shrilled its repetitious war-cry.

Sonia shivered. There was something cruel and dark in the silliness, something maliciously exultant in the eyes of the man facing her. What had he meant by, "Truth will out"? Had he discovered that Dicky was Guy's son? What of it? How could that hurt Michael? If only Guy Farr would write and acknowledge the boy! Why didn't he? Why didn't he? Sometimes she felt as if she must fly to South America and shake the truth out of him.

The boat rounded a point. The windows of Kingscourt twinkled in the dark. A light flashed on the pier, that narrow landing which led to safety and friends and welcome. Sonia's heart, which a sense of danger had set to quickstepping, quieted. She felt safe, a blissful sense of getting home. Two figures on the pier. Were Michael and Tom both waiting for her?

Brandt shipped his oars as the boat tossed toward the landing.

"Your bodyguard is on the job, Sonia."

Nash caught the bow to steady it against the pier and called:

"Hold everything!"

"Right on the job, aren't you, Nash?" Brandt jeered. "What are you afraid Miss Carson will do that you don't let her out of your sight?"

"You don't think I'd tell you, do you?" Tom's grin was wide and engaging. "Help the gal, Farr, this boat is bobbing to beat the band."

Michael steadied the jiggling stern.

"Grab my shoulder, Sonia. Steady!"

As she stepped to the pier, Michael gave the boat a mighty shove.

"There you are, Brandt. It's a sort of 'Here's your hat, what's your hurry?' but your boat will be knocked to pieces against this pier if you don't keep going."

Brandt picked up the oars. In the dim light his face seemed of a piece with his white clothes.

"Much obliged. Don't know how I've managed all these years to get girls home safely without your help, Farr. I'll meet you at the new house in the morning, Sonia."

Sonia watched the boat lurch and bob. "Do you think he is quite safe?"

"Safe!" Tom Nash's repetition was a hoot. "I'm telling you. But we didn't like having you galivanting round on that choppy water, Sonia. Gosh, what a quick change of weather! Farr and I had just decided to get out the speed boat and go after you when you rounded the point. Your dress is damp. Didn't that bozo have a wrap in the boat?"

"He did, but I wasn't cold and didn't need it. Getting darker and darker every minute, isn't it?"

Michael Farr caught her fingers. "Go on, Nash. Throw your flashlight on the path behind you, then Sonia can see where she is stepping."

As they came to the pool, Sonia freed her hand.

"I can see perfectly now, thank you. Tom, what's the rush?"

Nash looked over his shoulder and grinned.

"I've done my Boy Scout deed for the day. Rescuing you from the politician's jaws ought to get me a feather or a stripe or whatever they award for deeds of daring."

Sonia was conscious of Michael Farr close behind her as she ascended the garden path. Why didn't he speak? Was he angry because she had gone on the lake with his political rival? That reminded her! She stopped on the lower step of the terrace. He was so near that her shoulder brushed him as she turned. His eyes met hers. She demanded before she should lose courage:

"What sort of bomb can Donald Brandt explode at the last minute which will hurt your chances of election?"

"Bomb! Was that what he was talking about?"

"Not all the time. Among other things he told me that he had a wife."

"I have known that."

"Why didn't you tell me?" They were on the terrace.

"I thought of course you knew it. Would the fact that he is married have made any difference in your taking the commission?"

"N-no."

"Then why tell you? But about this bomb. Are you at liberty to reveal the exact nature of the explosives in it?"

"Don't laugh. If you had heard Donald Brandt's voice when he spoke of it, you wouldn't think it a joke."

"But what piece of publicity could he spread at the last moment? My life is an open book."

"No pages stuck together? No hoarded gold?"

"Not guilty. Do you care, Sonia, whether I win or lose?"

His eyes were like fingers at her throat, contracting it. With an effort she said lightly:

"Care! Of course. Think how thrilling it would be to have a relative—even an in-law—in Washington. Perhaps—breath-taking thought—perhaps you will some day get to the White House."

He held the door open. The glow from the room shone on his face, revealed the tenderness of his smile.

"Like to live in the White House, light-of-my-eyes? Like to be the wife of a President? I'll see what I can do about it."

"And that's all Donald Brandt's threat means to you," Sonia thought.

"Are you so sure?" she asked gravely.

His eyes were dark now and unsmiling.

"Sure of what? That I will be President, or that you will be my wife?"

"I am trying to warn you that trouble is looming ahead and you—you keep joking."

"Joking! I never was more serious in my life. Don't you believe it?"

"I don't believe anyone whose name is Farr!" Sonia flung over her shoulder before she entered the house.

In her room before the mirror she tried vainly to shut out the memory of his husky voice:

"Like to live in the White House, light-of-my-eyes? Like to be the wife of a President? I'll see what I can do about it."

Gorgeous fooling, of course, but devastatingly upsetting just the same. She couldn't get it out of her mind. He hadn't been alarmed by Donald Brandt's threat, not for a minute. What was the old bomb anyway?

She stopped in the process of unclasping the string of near-pearls about her throat. There was apprehension in the dark eyes which met the eyes of the looking-glass girl. Had her suspicion been correct? Could it be about Ruby and Dicky? Did Brandt intend to spread the news of that clandestine marriage over the front pages of the newspapers?

Chapter XIII

Michael Farr paced the floor of his office. Once he glanced at the brass-framed calendar on the broad desk. The last of October. Election but a few days distant. How different the summer had been from what he had planned the day Sonia Carson had come to Kingscourt for the first time. July had seen him in Washington and across the water following up loans the Trustees had made for the Farr Estate. August came and went while he was on the same business in the West. September and most of the present month had been absorbed by the Congressional campaign, meetings, speeches, more meetings, radio talks. Out of the whirl and heat and bitterness had come one satisfaction. People were interested in the working of the government as they had not been since eighteenth century days. Politics had become a personal matter to millions, who before had hardly known the first letter of the word. And millions of people had become a matter of personal concern to the politicians.

He gazed unseeingly at the single talisman rose in the slender crystal vase on his desk. Would he win out? Could he win against Brandt who had had the advantage of being in the district all summer? That wasn't the only advantage he had enjoyed. He had had Sonia's companionship. She had been absorbed in her work to the exclusion of everyone but Dicky and Serena and her boss. On the few evenings he had been at Kingscourt he had had opportunity for no more than a word or two with her. He had seen her but once since the evening when she had said:

"I don't believe anyone whose name is Farr!"

Had she avoided him? If she had, why? Was it her way of letting him know that she did not care for him? He had tried to appear indifferent to her moods. If she realized how passionately he loved her she might feel that she must leave his home. Now, he would make her stop, look, listen. The long expected letter from Guy had arrived.

He dropped into a chair at the broad desk and picked up the closely written sheets of paper which had come in the morning mail. He frowned as he read.

"Yours about Ruby Carson and the child at hand. Someone is stringing you, m'lad. I'll come clean. I did marry Ruby, but Ruby died. Because of opposition and complications, I went haywire, I guess; that's the only reason I can think of now which will account for my slipping on the ball-and-chain. Her sister Sonia stood between us every chance she could get. She didn't like me and—well, I finally persuaded Ruby to slip off to a Justice of the Peace. She was different from the girls I had played round with—ideals and all that, if you get what I mean. The sisters were a throwback to 1900 or thereabout in bringing-up—New England mother.

"Had the dickens of a fight persuading Ruby to keep the marriage secret for a time, even from her sister. It was the year Father was ill. I knew what would happen if he discovered that I had married without his consent. The old 'You're-no-longer-son-of-mine' patriarchs would have had nothing on him. Ruby began to be infernally jealous. Every time I saw her she would dissolve in tears. Now, I ask you! Never could I stand a sniffling woman. I stopped going. She wrote that a baby was coming. I figured that it was a trick to get me back. Then one day came a letter from the sister telling me that Ruby and the child had died.

"What was her object in writing that if it were not true? You say that old Lib recognized the boy as a Farr. She's a sentimental—"

The sentence remained unfinished. Further down the page the letter began again.

"As I was writing the above, something bit me. For weeks I didn't know anything. I'm ready to swear that once I heard the click of golden gates. My mistake. I doubt if I would have gone in that direction. It is more probable that I heard a red-hot iron grating clang. Well, I went neither up nor down. I am still on earth, thin as a rail and about as bloodless. They tell me that it will take several years before I stage a come-back. Imagine me a semi-invalid! It's a cockeyed world!

"Your second letter in which you stated that you were convinced of the justice of the boy's claim came while I was giving old man Death a run for his money. I can't believe it, Mike. What would be Sonia's object in writing that both Ruby and the child were gone? To be sure, she always detested me, but she had no money except what she earned. Of course you couldn't find a record of the marriage in that New York town— from your letter I judge that you turned the place upside down—I fixed that with the clerk. Couldn't take the risk of Father getting on to the ceremony.

"Quite a trick to keep Sonia and the boy at Kingscourt as new-found cousins. I'll bet the county tongues are hung in the middle and are clacking at both ends. We'll keep them guessing till I get back to make the dramatic announcement that he is my long lost che-ild. I will start for home as soon as I can get out of the jungle. While lying here in this tent I have nothing to do but think and plan. I want to see the boy. He's probably a spoiled kid. I want more to take him away from Sonia Carson—you say she is devoted to him—

it will even up for a few of the things she said to Ruby about me. I'll send him to our Prep School, give him all the money he wants, and bring him up to be the best sport in the country."

There was a page descriptive of his surroundings, another devoted to what the expedition had accomplished. At the end he wrote:

"Draw from my reserve for whatever money the boy needs. Put the skids under Sonia—on second thought wait till I get there. I'll take pleasure in doing it myself."

Michael slipped the letter into his pocket. Sonia had been right in her fear that if he knew of the boy Guy would take him away from her. How well she understood the man who had married her sister. And he had married her, there was no longer doubt of that. The child could take the Farr name; but he must not be separated from Sonia unless she thought it was wise. Could he make Guy listen to reason?

He crossed to the window. The days were shortening. Outside towers and spires were silhouetted against a crimson afterglow. A distant clock chimed. Lights appeared in tall buildings. The city was hooding its typewriters before starting for home.

The door opened. Linda Hale came quickly into the room and closed it behind her. Her tone was as crisp and vivid as the little red curl on her forehead.

"Mrs. D'Arcy is here."

"What Mrs. D'Arcy?"

Michael remembered that he had asked that same question once before in the same surprised voice. Was his secretary remembering also? Her lips twitched—was she laughing?

"Mrs. Bill D'Arcy."

"What does she want?"

"Shall I ask her?"

"No. Send her in."

What the dickens was Phyl's scheme now, he wondered, as he waited. He had become expert at dodging her, at turning down her invitations—they had been many. He didn't flatter himself that she cared for him; of course, she might visualize herself as a social leader in Washington—he had taken up the Congressional fight after she had run away with Bill D'Arcy—but the betting was that Brandt would win out.

Brandt! He had told Sonia that he had a bomb up his sleeve which would shatter his opponent's chances. A bomb! Ridiculous. He had been talking loud, wide, and handsome, the great mouthpiece!

"So good of you to see me, Michael," Phyllis D'Arcy acknowledged softly, as she crossed the room in a faint wave of perfume.

He knew the brand, he had purchased enough of it at twenty dollars per ounce. He looked at her in her black frock, which accentuated the soft gleam of her pearls; at her wide blue eyes and wistful red lips. He regarded her critically. Charming, perhaps, but bloodless. The woman standing there had for him not a particle of allure. Couldn't she sense his indifference? There was something cruel and cold about her, something intangible which repelled him. Had he been under a spell that he had not realized it before? She was as harmless to his emotions as old Sara Grimm; he had a hunch, though, that she might prove quite as irritating.

"What's the idea of coming here, Phyl?"

She perched on one corner of his desk.

"Sit down, Michael. Don't prowl. I was detained in the city and I thought you might be noble enough to take a lonely lady out for tea. But, first, I have something on my mind and I want your undivided attention." She leaned toward him as he pulled out the chair opposite. "What do you really know about those Nash people, Michael?" The question was drenched with innuendo.

"What do you mean by 'know'?"

She hunched her shoulders in the motion he detested.

"Don't snap. I mean just what I said. What do you know about the strange couple Miss Serena picked up? The wife has a certain veneer but he is the original rough diamond, or a well thought-out imitation. Just because they are alleged cousins of Sonia Carson doesn't prove anything. I think they will bear watching."

"If that absurd suspicion is what you came here to tell me, now that you have it off your mind I suggest that this is my busy day, Phyllis. Sorry, but I can't take you to tea. I have an important date. You'd better go."

"That is just the beginning. I came also to warn you to watch out for trouble. There is a rumor started about you as a candidate which you should know."

Tipped back in the swivel chair, Michael frowned at her. Was her mysterious manner simply good theatre or had she heard something? She was friendly with Brandt. Had he confided to her as he had to Sonia that he had a bomb up his sleeve?

"Shoot! If this startling revelation has no more sense than your other phony suggestion, you have wasted your time, to say nothing of mine, by coming here, Phyllis."

Her eyes were on her pink-tipped white hand from which she had drawn the glove, the left hand upon which a narrow circlet of diamonds glittered. She outlined a design on the green blotter with a slim finger.

"Have you any idea the amount of talk that Miss Carson living at Kingscourt with that child has started?"

The question brought him to his feet.

"What do you mean?"

She shrugged. "Only that people suspect that the boy, who is so unmistakably a Farr, is yours."

"Mine! What rot! If he were mine why wouldn't I say so?"

"Don't ask me."

"Phyl, if you shrug your shoulders again, I'll—I'll—oh, never mind. What has all this stuff to do with my candidacy? Is this the warning you came to hand me?"

"Yes, but you needn't bite my head off—when I am here to help. You are not very sympathetic, Michael. The day that horrid Nash woman pushed me into the pool, you laughed. I saw you." Her long lashes swept up, her lips trembled.

"Old stuff, Phyl. You'll be surprised. It doesn't click any more. Get on with the warning."

She swallowed and dabbed at her eyes. "How you have changed."

He loomed over her as she perched on the end of the desk.

"Was that what you came here to tell me? Be as ingenue as you please, but get on with your real reason for coming."

"You are brutal, Michael. You don't deserve to know that Brandt's campaign manager means to—"

In response to the buzzer, Michael picked up the desk phone.

"Who? Brandt? Tell him I'm busy. . . . Hold the line." He put his hand over the receiver.

"Where are you going, Phyl?"

"Out your private door. I wouldn't have Don Brandt find me here for worlds."

"Come back! Don't slip out as if you were doing something—"

He ground a forcible exclamation between his teeth as the door closed softly behind her. Was she trying to give the effect of something clandestine? He uncovered the receiver.

"Brandt still there, Miss Hale? . . . Send him in."

"This is luck, to find you in and at leisure, Farr," Donald Brandt boomed, as he entered the room. He stopped for an instant near the threshold. Michael would have sworn that he sniffed. Did he recognize the scent of Phyl's perfume. Why had she come? Having come, why the dickens had she sneaked out?

"Won't you sit down?"

"I won't detain you but a moment; afraid I have interrupted more important business."

Michael, with difficulty, controlled a savage urge to twist his fingers in the silvery white hair and yank until his victim yelled for mercy. Collegiate stuff. Hadn't he outgrown that phase? He detested having his business office hazy with smoke but he pushed forward a bronze box.

"Smoke?"

"No, thanks, I'm not a smoker."

"Or a swimmer?"

Michael never had seen a skin turn so dark a red.

"I'm glad for a chance to explain about the night D'Arcy went overboard, Farr. I didn't feel called upon to risk my life to save a drunk. If it had been daylight—"

"It was dark, wasn't it, but not too dark to see his face the first time he came up."

"Are you implying—"

"I'm implying nothing. I'm saying things."

"Are you planning to say those things at the rally?"

"That would be a talking point, wouldn't it?—but I don't have to depend on personalities to win."

"You don't! I have no such scruples. I'm out to win this fight—watch me, just watch me."

Tom Nash's words flashed into Michael's mind:

"I'll bet some personality expert tipped Brandt off that he had personality-plus."

Michael's lips twitched. Brandt certainly had his personality running on high now. He glanced at the clock on the wall.

"All right, I'll watch you. If that is all you came to tell me, I'll remind you that I'm busy."

"I suspected that when I came in. Your secretary said you were in conference." Brandt picked up his hat.

"What I really came to say was that my campaign manager has the goods on you, Farr."

"What do you mean, 'goods'? Are you starting a broadcasting system? What are the initials of your network?" Michael's voice reflected his amused scorn. "I suppose he's been looking up my tax returns, what? That stunt, like the poor, is always with us."

"No. He has put the Farr estate returns through a fine sieve. Nothing doing there—but—*

"Do you know, you are getting on my nerves." Michael flexed his arms suggestively. "I'm not an entirely responsible person when my nerves go ragged."

With his hand on the knob of the door Brandt smiled.

"As I was suggesting—better withdraw from the fight and withdraw quick. If you don't—"

"And if I don't?"

"I shall hate of course to do it, admiring Miss Carson as I do—"

"Leave Miss Carson out of this!" Fury hoarsened Michael's voice.

"How can I? It wouldn't be honest to the voters not to let them know your aunt who ran away never was married, that this long lost relative stuff is a blind, that the boy is yours—that . . . I guess you're keen enough to realize from what I've suggested that you're washed up for good, Farr."

Michael's eyes burned with anger. So Brandt and his dirty gang thought Dicky was his boy. He had Guy's letter. Should he produce it? No. It was up to Guy to acknowledge his son. He laughed.

"I washed up! There's no such thing as being washed up for good while I'm alive, Brandt. Don't fool yourself. As for that bomb! Before you drop it you'd better be mighty sure that it isn't a dud."

Chapter XIV

October was going out in a blaze of color. Foliage, brown, crimson, with flashes of flame, still fluttered on the trees like thousands of gay little flags flying. Grass was tinged with rust. The ultramarine lake rippled with gold where the sunlight touched it. A light breeze which rose and fell brushed its surface with rhythmic sound. Gauzy mists lay in the coves. Far-away hills fused into an amethyst sky. One fleecy cloud snuggled on a purple hilltop like an ermine collar pulled close about the throat of a lovely woman.

"What a background!" Michael Farr thought, as seated

in his black roadster his eyes came back to the recently completed house.

It was not only attractive, it was wistfully appealing. Its windows were clear and gleaming, its open door inviting. Its early American plan was perfect for the location; the great maple near it divinely designed to set off the brick chimney, its sun-checkered red-brown roof and its natural colored clapboards. A small bird was dusting itself in the drive. A bicycle leaning against the porch gave it a lived-in look.

"And the Lord God said, It is not good that the man should be alone; I will make him an helpmeet for him."

Had the sight of the house sent those words bubbling to the top of his mind? When had he stored that bit of Holy Writ in his subconscious, Michael asked himself.

With potted plants and a vase of flowers hugged tight against her rusty-orange knit suit, Sonia Carson came around a corner of the house. She stopped in surprise as Michael approached.

"You! How long have you been here?"

"Long enough to realize that your house is a knockout."

"Then you are not sorry you sold us the land?"

Michael flinched at "us" but responded cordially:

"Not for a minute. Even if I were, I never hold postmortems over decisions. When a thing is done, it's done, with me. Look out!"

He caught the blue vase, which, with that lack of a sense of the timely so characteristic of inanimate things, had slipped from her arm.

"Why do you load yourself up with all this stuff? Aren't there men enough at Kingscourt to do this sort of work?"

"Don't growl. I only brought them around the corner." She looked at the house, then up at Michael. "Like it?"

"It's a winner. Finished?"

"The house is. Pools and stable, tennis court and gardens are still on paper. I would advise no landscaping until the purchaser moves in, then the family can study the views and decide what features it wants to emphasize and get the full artistic value from the natural beauty of the place. All it needs now is a woman to purchase, adore and complete. Won't you come in?"

He followed as she entered the spacious living-room walled in knotty pine. She set her burden, plant by plant, on the shelves in the double window corner which was already stocked with ferns, ivy, and salmon pink geraniums. She stood back to regard them.

"It's astonishing what a vivid effect the living green gives to this unfurnished room, isn't it? That window is one of my selling points. I borrowed the plants from your greenhouse; one of the men brought them over. I hope you don't mind."

"Mind! Don't be foolish."

"You needn't clutch that blue vase any longer. Set it on the mantel. I suppose you think me a little mad to fill those shelves, but, having been brought up to be a perfect gentleman, you aren't saying so."

His arm on the pine mantel, Michael watched her as humming happily she rearranged the plants. She was gay, vivid, beautiful. A glowing human being. She appeared to be without a care in the world. Would the letter in his pocket cast a spell over her light-heartedness? She need not know at present of Guy's threat to take his son. Perhaps she need never know. He doubtless wrote that on impulse. When he thought the matter over he would side-step responsibility— if he knew him, and no one knew him better. He might not return to civilization for years.

As if she felt Michael's appraising regard, Sonia looked up.

"Why are you scowling? You are the answer to a screen director's prayer with that expression—Cousin Michael."

Her gayety of spirit was a revelation. He had seen flashes of it but nothing like this; it set his blood quick-stepping.

"I was thinking that you are an entirely different person from the girl who came to Kingscourt last June; you are so vivid, so tinglingly alive."

"But this is such an on-tiptoes morning! It is so crisp, so cool, so stimulating, how can one help being tinglingly alive? Don't you feel it?"

"Sure, I feel it. Love this work, don't you?"

"I do. Always have loved houses. Never could pass an attractive one without an impulse to pat it. I hope someone will like this. It is a lovable house. Like the lady of Words-worth's poem, 'Not too bright or good for human nature's daily food.' Would you—would you care to look it over?"

She asked the question diffidently with a slight increase of color.

"Care! Of course I want to see it. Any nibbles yet?" Michael asked, as he followed her into the soft yellow walled dining-room.

She set the blue vase with tall stalks of purple and lavender salpiglosis and red amaryllis against the gold lining of the corner cupboard.

"Isn't that perfect? The woman who can resist that deserves to be sentenced to a two-room-and-bath walk-up for life. Yes, one prospect already. A bride and groom came while I was here yesterday. He sounded like business, he asked all sorts of questions about costs. Her pet line is, apparently, 'Yes, Sam,' 'Just as you say, Sam.' She's a hangover from that dark age when woman's place was in the home—only."

"Go on, tell me more about them," Michael encouraged, as he preceded her up the charming stairway. Not that he cared about the bride and groom, but he wanted to keep this fascinating Sonia Carson talking.

"Not much more to tell. He shook his shiny, black lacquered head over the heating plant; said he was afraid it would lap up a lot of oil. I'll wager he is the sort who will check up on the amount of butter and eggs she uses and ask her what she did with the last dollar he gave her. She will bear down heavily with bridge lamps and petit point in the décor, but what have you? If their social recommendations are all right, the building and architect want to sell. People are just beginning to be house-conscious again. They have to be tended and coaxed along like a baby learning to walk."

"Have you had that payment on account yet?"

"I have. Notice that I have planned two so-called master's bedrooms with baths? Being crowded into close quarters wrecks more marriages, I believe, than any other cause. Life is much more of an adventure if a man dashes into his wife's room for her to slip in his cuff links than if he is fussing and fuming about them at his dresser in the same room."

"You know a lot about men for one so young."

He watched her slow color rise as her eyes met his.

"I know a lot about their behavior patterns. Where were we when I digressed with my monologue on the perils of matrimony?"

"At the master's bedrooms."

"Oh yes—notice the window seat built over the radiator? Three closets. Shoe shelves, so that the Head of the House won't have to fumble round on the floor for his shoes. I'm quite mad about those mirror-back shelves for decorative bottles and jars in that smart black and flame bathroom. Isn't it a triumph of modernity? If a woman is as old as she looks, a house is as old as its bathrooms. That slogan popped to the surface of my mind in the middle of last night."

"You have missed your vocation. Instead of an architect, you should be a real estate agent. My fingers are itching to sign on the dotted line of the deed of this house."

"Then you like it really?"

"I told you, it's a knockout. And what a view!"

They stood side by side at an upper window. Far off loomed purple ridges, their foothills lightly brushed with green. The lake glinted like a huge mirror, deeply tranquil in the middle, but frilled with white along the shore where its ripples encountered rock or bar. Sunshine lay warmly on its shallows. Birds were flitting, darting, planing through the branches of a mammoth hemlock which dominated the foreground with an air of sombre mystery.

Michael turned away from the window.

"The house is perfect."

"It may not be perfect, but it is soundly constructed, it has insulation and fire-stopping, air-conditioning, rust-proof gutters and flashings. It is built on honor for durability, convenience, and comfort. It is surprising how new methods and new materials are bringing building costs down."

"You have put a lot of yourself into this house, haven't you? I hope you put the deal across today."

"I am not selling it. That is the agent's job. I wish I were buying it."

As they reached the living-room door, she said: "See the sun streaming into that plant corner! See how it accentuates the green of the leaves, the pink of the blossoms? I would like to live here myself."

"Like it better than Kingscourt?" Michael demanded jealously.

"Don't be absurd. Comparing this house with yours is like comparing an igloo with Buckingham Palace. But I believe that a home like this helps keep a man and woman together, it gets to be an expression of their personalities. Not that Kingscourt isn't perfect; life there is so harmonious. No clashing of temperaments, no creaking of domestic machinery. It's a heavenly atmosphere. I would not have believed that daily living could be so smooth. A mansion like Kingscourt reflects the personalities of past generations."

"Just at present it is reflecting a modern of the moderns."

"I don't suppose you would care to see the kitchen?" Sonia asked quickly.

Did she realize that he had been thinking of the changes in décor Phyllis had made in his home?

"Of course I want to see the kitchen. Want to see it all. Otherwise how can I recommend you as an architect?"

"Thinking of employing me?" she asked gaily from the threshold of the green and white room. "Then I must polish up my line.

"See that ventilator? It carries off the odor of cooking

so it can't penetrate to living-room and hall. Been done in large houses but not much in smaller ones where it is needed more. Here's the built-in ironing board with electric plug, and here is the breakfast room, off the dining-room. See the windows? Morning sun. Man of the house eats breakfast here and starts off for town all comfy within and lighted up with courage."

"You have thought of everything, haven't you, even of the intangibles. Love it, don't you? You said you would like to live here. Anyone particularly in mind as a companion?" Michael probed in a voice he tried to keep light but which betrayed him with one break.

What a wonderful face she had, he thought, as her laughing, radiant eyes met his. With an attempt at shaping her lips into a wistful line, she sighed.

"I can't answer that. My love life has had a terrible shovin' round. This real estate agent! His irresistible eyes have done things to my heart. The eagle look!"

The effort to keep from silencing her tormenting lips with his sent the color in a dark tide to Michael's hair. Were Brandt's eyes, not the agents, irresistible?

Sonia started for the door. Did she feel the electricity in the atmosphere?

"I must get away before the agent arrives. Close the door. It locks itself."

"I will drive you back."

"But my bicycle is here. Lucky for me they are in fashion. I have saved gallons of gas in my trips back and forth from Kingscourt."

"We'll bundle the bike into the rumble. I want to talk with you."

She looked up at him. Her eyes shadowed.

"Your voice sets my nerves prickling. Have you—have you—" Her question thinned to a whisper.

"I have heard from Guy. Hop in."

He wheeled the bicycle along the flagged walk and lifted it into the roadster.

Sonia's gayety and exuberance had vanished as completely as a snuffed-out candle flame. All sparkle and color had gone from her voice. She was the troubled, on-the-defense girl who had come to his office that never to be forgotten June day. That letter had been the killjoy. Was she gay and light-hearted with Brandt as she had been with him this morning before Guy had cast his shadow? Brandt! Would he dare bring Sonia and the boy into the political fight? Little as he liked the man he couldn't believe that of him.

Beside him in the roadster, Sonia confided with an apparent effort to give her words the light touch:

"You have no idea how many extras slink in after one has a house planned. The moment I think of a thing I visualize it. If I see a frock I like, I dramatize myself in it. Imagination is a fearsome thing. Why am I chattering? Let's get it over. What have you to tell me?"

"I can't tell you here. We'll drive to your workroom; there we can talk without interruption."

The thought of all he wanted to say that had no relation to Guy and the boy rushed over him like a high and dangerous wave. The speedometer shot to 70. As Sonia clutched her soft beret it slid back to 45.

"Sorry."

Sunlight patched the road, the shining black road which was taking them to Kingscourt. The swish of the car stirred up little spiral pillars of whirling leaves. A powdery haze, opal and faintly pink, hung about the dark tree-tops; there was a scent of wood smoke in the air, a murmur of unseen life in the shrubbery. Sunlight lay on the hilltops, purple shadows in the valleys.

Michael's thoughts kept pace with the wheels. Why should he be so low in his mind about winning Sonia when he was so sure, in spite of head waggings and warnings, that he would win out in the Congressional fight?

"No man has earned a woman till he has put up a no-surrender battle, has doggedly hitched his wagon to her particular star," he reminded himself, with the result that his spirit picked up. The sunlight became warmer, the sky bluer, trees and shrubs stood out clearer in air which quivered with life. He felt a swift, tumultuous certainty that the girl beside him would be his.

"Far be it from me to suggest to such a superb driver," Sonia broke in on his thoughts, "but the temperamental spurts of this roadster are making me dizzy."

He fought the impulse to tell her what he had been thinking, held back the lover ready to leap into his voice and eyes.

"Sorry; must have been rehearsing an impromptu speech for the last rally next week. Brandt and I are speaking on the same platform, in a town from which he has been ordering building supplies. Add that up. He will be as irresistible as a band. Perhaps he will have one there."

"You don't seem particularly depressed about it."

"Oh, I'm keeping my powder dry. What the dickens—"

He brought the roadster to a sudden stop in the drive behind the sportshouse. On the broad terrace, with its background of curtainless mullioned windows, sat Dicky in golden-tan blouse and shorts. His dimpled legs were spread wide. Between them he clutched the wriggling Sealyham with one hand. With a long brush he was absorbed in adding the finishing touches to the dog's stubby tail. Shreddy's body was already striped with green paint till it looked like nothing so much as a scrap of awning cloth. A daub on the tip of the boy's nose glowed like a huge emerald against his rose-leaf skin.

"Dicky! What in the world—" Sonia's voice bubbled into an infectious ripple.

The startled child looked up. The dog took advantage of his diverted attention and broke away to whirl into a merry-go-round gone mad as he attempted to lick the paint from his tail. Sturdily, on feet spread wide apart, the boy regarded the man and girl who had left the roadster.

"H'loa." He hopped up and down in suspense. "Sonia won't let me say, 'Did you bwing me a pwesent, Cousin Mike.' So you must say, 'What do you fink I bwought you, Dicky?'"

Michael threw back his head and shouted with laughter.

"Don't laugh at him, don't! Dicky! That is just the same as asking for presents," Sonia reproved sternly. "Where is Nanette?" She took the brush dripping with paint from the boy's hand.

"Weadin'. She's alwus weadin'. I found the paint in your workwoom, Sonia. There she is!"

"Well, for the love of Pete!"

Even her startled exclamation did not disturb the Oriental impassivity of the face of the little maid in the doorway.

"Nanette, take poor Shreddy to the garage and ask Johnny to clean him," Michael Farr directed.

"I can see where we will be unpopular with Johnny," Sonia commented. "After you have left the dog, Nanette, take Dicky to the house and remove the paint from him."

As the maid and boy and wriggling dog disappeared around a corner of the sportshouse, Dicky's voice drifted back.

"Will the paint stay on al-wus, Nanette?"

"I guess so, unless that Filipino Johnny gives Shreddy a bob. Always pulling some crazy stunt, aren't you, Dicky Carson?"

"That seems to be that. I ought to be the stern disciplinarian; instead, I can't help seeing the funny side of it.

Please, please do not bring Dicky another present for weeks," Sonia pleaded. "He expects a gift every time you appear."

"I have brought him roller-skates this time and a pair for Nanette. Think him too young for them?"

"No, but you are spoiling him." With a quick change of tone, she commanded:

"Now tell me!"

She pulled forward a peacock chair on the flagged terrace. She leaned her head against the spreading back of fine wicker and looked up at him.

What uselessly long lashes, Michael thought, as he faced her. With an effort he averted his eyes and regarded the path which meandered through russet-tinged fields to the lake, still now as a mirror shining like molten metal. Somewhere near a bee hummed. From a field came the call,

"Bob White! Bob White!"

Michael's eyes came back to Sonia.

"Tell me, quick! What did your brother write?"

Her voice was barely more than a whisper. Her dark eyes seemed like big, velvety pansies. Old stuff, that had been thought and said before, Michael reminded himself. Her long, graceful fingers gripped the arms of the chair till the nails showed white under the pink lacquer.

"What did he write?" she repeated.

"Don't be so breathless, dear. He admits the marriage."

She drew a long, sobbing breath; then bit her lips as if to steady them.

"He has taken his time in replying, hasn't he?"

"He has been ill. He is coming home."

"Home! To Kingscourt?"

"He is eager to see his son."

"Guy Farr eager to see the boy! I don't believe it. You are making that up to give a good impression of your brother."

"Play fair, Sonia. That isn't true and you know it." He took a letter from his pocket, and turned the pages. "He writes:

> " 'I'll start for home as soon as I can get out of the jungle. While lying here in this tent I have nothing to do but think and plan. I want to see the boy.' "

Michael folded the letter. His color rose as he met Sonia's intent eyes.

"What did you skip?"

"Just something about drawing from his reserve for money."

"Now it's my turn to say, "Play fair." He intends to take Dicky away from me, doesn't he? It would be like him. He hated me. I tried to move my little heaven and my little earth to prevent Ruby from marrying him. He is the kind who wouldn't forget."

"Steady, Sonia. Guy may think he wants the boy now, but he won't stand for the responsibility. He—"

"He won't have a chance to stand for it!"

She was on her feet. Her color had ebbed away under her tan.

"He won't get it. Before he can reach home, Dicky and I will be so far away that he never will find us. We—"

"Better get going, then," advised a voice behind them.

Sonia stared incredulously at the thin, gaunt man in the doorway. Guy Farr! Could it be? He had been so gay, so debonair; now there was no youth left in his face.

Michael gripped his hand.

"Guy! When did you come?"

The drooping eyelid half covered one icy blue eye as Guy Farr drawled:

"Flew. Couldn't wait to see the boy and—Sister Sonia."

Chapter XV

A terrifying moment. A moment at the crossroads. A moment patched with the grim shadows of possible mistakes and the glitter of traps for her hesitant feet. Everything was bound to change and never be the same again. Should she show Guy Farr how she detested him, or should she be politic for the sake of Ruby's son? Sonia demanded of herself.

"Diplomacy, woman, diplomacy," she decided. "What you say or do now may make or mar Dicky's future."

With hands extended, she welcomed breathlessly:

"You! You! What a relief! What an unbelievable relief! Now there will be someone to share the responsibility of the boy!"

If that saccharine greeting hadn't drawn his fangs, nothing would. If she lived to be a hundred she would not forget the swift change in the man's eyes from malicious triumph of incredulity. Without looking, she was aware of Michael's attitude of icy unbelief. Guy Farr was the first to rally. He seized the outstretched hands.

"This is a welcome worth flying thousands of miles to get. You are even lovelier than I remembered you, Sonia, and you may remember that I thought you beautiful?" There was a hint of daring in his voice and more than a hint of innuendo.

As he lingeringly released her hands to slip his arm within the unresponsive arm of his brother, Sonia told herself that one might think from tone and impassioned manner that she was a long lost love instead of a girl who never had hesitated to show her dislike of him. Could she keep up the appearance of cordiality tinged with interest which was a smoke-screen to hide her detestation? Could she! No question of could. She must. For Dicky's sake. What would Michael think of her swift change of heart? He knew that she had fought against Guy when he wanted to marry her sister. Would he be keen enough to recognize the reason for her present tactics, or would he think that she had opposed their marriage because she wanted his priceless brother herself? That was a thought! What fiend had sent it flashing through her mind?

Her throat ached, her eyes burned from emotion held in leash as she looked at the brothers. Was she up against defeat? Would those two men stand together against her and take the boy? What was she to them? Nothing. They were linked by kinship and tradition, heavenly twins which would unite them solidly against her. Was it worth while to go on fighting for Dicky? It seemed as if she had been fighting against or for something for years. Without him she could go anywhere, travel anywhere in the interest of her profession.

"But I don't want to go without him," she told herself passionately. "I want to help him grow to be a fine man."

Michael's voice brought her thoughts back to the present.

"You almost beat your letter, Guy. That arrived yesterday."

"As I said, m'lad, I had a chance to hop it; the letter came by boat. Sit down, Sonia. Don't keep the gentlemen standing. I'm about all in. I am still feeling the effects of that infernal bite."

His voice weakened. His face was white; lassitude enveloped him like a crumpled garment. He drooped. Michael caught his arm.

"Get into my car. I will drive you to the house. Better not try to walk back through the garden."

He half lifted Guy into the roadster.

"Shall I leave the bike here, Sonia?"

"Please."

"Aren't you coming?" Guy Farr demanded.

"Later. This is my workshop. I will be up for luncheon."

She watched the car until it was out of sight. Michael had looked at her but once. Without closing her eyes, she could see his, clear and clean and about as warming as two ice-cubes. Did he think that she was a victim of his brother's charm? If he did, so much the better. If only in some way she could commit Guy to giving her the guardianship of the boy. Not that she thought herself infallible as guide, philosopher, and friend, but she was better than his father, a whole lot better.

She entered the main room of the sportshouse, only to wander restlessly from one uncurtained mullioned window which presented a picture of the sparkling lake set like a gigantic mirror in a huge mosaic of browns and reds and scarlet, to one which framed a view of the heavenly-blue tiled swimming pool.

How cool and refreshing the water looked, splashed with gold where the sunlight touched it on this Indian summer day. Had she time for a dip before luncheon? She glanced at the clock. Time to swim back and forth, at least. The exercise would help restore physical and mental balance.

Every nerve and muscle in her body had been tense since the moment Michael Farr had told her that the letter from his brother had arrived. She had been fanning wings of exuberant satisfaction over her house when he had appeared. Was life always like that? Peaks of enthusiasm, hollows of discouragement and disillusion?

A few moments later on the edge of the pool she pulled a cap tight over her hair.

"Wonder if it's cold?"

She shivered. Dived.

Under the water she slid like a red and ivory arrow. Half way across she came to the surface, swam lazily, loving the sun on her bare shoulders and arms. With a quick turn she started back. As she clutched the rungs to pull herself out, a voice boomed:

"Need any help?"

She almost dropped back into the water as Donald Brandt in riding clothes approached the pool. She was reminded of Paris in A Tale of Troy.

"A panther's eye and a peacock air," she quoted to herself.

"What's the joke, Sonia?" Brandt demanded.

"Shouldn't a lady smile when she sees you?" she parried. No use quoting John Masefield to him; probably he never had heard of the poet. Why had he come? She shook moisture from her eyes and climbed to the coping. Seated there with her toes in the water, she tugged off her red cap and shook back her curling black hair.

"That was purely a rhetorical question, wasn't it? You dropped into that chair as if you never intended to move again."

"I can move if I have sufficient inducement, and what bigger one could I have than you?" He pulled the chair close to her.

For the first time in her grown-up life, Sonia was uncomfortably conscious of the brevity of her swim-suit. She felt like a centipede, all bare arms and legs. She was getting provincial. Didn't every woman wear this sort of thing? To bridge what was getting to be an uncomfortable silence, she asked eagerly:

"Why are you here at this time of day? Did the bride and groom buy?"

"Haven't heard. Do you ever think of anything or anyone besides houses and Dicky?"

"Occasionally, but business for business hours is my slogan. My business hours are from 9 to 5."

"You are a maddening person. I feel as if I never probed beneath the surface of your mind. You are always glitteringly light-hearted—"

"'I only mark the hours that shine,'" Sonia quoted glibly. "If you didn't come to tell me that our prospects have signed on the dotted line, what did you come for?"

"I might say that I came to see you."

"Don't, for I shouldn't believe you."

"I came to ask you a question."

"Ask on. There are no secrets in my young life."

Secrets. She felt her face warm with color as she mentally repeated the word. Hadn't the real reason of her being at Kingscourt been carefully guarded? No necessity of that after today. Guy Farr had returned to acknowledged and claim his son.

Brandt appeared absorbed in a pattern he was tracing on the stone coping.

"I called on Michael Farr at his office yesterday. I was rather unfortunate in the time I chose. Mrs. D'Arcy slipped out of his private door as I entered."

Phyllis D'Arcy "slipping"—horrid word—out of Michael's office! Had Serena been right? Was she trying to attract him again? He had been at home so little that she had had no opportunity of judging. He had been light-hearted enough the night of Bill D'Arcy's accident. So light-hearted that he had laughed: "You couldn't say, 'Good-night, Mos'

118

Dear,' to me, could you?" She remembered her impulse to draw his head against her shoulder, the haggard lines in his face had been so at odds with his voice and manner.

"Has the fact that Phyllis D'Arcy was at Farr's office struck you dumb?"

Had she appeared as if in a trance, Sonia wondered, in the instant before she protested:

"Don't call me dumb! I don't like it. Why so theatrical? The stage lost a grand leading man when you went in for construction. You would make thousands of women who saw you on the screen discontented with their prosaic and hard-working husbands. Wouldn't that be a triumph? I was amazed that you spoke of dropping in upon Michael Farr as if it were an epoch-making event—something like calling at the White House. I was thinking of that, not of the glamorous D'Arcy. Haven't you been at his office before to talk land?"

"This time I went to talk politics."

There was an implication in his voice which started a premonitory pricking in Sonia's submerged pink toes.

"Politics!" She crinkled her brows as if never before had she heard the word. "Do opponents usually get together to talk things over?"

"This is not a usual situation. I went to advise Farr to withdraw from the fight."

"Withdraw! Just why would you advise him to withdraw?"

Brandt tapped one polished legging with his riding-crop.

"Remember that the night we were on the lake I mentioned a bomb? That's the reason. The consequences will be rather unpleasant for you, if it goes off."

"For me!" She stared at his smooth, unlined face; met his cool, appraising eyes, strikingly dark in contrast to the silvery whiteness of his hair. "In what way can Michael Farr's candidacy possibly affect me?" she asked in honest amazement.

He smiled. She hated the smile. Had the man she had once liked vanished and left this suave, super-suave individual in his place? There was something rather terrifying about this one.

"Answer," she commanded impatiently. "Don't sit there grinning to yourself like the Cheshire Cat."

She knew from the sparks which glowed and faded in his eyes that she shouldn't have said that. Would she ever learn to be tactful?

"I'll answer all right if you are sure you can stand it.

My campaign manager has been making inquiries about the child at Kingscourt. Curiously, he can't find that a Farr daughter ever married a man named Carson."

Sonia swallowed an exclamation of dismay. Her fleeting suspicion that the "bomb" of which Brandt had been bragging had to do with Dicky and Ruby had been right! Had her heart parked in her throat forever? Its thump was choking her. No mistaking Donald Brandt's meaning. In some way he and his smart manager intended to trap Michael Farr in a coil of scandal. She would be responsible. If she had kept her promise to Ruby, he never would have known about the boy. Guy—

Guy! Guy was here. Here to claim his son. The relief! The unbelievable relief! No more secrecy! No chance now of Michael's paying the piper for his brother. Should she tell Brandt the truth? At the crossroads of decision. No. That must come from the Farrs.

Gayety, the zest for living swept her in a buoyant tide. She laughed.

"Is that what you came to tell me? Isn't it absurd for you and me to go into a huddle to decide something which will be left to the voters in a day or two? There's the Japanese gong! Isn't the tone heavenly? That means luncheon. I must dress."

Donald Brandt blocked her way as she started for the sportshouse.

"You're a grand little bluffer but you are not going until I have finished what I have to say."

"Really. Who will stop me?"

"I will."

He moved a step nearer. Sonia looked over his shoulder at the sportshouse. It wouldn't do her much good if she reached that. He might block her exit. There was one other way to escape.

She took a quick step, turned a back flip into the pool. Hand over hand she cut through the water. Would he race around to stop her? He wouldn't dare. She kept her eyes over her shoulder until she pulled herself to the coping. Donald Brandt, with her red cap in his hand, was standing at the other end where she had left him.

She brushed her dripping hair from her eyes, waved, and called:

"So sorry I can't ask you to stay for luncheon."

With a laugh she turned—almost into the arms of Michael Farr.

"Were you running away from Brandt?" he demanded.

Sonia dug into the soft grass with her bare toes.

"I wouldn't exactly call it running, would you? That moving-picture should be captioned, 'Girl Swimming,' and how!" she added flippantly.

"You know what I mean. What was he saying to you?"

Better not tell him. Relations between the two men were strained enough. She would tell Guy that he must acknowledge the boy at once for his brother's sake—meanwhile—

"Do you mean to keep me here—s-shivering while you c-cross-examine me as to my b-business deals?" she asked insouciantly. "Remember, this is Oc-tober—the last of it." The shivers had been well done, she congratulated herself. Perhaps she had mistaken her vocation, perhaps she would have been a better actress than architect.

"Slip this on—quick!"

"I don't need your coat. Put it on again. I will be at the house in a moment."

She was off like a flash, between the lacelike iron gates, up the flagged walk between the perennial borders still colorful with late chrysanthemums, shafts of purple and pink asters, a few mammoth rose-color dahlias. Up the terrace steps. She stopped. Guy Farr was smiling at her from a chaise longue.

"Where's the fire?"

"In here." Sonia tapped her forehead as she approached him. "You know, don't you, that your brother is running for Congress?"

"Why are you whispering? Of course I know. Sit down. If you don't, being a perfect gentleman, I shall have to get up and I doubt if I can make it."

"Never mind that now. Brandt, his opponent, is planning to—to mix him up in a scandal."

"Scandal! Mike!"

Surprise brought Guy Farr to his feet. He closed his eyes for a moment and clutched at the back of the chaise longue. Sonia caught his arm to steady him.

"Are you faint?"

He shook himself as if throwing off a spell.

"No. No. Have to be careful about moving quickly. Where did you get that fool idea about Michael and scandal? I should as soon expect to find the angel Gabriel on the Public Enemies list."

"Someone hinted it. Don't you see? Don't you understand?" Sonia glanced over her shoulder. Michael Farr would mount the terrace steps in a moment. She clenched her hands behind her to keep them from shaking Guy Farr's shoulders in her impatience.

"I don't."

"It is Dicky!"

"Dicky! Who the dickens is Dicky?"

"Your child! Your son! They intend to broadcast the lie that he is your brother's and that Michael has been hiding—"

"You'll get stronger every minute in this glorious air. But I wish you wouldn't stand because I have been selfish enough to stop and chatter, Guy."

Sonia kept her tone light as she switched subject matter, but her eyes flashed a warning. Would he be bright enough to understand that his brother must not know what she had told him? He had been dumb enough so far.

"Better have Elkins serve your luncheon here on the terrace, Guy," Michael Farr suggested, as he approached. "Here comes Serena with—with your son."

The Sealyham, his wet coat a pale pea-green, dashed onto the terrace from the French window of the library. Serena Farr followed, hand in hand with Dicky, who hopped and skipped beside her. His hair had been brushed until it shone like wavy copper, his skin had the pinky appearance of recent and drastic scrubbing, his eyes were wide and blue and merry.

"Guy! When did you arrive?" The woman's hand tightened on the child's.

"An hour—it seemes like a year ago, Serena. You look younger than ever. Get off, you cur!" He struck at the Sealyham who was attempting to dry his wet coat against his trousers. The dog yelped and ran down the steps.

"So this is the boy! Hullo, Dicky." He held out his hand. "Come and say howdy to—"

Suspense held Sonia's breath. His acknowledgment of the child would solve one of Michael's problems.

"—your cousin Guy."

Cousin! Had he said that, or was she hearing it in a nightmare. Now that he had seen the boy, did he doubt that he was his?

Dicky dug one stubbed shoe into the flagstones.

"Michael's my cousin. Don't want anuver."

He dropped Serena Farr's hand and flung himself at Michael. "Wide me to lunch, Mikey! Wide me to lunch!"

Michael held him by the shoulders.

"First shake hands with your—new cousin, Dicky."

There was a tinge of anger in his voice and not a little contempt. The boy looked up.

"But I don't like him, Cousin Michael. He hit Shweddy. Shweddy cwied."

"Let the kid alone!" Guy flung himself onto the chaise

longue. "He's been spoiled all right. Easy enough to see that he has been brought up by a woman. Send Elkins out with lunch. I'm all in."

Sonia's eyes met Michael's. He lifted the boy to his shoulder and said as if in answer to her wordless appeal:

"Unless you intend to lunch in that swim-suit, Sonia, you'd better change quickly."

Even Sonia's ears burned as she entered the cool, darkened library where a fire was blazing on the hearth. She had forgotten the scantiness of her costume. Curious that Donald Brandt was the only one of the three men who had made her flesh-conscious. She felt like a small girl being sent to her room. What had she done to turn Michael Farr's anger against herself? As "Cousin Guy" Guy Farr had introduced himself to his own son. Did he intend to let it go at that, intend to allow his brother's candidacy to be messed up because of him?

Behind her at the window she heard Michael's voice:

"After you, Serena. Duck you head, Dicky. You are getting heavier every day—and wiser, my boy, wiser."

Chapter XVI

Sonia heard the rattle of rollers on the terrace below her window, an intermittent sound as if the person on skates were learning. Dicky, of course. She could hear his excited voice and the Sealyham's sharp, staccato bark. What a day! An almost cloudless sky, clear and brilliantly blue. The purple hills seemed bound together like an endless chain of rough amethysts; the foliage on the shore of the lake resembled nothing so much as the colors in a once gorgeous, now somewhat faded, Persian rug.

It promised to be a perfect week-end as to weather. Almost too warm for the first of November. If only it would keep fair until after election day, Sonia thought, as she buckled the belt of her red knit frock and turned to note the effect in the mirror; so many voters were like cats, they hated to step out in the wet. A grand idea of Serena's to fill the house with guests, guests friendly to Michael's candidacy, who would motor to the rally tomorrow night and back him up in his final speech. Amusing of her to include Donald Brandt in the party. Of course he had accepted. Phyllis D'Arcy was to be among the guests, too. She—

What was that? Dicky? Crying? He wasn't crying. He was yelling with fright or rage. Never had she heard his voice raised like that before. Had Shreddy bitten him? Perhaps—

"Nanette!" she called to the little maid in the next room.

She heard the girl behind her as she flew down the stairs. At the door to the terrace she stopped in consternation. Guy Farr, seated on the edge of a chair, was laughing uproariously. Dicky, on skates, was trying desperately to keep his balance. His eyes were hot blue stars of rage, his cheeks flaunted red flags of anger. The rollers rattled as he stamped and screamed shrilly:

"Don't do that! I don't like you, Cousin Guy! Don't do it!"

In answer Guy gave him a rough push. The yelping Sealyham dashed after the boy who caught a chair and steadied himself. Sonia came swiftly forward. Dicky flung himself against her and clutched her skirt.

"He keeps pushin' me down—when I'm twyin' to—to learn to skate." His angry, childish voice caught in a sob.

Sonia dropped to her knees beside him.

"Be a good sport, Most Dear. Everybody falls down when he is learning. Lean against me. I'll take off the skates. There! Now you are steady, aren't you? Look at Shreddy with his head on one side, tongue hanging, panting for breath. He's watching you. Isn't he funny?"

A smile broke through the tears in the boy's eyes.

"Shweddy's laughin'."

The sobbing catch in his voice twisted Sonia's heart. He was so little to be hurt. She was conscious of Guy Farr's sardonic eyes above his cigarette.

"Here is Nanette. Go and get bathed for luncheon, Most Dear. Remember that Aunt Serena said there would be ice cream especially for you?"

"Pink ice cream?" The child's world was turning rose-color.

"Pink, I am sure. Run along, honey. Nanette, put a fresh suit on Dicky."

"But that suit was fresh this morning, Miss Sonia."

"I know, but he has been unhappy in it. Change it, Nanette."

"Sure. Come on, Dicky. You been unhappy, you poor little kid?"

Sonia saw the boy slip his hand in hers, saw him look up at her and laugh with all his pearly teeth in evidence.

"Shweddy watched me skate, Nanette. He twied to bite the wollers an' he barked an' barked."

The voice, still sob-shaken, dwindled to a murmur and thinned into the distance. Sonia's spirit rose in a fury of

124

rage as she looked at Guy Farr who was regarding her with sardonic amusement.

"Watch your step! Watch your step!" she warned herself. "He is waiting to trap you."

She dropped into a fan-back chair and observed lightly:

"Nanette is about as responsive as one of those lead nymphs in the garden, but she must be what the Spanish call *simpática* when she is alone with Dicky or he wouldn't love her as he does." She abandoned diplomacy.

"Why did you push him down?"

"It was fun to see him pull himself up. First only his face would get red. Then he began to stamp his foot and yell."

"A child should not be tormented."

"Good discipline."

"Do you realize that he is little more than three years old?"

"You are rather amusing yourself when you fly into a rage, Sonia. The boy is more like you than his mother or —or me."

"Thank God he is—" Sonia caught herself in time and finished lamely, "stronger than his mother." Almost she had said, "isn't like you." "I am glad to hear you acknowledge that he is your son."

"That acknowledgment is not to be made public yet, get me? There are strings attached."

"Strings! What do you mean? Either the child is yours or he isn't."

Guy Farr drew a chair close to hers. As he bent his head to pick up the lighter he had dropped, she noticed the thinness of his hair on top, its one time glint of gold was tarnished.

"Never had much use for me, had you, Sonia?"

"As much use as I had for any of the men in Ruby's stag line. It was a long one."

He flung his cigarette over the parapet and leaned forward.

"All this chatter isn't getting us anywhere. I had plenty of time to think lying in my tent in that confounded jungle. And I thought of you, Sonia, of coming back to you, and of how we would make a home for the boy—together."

"Together! You don't mean—"

"I mean that I want you to marry me. Sit down! Wait until I'm through!

"You see how much I need you. Women like to fuss over a man. You'll have enough of that. It may take several years before I am back to normal—though the few days I have been at Kingscourt have been better than a tonic. I'll buy that house you have planned for Brandt and we will settle down there with the boy."

Settle down! Sonia hoped that her face was not playing telltale and showing her contempt. Now that Guy Farr was incapacitated for a gay life, he was willing to settle down and let a wife take care of him. She appeared concerned as to the smoothness of the lacquer on her pink nails.

"Suppose I do not care to settle down?"

He leaned back in his chair and blew smoke-rings.

"There are others—who are keen to look after me and would put up with the boy for my sake."

"Put up with Dicky! You wouldn't take him, would you?"

"Sure thing. Think I would let you bring up my son without me as a balance wheel?"

"Balance wheel! That's the funniest thing I ever heard. Then you acknowledge him as your son." She turned triumphantly to Serena Farr who was approaching. "You heard Guy say that Dicky is his son, didn't you?"

"Of course I heard. I'm glad you have had the decency to drop that cousin pose, Guy. You know that I don't like you, but I'll forgive you a lot for bringing Sonia into our lives. She has come into this old house like a fresh breeze in a heat-weary world. Be a man. Rise to your responsibilities for once. Make the announcement that the child is yours at tea this afternoon when our guests are together in the hall. If you don't, I will. There is a lot of whispering going about which may hurt Michael in his campaign."

Guy Farr's face was colorless. Even his lips under his slight mustache were pale. The diamond on the thin, unsteady hand which held a cigarette glinted like a sinister eye.

"Michael! Always Michael with you, Serena. Well, you are not the only one who thinks he is the finest thing on earth. As to helping him in his campaign—you'll be surprised what I can do. I meant all I said to you, Sonia. Think it over."

Serena Farr's eyes followed her nephew until he vanished into the dusk of the room.

"You know, I'm terribly sorry for a born fool but I hate a darn fool." She left that for Sonia to interpret. "I heard Dicky screaming with rage and hurried down. He has not cried before since he came to Kingscourt, has he? I was not surprised to find Guy here with the boy. He can stir the most peaceful situation into a boiling, bubbling volcano, spitting red-hot lava. It's a gift. You have a laugh like a soft silver bell, Sonia, but don't dare laugh at me."

Sonia's voice rippled. "I can't help it, Serena, when you indulge in slang. It's so—so f-funny with your exquisite self."

"It may be funny but it is expressive. You see, I am reacting to my nephew's technic already."

"Do you think he can help Michael in his campaign?" His voice was gruff with feeling when he spoke of him."

"He is fond enough of Michael, Michael is the only person who has the slightest influence with him, but how can he help? The district knows him for what he is, an unreliable, attractive playboy. If he were to champion his brother in public he would be laughed at. Not that people think he would steal or be dishonest, but to see Guy Farr taking the stump for the prevention of crime when he has broken every small law that there is to break would be a joke, nothing less than a joke."

"But he hasn't the strength to go about speaking, dear."

"There is one more rally only. I'm not so sure that he couldn't manage that. He does what he wants to do, always. He has picked up wonderfully in the few days he has been at home. If he hadn't, I would not have planned this house party."

"You are putting a lot of strength and time into it, Serena."

"Perhaps I am, but I adore giving parties. Tom and Jane are helping. Nice of them to come a day ahead. They have written and planted all the directions for the treasure hunt tonight. We have planned to have tea at five—dinner would take too long—the hunt, and then a supper with all sorts of hot dishes, and the prizes."

"How exciting!"

"You will think it exciting when you see the prizes. The girls in this community haven't had many luxuries these last years, so I decided to put a few of my treasures into circulation. I might as well have the fun of disposing of them while I'm alive. I have found a girl who will play the flute. She warned me that it might be a flop, that outdoor air was bad for the delicate instrument. She will have to keep it wrapped in her cape when not in use, but it is worth trying. It has been one of the dreams of my life to give a party and have a flute played in the garden. She is to move about and play, a sort of will o' the wisp effect, to lead the hunters on."

"It sounds enchanting. Why waste your talent on festivities at Kingscourt? You ought to be a motion-picture director, Serena." Would Guy Farr's cryptic reminder ever stop going round and round in her mind?

"I meant all I said to you, Sonia. Think it over."

"What were you saying, Serena dear?" She must keep the man and his maddening proposal out of her thoughts.

"Michael will get here only in time for tea. I don't know what he will say when he finds that I have invited Phyllis D'Arcy and Donald Brandt to join the house party for the treasure hunt. He won't understand that I am hoping that they will decide to marry each other—Brandt has started divorce proceedings against his wife, I hear—and set you and Michael 'at liberty,' as the actors advertise when they are out of a job."

"Me! At liberty! Where did you get the idea that I am not? I couldn't be much more at liberty than I am, Serena.

" 'I care for nobody, no, not I,
    And nobody cares for me.' "

she chanted as they entered the library. Elkins looked up from the telephone.

"Call for you, Miss Serena."

"Wait, Sonia. I want to tell you something about tonight." Serena Farr spoke into the receiver:

"Miss Farr speaking.—Jim! Jim!—When?—A week ago! —Of course I understand—Can I help you?—Good-bye!"

Serena Farr's face was colorless, her hand shook as she replaced the instrument on its stand.

"Jim Neville's wife died last week. He had been called to San Francisco in consultation. That is why I haven't heard." Her voice was high and strained. "I—" Her teeth chattered, her body shook as if from a nervous chill. Sonia flung an arm about her shoulders.

"Can I help you, dear?"

Serena Farr made a valiant effort to control her shaking body. "No—no. I'll be all right in a minute. It—has come so suddenly. Jim and I were engaged. Father broke it off. Jim married and after a year his wife lost her mind. She was a child again. He couldn't desert her then. The years have gone on and on—such long years. And now—"

She put her hand to her contracted throat and said in a husky whisper:

"I'll be steady in a minute, Sonia. Don't come with me."

Sonia watched her as she left the room. Emotion stung her throat and eyes as Serena's breathless words echoed through her mind.

"The years have gone on and on—such long years."

How many women would love and wait for a man for years? Thousands of them, Sonia answered her own question. She couldn't see herself marrying one man while she loved another. What would happen now? Would Doctor Jim and Serena marry?

The question was uppermost in her thoughts during the rest of the afternoon. Not until she entered the hall at tea time did she remember that this was the time and place Serena had selected for Guy's acknowledgment of his son. She might have known that he would side-step, she told herself bitterly, as she looked for him among the guests assembled. He was not present. The galleries and beamed ceilings were mysterious and picturesque as the flames from two fireplaces patterned them with flickering shadows. The glow from softly shaded lamps brought out the colors in the sports frocks of the girls, threw a glamorous light on the tweeds, the shabby tweeds of the men.

The party was hitting on all cylinders. Everyone gay. Everyone laughing. Everyone keyed up to excitement pitch. The champagne blonde beside Sonia whispered:

"Michael seems to be getting that way about Phyl again, doesn't he? She has him eating out of her hand."

The man on the arm of her chair glanced over his shoulder at Phyllis D'Arcy and Michael seated on the Martha Washington settle. He had a wintry face. Tight eyes. Tight lips even when they stirred in a sardonic smile as he answered:

"Mebbe so. Mebbe so. But I'd advise Phyl to watch out. She may get that white hand bitten off. I know the King of Kingscourt. He's not an easy mark. Ever heard that one about fooling some of the people some of the time and—"

"Of course I have, foolish. This is some party. I hear that the two prizes for the women are pieces of Miss Serena's jewelry. That woman doesn't own anything that isn't choice. I'm cold with excitement. Suppose I should win one! Look at her pearls! Isn't she marvelous herself? She must be in the fifties. She looks early-fortyish."

Sonia's eyes followed the girl's to where Serena Farr was presiding at a table laden with choice old silver. She was gay, laughing, there was no trace on her face of the emotion which had shaken her in the library. Only the unevenness of her voice betrayed her.

Michael had left Phyllis D'Arcy and with Tom Nash was talking to his aunt whose eyes were as brilliant as if a fire were lighted behind them. She had threatened to announce the truth of Dicky's parentage if Guy did not. Had the news she had received banished all else from her mind? She was saying something to Michael. He shook his head emphatically. Sonia drew a little sigh of relief. Much as she wanted Dicky acknowledged, she didn't want it done in a melodramatic way.

Serena spoke to Tom Nash. He tapped a teaspoon against the silver tray. Immediately the guests were tensely still. His short neck was boiled-lobster red as cheers and applause greeted him. His color accentuated the whiteness of his lashes. His eyes twinkled. He ran a stubby finger under his collar.

"Miss Serena has asked me to explain the plan for the treasure hunt. On the large table are envelopes clipped together in pairs. The name of a man is on one, the name of his hunting partner—girl, of course—on the other. Each pair has a number, Couple I, Couple II, and so on. Inside are directions for finding the first clue. They go like this:

" 'My first runs for miles without moving to my second, near silver lately capped with gold; Indians made boats of them, lovers carved trysts on them. Behind my third, with its red-brown hat, stands a tree whose leaves will hang white and square when the maid goes into the garden. Dig at the root.'

"What runs for miles without moving?"

"I think I know! I think I know!"

"Quick! Let's get going!"

Nash held up his hand to silence the excited voices.

"Hey! Hold everything! Get the rest of it. Couple I leaves first. Five minutes later Couple II starts, and so on. When you find a bunch of clues, take out the envelope bearing your number, it will contain the next clue—and leave the others where you found them. Leave the others. I'll check up on your time when you return. The couple which collects all the clues in the shortest time gets first prizes. Thomas Nash announcing. Go!"

A billow of color and tweeds surged toward the table. Someone called:

"There's Guy!"

"Hi, Guy!"

"When did you get back from the jungle, stout fella?"

Sonia looked up. Guy Farr stood half-way down the stairway. He seemed pathetically thin and insignificant under the galleries and the raftered roof which loomed above him. He waved a clawlike hand in response to the hails.

"Looks like Old Clothes Week, boys and girls. Where'd you dig 'em up? Sorry I couldn't take tea with you. Have to go slow for a while. Came down to see the start. I'll be here when the prizes are awarded. What's the trouble?"

Sonia did not need his question to realize that in the tick of the old clock the party had been de-fizzed. It was

130

as flat as sparkling Burgundy left standing in a glass. Camaraderie had gone. Laughter had stilled. Thrilled excitement had evaporated. Girls frowned at men who glared at the cards in their hands; turned shoulders on men who were apologetic; smiled sportingly at men who played up in return. The tight-faced man was staring in consternation at Phyllis D'Arcy; Donald Brandt was giving an excellent imitation of a pillar of stone as he stood beside the champagne blonde.

What was the matter? Had the party gone suddenly haywire? Sonia looked at Michael Farr. Had he felt the sudden drop in temperature? She saw two little lines cut deep between his brows as his eyes traveled from couple to couple, then flash to his brother on the stairs. Guy's face was alight with malicious satisfaction. Michael laughed.

"I'll bet someone has mixed the signals as a means of self-expression. Match up the envelopes as they were, Jane. It won't take but a minute."

In the confusion and hubbub, Donald Brandt approached Sonia. There was nothing old about his tweeds, they were as fresh and unworn as if they had recently left the tailor.

"You are hunting with me, Sonia," he announced in a voice which seemed to echo among the rafters.

"Must have read your card wrong, Brandt," Michael Farr suggested crisply. "She is hunting with me."

The assurance in his voice brought the blonde girl's words surging through Sonia's mind.

"Michael seems to be getting that way about Phyl again, doesn't he?"

She slipped her arm within Brandt's.

"Do you know, I think I'm going to adore hunting with you, Don. What is our card-index number?"

Chapter XVII

"Keen about the treasure hunt, Sonia?" Donald Brandt inquired, as he sent his smart maroon convertible down the drive.

"Keen! I'm mad about it." She flashed a pocket light on the card in her hand. "What runs for miles without moving?"

"One guess is as good as another, but I'd say a road."

"Of course. I am dense. It runs 'to my second, near silver lately capped with gold'—silver lately capped with gold—'Indians made boats of them'—what did Indians make boats of?"

"They made birch canoes, didn't they?"

"I have it! I have it! The clue is hidden at our house near the silver birches! That has a red-brown hat, the roof. And the tree whose leaves will hang white and square when the maid goes into the garden is the clothes pole. Remember? 'The maid was in the garden hanging out the clothes.' Hurry! Hurry!"

"You are keyed up, aren't you? It's going to be one grand night. Pity to waste it on this silly hunt stuff. There comes the moon."

Sonia watched the golden rim rise above the horizon. If Donald Brandt kept on in his present mood he would scrape all the icing from the party and this heavenly evening.

"Stop a moment! Please!"

The whirring wheels of the car stilled. Music, borne by the wind, soared in the fragrant dusk like the sudden, surprising song of a bird in a dark pine. All the sweetness of the flute, all the magic of the player's art was in it.

"How exquisite! Makes me think of the winged flight of an angel. It stirs the deeps of my heart and soul." Sonia blinked wet lashes and cleared the husk from her voice. "Go on."

"What an emotional person you are." There was more than a tinge of amused patronage in Brandt's voice and eyes.

"Mebbe so, mebbe so, but you will have to admit that I am practical also." Her voice was clear and cool again. "Didn't I keep that house within the figures you gave me?"

"You did, but why talk business on a night like this?"

Sonia edged away from him. He had used that tone the evening on the lake and she hated it—from him—especially if it were true that he was divorcing his wife.

"What better can we talk about? How soon will we be able to start another house?"

"Just as soon as this one is sold. I have news for you. Nash is seriously considering buying it."

He was all eagerness. Sonia relaxed. She had steered the conversation safely round one skiddy curve.

"Tom! Would he and Jane want a place so small?"

"Ten acres isn't what you would call a patch of ground. He says that he is sold on the neighborhood, that he and the missus—that is his cultured term, not mine—"

"Don't sneer at Tom!"

"Firebrand! I'm not sneering. I'm quoting. He said that they were tired of running a boarding house for servants."

Sonia snuggled into the corner of the luxurious seat. With eyes on the shining lake, so like a huge rounded mirror which might have been dropped and forgotten by a lovely goddess straying from Olympus, she visualized Jane and Tom in the house she had planned. She had supposed that they would want more splash, but apparently they were following the trend for small places. They would have plenty of money to complete the layout and make a gem of it. What grand advertising for the architect. It was evident that they liked the neighbors. Why not, when they had been cordially welcomed? It also was abundantly evident that they loved Serena Farr and admired Michael extravagantly.

Michael. What had he thought when she had turned him down for Donald Brandt? She had met his eyes for a moment. There had been a curious, biding-my-time glint in them that had started little red-hot darts pricking through her veins. Why had she done it? He would have been heaps more fun as a hunting mate; he had demonstrated his capacity for good-comradeship that night in the pantry. With whom was he paired this heavenly evening? The enticing and yielding Phyllis?

She straightened as if an ice-cube had slid down her spinal column hitting on every vertebrae. Brandt looked at her.

"Thought you were asleep. I was about to offer a most comfortable shoulder."

Sonia regarded the one near her critically.

"I'm not so sure. That tweed looks prickly."

"Had a lot of experience with tweed against your cheek?"

Sonia frowned reflectively before she glanced up under sweeping lashes. Her eyes brimmed with laughter.

"If you ask me, I might say. I have had more with dinner jackets. I am a working woman. I don't get much chance to play in tweed hours. There's our house! Isn't it adorable in this dusky light?"

As the car turned into the drive, a roadster shot past. Someone leaned out and waved a white envelope, Sonia exclaimed breathlessly:

"They've found it! Hurry! Hurry! We must get our clue before the next couple arrives."

"This place will look as if a horde of cattle had tramped it, when the hunt is over. Nash is responsible. If he buys he'll have the fun of restoring it. I'll make him come across whether he buys or not," Brandt growled.

His annoyed comments accompanied their progress like an off-stage chant as he followed Sonia. She dashed to the latticed yard. Pointed to the galvanized iron contraption which had been sunk to hold the clothes pole.

"Open it! Open it! Wouldn't you call that the root of the clothes tree?"

Brandt's impatience boiled up and over as on his knees he broke a finger nail prying up the iron cover.

"Here is the fool envelope! Of all the kid games, this is the limit."

"Be a sport. I think it's grand." Sonia was reading the clue card by the light of her pocket flash. "I know where the next one is! Let's go!"

As their car skidded around a curve of the drive, Brandt exclaimed:

"Here comes Farr with Phyl D'Arcy. We've beaten them to it."

From the corner of her eye, Sonia glimpsed the man and woman in the approaching roadster. Would they be just behind Donald Brandt and herself all through the hunt? She didn't care much for that, but apparently their proximity had a beneficent effect on her companion. He exulted:

"From now on I'm with you, Sonia. I'll beat Farr in this hunt as I will beat him at the polls."

"Don't shout! Do you want him to hear you? There are times when I suspect that you think more of beating the man than winning an election by which you may be able to do much for this district."

"I like a fight. Where do we go from here?"

They sped from clue to clue sometimes arriving in the midst of a giggling, hunting group of men and girls, sometimes departing first, sometimes the last to leave, but always a mere lap ahead of Michael Farr's shining black roadster.

Brandt cut off the engine near a towering pine beside the road.

"Sure this is the place? No one else here. Read that foolish clue again."

"Foolish! I think Jane and Tom were wonders to write all these." She flashed on her pocket light.

" 'Where the Scotchman's highway'—you said that was the mac-adam road—'gives way to sand, follow Greeley's advice to the youth of the land.' I know that, 'Go west, young man.' 'Take the sinister fork'—we decided that meant left—'where the swallows fly'—that was the tumble-down barn—'to a tall black shadow against the sky. Not at its foot, but beneath its shade, in pitch and tin will the clue be laid.'

"The all black shadow must be this pine and I'd say

that the clues were hidden in the branches. Listen! The flute. That was to be a clue, too."

A passionately ascending note soared like a freed spirit crying to the sleeping world below.

"Awake! Awake!"

It descended and became all hymn and prayer until it breathed away in a soft sigh. A night bird winged across the moon.

With difficulty Sonia cast off the net of melancholy woven about her spirit by the music and the fragrant night.

"Let's get busy. Look! Look! What's that? See? Tucked in that crotch above your head! Watch my light!"

"I see it. I can't reach. Hold on, I'll fix it."

Brandt brought cushions from the roadster and piled them at the base of the tree. Standing on them, he tugged at a small tin box.

"Hang it! Whoever put that there wedged it for keeps!"

"Hurry! Hurry! I hear a motor. We must hide the box again after we open it. You'll have it in a minute! I saw it move!"

"Hold that light steady. Don't jiggle it. Don't jig—"

The box came away so suddenly that he lost his balance. The cushions slid. He jumped.

"Take it! Get our envelope. Quick! Stop giggling. Nice hunting pal you are."

"I'm s-sorry—but you have such a g-grand manner and to see your arms w-waving like a wind-windmill in a cy-cyclone was too funny. Here's our envelope. Only one left. The others have been ahead of us. Put that box back. Quick! If you don't, it will be too easy for the last couple. I hear a car!"

"Read directions while I'm putting this up."

Sonia pulled a card from the envelope and read aloud:

> " 'No home, but a house
>   As nice as you'd wish
>   Where a worker earns her fee.
>   No hook but a line
>   For an azure fish
>   Beneath an azure sea.' "

Brandt jumped to the ground and picked up a cushion.

"I'll bet it will take time to pry that box loose. What do you make of that azure sea stuff? The lake?"

"No. 'No home but a house where a worker earns her fee'—that's me—is the sportshouse, and the azure boat beneath an azure sea must be a blue glass bottle on the end of a line in the swimming pool. That would bring the hunting party back to the big house."

"Sounds reasonable. It must be the last clue. That's a break!"

"Don't be such a kill joy. I'm having the time of my— here comes a car!"

"Farr, I'll bet a hat." Brandt pulled on his gloves. "If they see my pitchy fingers they will be on to the hiding place."

Michael Farr brought his roadster to a stop with a theatrical flourish, jumped to the ground and held out his hand to Phyllis D'Arcy.

"Come on. I told you I thought this was the place, Phyl. Now I know it. Brandt looks as if he were about to burst with satisfaction. We would have been a lap or two ahead of him if my engine hadn't gone on the blink."

He jerked up the hood of the roadster and frowned and poked at its internals.

"Is he pretending that he hasn't seen me? Is he still furious?" Sonia asked herself.

Phyllis D'Arcy's face, in contrast to her dead black knit suit, was chalky. The muscles of her throat worked convulsively. She turned petulantly to the man who was tinkering with the engine.

"You and that poisonous roadster, Michael. You've been fussing over it ever since we left the house. I want to win that first prize. It's a diamond and ruby ring, someone said. I could care for that. I shan't be in mourning always. Don, your car is running perfectly, isn't it? Take me with you. The first prize for men isn't to be sneezed at."

Was Michael's head so far under the hood that he didn't hear the spoiled-child voice? Sonia had time only to wonder before Donald Brandt caught her arm.

"Let's get going! Sorry, Phyl, but—"

Michael Farr's head and shoulders came up with a jerk. He wiped his hands on a bunch of waste.

"That's a whale of an idea of yours, to go on with Brandt, Phyl. As Sonia and I are really family, it would be a social blunder if either of us were one of the prize winners. I don't want the man's prize, anyway. Rare gold coins are nothing in my young life."

"What's that?" Brandt boomed.

Michael stuffed the waste into a pocket.

"I shouldn't have given away Serena's secret, but now that I have, might as well tell all. It's that corking mint copy of the $5 gold piece of 1826. Noble of her to part with her treasures. Phyl, if Brandt won't take you, we'd better get busy hunting for that clue."

"Hold on, Farr. Mind if I go on with Phyllis, Sonia?"

Sonia felt her cheeks grow hot, but she kept her voice light.

"Mind? Why should I? Keep on the gold standard by all means. Who am I to expect to compete with a gold coin? Everybody's collecting them, rare or modern. Take this clue. Apparently I won't need it."

"Give me the card." Phyllis snatched it from Sonia's hand. "Hurry, Don! We'll figure this out after we start."

Brandt looked back at Sonia standing in the middle of a road burnished to copper by the headlights.

"I'll make it up to you, Sonia," he called. "Save me the supper dance." The tail light of his car faded into the distance like a red star.

"You had this coming to you for turning me down in the hall. You and I had been paired together," Michael Farr informed Sonia coolly. "Hop in."

"You might have allowed me the fun of hunting, even if it would be a social blunder for me to win that adorable diamond and ruby ring," she protested as she took her seat.

"Like rings?"

"I don't know. I never owned one."

The roadster shot forward. It seemed to Sonia that they drove miles and miles without speaking. She knew that Michael looked down at her from time to time, but she kept her eyes on his hands on the wheel. Wonderful hands. Strong, flexible, with a faint shadow of hair on them. Not too white, the nails not too polished. They looked as if they might be hands to grip in an emergency. She loved them. Loved! She caught her breath and straightened.

"Cold?"

"No. The air is positvely warm. See that moonbeam? Looks like a golden toboggan slide from the heavens to the earth, doesn't it, or reversed, a stairway to the stars?"

"Why did you make that queer sound in your throat? Still regretting the ring? Don't waste a sigh on that. I have one which was Mother's that has Serena's beaten to a frazzle. Some day I'll show it to you. I want to talk to you."

"The air is yours."

"What has Guy been saying to trouble you?"

Should she tell him that his brother threatened to take Dicky away from her unless she married him? Better not. She must keep Guy guessing her answer until she had thought out a way of retaining the boy and her freedom.

"G-Guy?"

"Take your time, take your time. I had a hunch that he had been up to some of his infernal mischief, and now I know. Sometimes you have little-girl eyes, Beautiful. Where shall we go now? We didn't hunt for the clue at the pine. I forgot about it."

"Aren't we taking a round-about way home? We ought to hear voices at the pool, but there isn't a sound. Have the others reached the house so soon? We are all to change for supper."

"You don't like me much tonight, do you?"

She resented the hint of amusement in his voice.

"Have I ever liked you—much?"

"*Touché*. My mistake. Here we are at Kingscourt. You won't have to endure me much longer. What the dickens— The gate lights are out!"

The roadster took the incline like a creature on wings.

"The windows are dark!"

Michael swung Sonia from the car when it stopped. He caught her hand. Inexplicably her heart was pounding with excitement as they ran up the steps. Elkins swung open the door.

They stopped in the hall. It was in darkness except for candle lights which were darting about the galleries like overgrown fireflies to the accompaniment of laughter and excited voices.

"Everybody's back! I thought we were a long time on the road. I don't think much of that roadster of yours."

Sonia's half laughing, half serious comment missed its mark. Michael Farr was frowning at the darting spears of flame.

"What's happened to the lights, Elkins?"

It was apparent that the butler's spirit was wringing its hands.

"I don't know, Mr. Michael. The electricity went off. Soon after the last couple left to hunt."

"Why didn't you phone the garage for the mechanic?"

"I was so flustered, Mr. Michael, I never thought of him. I supposed something had happened at the main power-house."

"Get him now."

Michael smiled at Sonia. "Elkins is devoted but not too quick on the mental trigger. I—"

"My pearls! My pearls!"

The wail echoed through the domed hall.

"My pearls! Gone!"

Chapter XVIII

The hall resounded with shrieks. They followed one another with the speed and explosiveness of firecrackers going off after the first of the bunch had fizzed to fragments. Men, knotting the cord of a lounge coat about their waist with one hand, candle held high in the other darted from doors and bumped into girls running for the stairs.

"My rings! Gone!"

"Someone's snitched my diamond bracelet!"

"My earrings! My adorable earrings!"

Michael Farr stared up at the flitting lights in the galleries. Nightmare? Must be. Like something out of Van Dine. Wholesale robbery couldn't be pulled off in his house. He set his teeth savagely, to break the spell. He was awake all right. He could hear the monotonous tick of the tall clock. He could smell the roses on the table. First thing to do was to stop the crazy yelling. He released Sonia's hand. Wonder he hadn't broken the bones in it. He shouted to make himself heard above the hysterical sobs and exclamations.

"Be quiet! Everybody!"

Tomblike stillness prevailed. Guy Farr appeared on the threshold of the library. He brushed his hand across blinking eyes.

"For Pete's sake, what has happened? I waked out of a sound sleep. Thought someone was being murdered."

"Murdered!" an hysterical voice echoed from the stairs. "Might as well be! We've been robbed! Send for the police, Michael!"

"Wait a minute!"

Michael caught the phone from the hand of the man who had grabbed it. "We won't call for police help yet. Come down here, girls. All of you."

They pelted down the curved stairway, some already in colorful evening frocks, some in elaborate house coats. Two were sniffling, others were agog with excitement. Serena Farr, in a violet gown, hurried in from the dining room. Her pearls gleamed about her throat, Michael noticed. What a tough break to have the guests robbed and not the hostess!

"What's the trouble?" she demanded. "I was in the pantry, the maids lost their heads when the lights went out. I sent candles upstairs when I heard—What is the matter? What has happened?"

Guy Farr approached his aunt. "Pull yourself together, Serena. There's a rumor that a light-fingered gent—or gents —got busy upstairs. Had a little treasure hunt on his own. It's a trend."

"Talk sense, Guy. Do you mean—something has been stolen?"

"That seems to be the consensus of opinion. Looks as if a bunch of bandits were by way of thumbing their noses at our Congressional candidate who is running on the prevention-of-crime platform, what?"

"Say, cut the comedy!" Tom Nash glowered at Guy. "Can't you see these girls are about all in? What do we do next, Michael?"

Next! The word mocked Michael as he turned from the excited group of men with whom he had been conferring. Nothing had been done yet. It seemed ages since the first wail. It wasn't. It was only five minutes by the clock. He must keep cool. Everyone else seemed on the verge of hysterics.

"Elkins will lock all downstairs doors. He'll bring the keys to you, Guy. Keep him here. Brandt, you'd better stay with the girls. The rest of us men will cover every inch of ground above the hall. We will hunt in pairs. Nash, you'll be my side-kick. Don't come, Sonia! Stay here."

Michael spoke sharply to the girl whose foot was on the lowest stair. Her dark eyes were wide with anxiety.

"I must go up! Dicky may be hurt! Frightened!"

"If he were he would be out in the gallery, he would have run down to you. Wait—please—Sonia, till we have been through your rooms."

Her throat contracted as if she were swallowing a sob of terror.

"All right. I'll wait. Call me the minute—"

She dropped to the lowest stair and clenched her hands on her knees.

Michael saw his brother's blond head bend over hers before he took the stairs two at a time. She had evaded answering when he had asked her if Guy had been troubling her. Perhaps she liked him after all. Perhaps she had succumbed to what she had called "his fatal charm." That thought didn't help keep his mind on the thief hunt.

The men ahead of him separated and went in different directions as had been planned. He motioned to Tom Nash to remain outside as he softly opened the door of the boy's room. His eyes followed the spot of light from his flash as it traveled. He switched it quickly from the curly red gold hair on the pillow.

Safe! The boy was safe! He hadn't even been wakened by the racket. He closed the door softly. The stiffening seemed to have gone out of his legs. He had lived through years of fear while his eyes had followed that moving light. Kidnaping had threatened to become a major industry. He leaned over the balustrade and called:

"Dicky's all right, Sonia! Sound asleep!"

Even at that distance he could see the sudden change in her face, could see color creeping back to it.

"Oh, thank you! Thank you!"

He saw her join the group of chattering, shivering girls in the center of the hall before he turned away. Nothing to trouble her, thank God.

The radiance of her dark eyes lingered in his heart as he went from room to room occupied by the women guests. Dressing-case drawers were pulled out; bed pillows had been flung to the floor. Desks had been rifled. The thief or thieves must have swept through like a cyclone. How could so much have been done in a short time? But was it so short? The treasure hunt had taken nearly four hours. Experts could pile up considerable loot in four hours.

Sonia's rooms were undisturbed. Curious. Had the thieves known that they were hers? Had they been tipped off that she had no jewels? Was this an inside case? The prospective treasure hunt must have been talked of for days in the neighboring houses, upstairs and down. Had someone in the house furnished information?

Tom Nash was waiting for Michael in the gallery. He beckoned. They entered a room together. A breeze rattled a French window which opened on a balcony. Nash reached for the handle.

"Don't touch it without your hand covered! Fingerprints! Think they escaped this way?"

Nash pushed open the window with his foot.

"Look!"

Michael's eyes followed his flashlight. On the floor of the balcony, blinking its hundreds of colorful eyes, glittered a diamond clip.

"Must have heard something that sent him off in a hurry," Nash whispered.

Michael nodded. Whose clip was it? Had he ever seen it on one of the guests? He couldn't remember. He picked the sparkling thing up in his handkerchief and dropped it into his pocket.

"Must have made his get-away here."

At the imminent risk of breaking his neck, Tom Nash doubled like a jackknife over the wrought-iron railing.

"See! The vine is broken. This balcony juts over a lot of shrubbery, doesn't it? Our bad boy must have dropped. I'll shoot down and see if the ground is trampled."

The lights in the room flashed on.

"Guess your mechanic is on his job. Just like the darned juice to take an evening off when most needed. I'll give you the high sign when I come in. You nosey along to the library and I'll report."

Michael stood for an instant in the middle of the disordered room. Was this a case for the police? Police meant glaring headlines and perhaps hourly radio reports of the progress of the case. Could he and Nash handle it themselves? Tom seemed to have the sleuth instinct. Every suggestion he had made had been to the point. Police or not, the first move was to search every inch of this floor and the floor above. Meanwhile, the servants must be kept in the kitchen and pantry.

His eyes sought Sonia as he went slowly down the stairs. Easy enough to pick out her rust-color sports suit among the evening frocks and elaborately embroidered house coats. She was talking earnestly with Brandt. He was laughing. Big stiff! Of course he would laugh. It wasn't his house which had been broken into and entered, his guests who had been robbed. In some way he would twist this unfortunate episode to his political account. Political! And the last rally tomorrow night! Doubtless he himself would be so entangled in the machinery of the law that he wouldn't get a look-in at the speaking.

"See anyone, Michael?"

"Find anything?"

"Hear a sound, Mike?"

"Don't the rooms look as if a tropical tornado had broken loose?"

The questions rattled against Michael with the staccato rapidity of machine gun fire. Phyllis D'Arcy darted forward and pressed her face against his sleeve.

"I was afraid—afraid for you, Michael darling! They might have shot—" She shivered.

Michael firmly and not too gently freed his arm. Evidently she had forgotten her anger at him and his balky roadster. Had Sonia seen and heard and misunderstood his late fiancée's demonstration? She had. He knew by her eyes as they met his. It was to be expected as part of this nightmarish evening. He laughed. It was not a merry burst of sound, he realized, but it passed.

"Don't go Hollywood, Phyl. Where's Guy, Sonia?"

"He said something about guarding the terrace door."

"Find him, will you." That would take her away from Brandt. "Tell him I want him. Not afraid, are you, now that the lights are on?"

"I'll go with you."

Sonia shook her head. "No, Mr. Brandt, you are needed more here. No chance of meeting our burglar, he wouldn't hang around in this turmoil." Her smile as she looked up at the white-haired man gazing back at her made Michael see red. "Though, if I don't return in five minutes you'd better come and look me up."

Brandt pushed back his coat sleeve. "Five minutes. I'll hold a stop-watch on you."

"That's about enough of that," Michael growled to himself. Aloud he said:

"To whom does this belong?"

He held out his hand. On a handkerchief spread over his palm sparkled the clip he had picked up near the rail of the balcony.

A dozen heads, blonde, chestnut, dark, bent forward. A dozen pairs of eyes stared at the jewels as if their glitter held them like a mesmeric eye. Slowly, reluctantly, a dozen heads shook in denial. A dozen voices chorused:

"Never saw it before."

Was that the truth? Michael's keen glance swept from face to face. Not a woman guest was missing from this group and yet not one of them claimed the clip. It was incredible. That piece of jewelry was part of the loot. The thief had dropped it in his flight. Did it mean that Kingscourt was the second stop on the burglar's jewel snatching expedition? 'Twas an ill wind that blew nobody good. If another household had been victimized, it might stir the citizens of this district to an interest in crime prevention. Hadn't Guy said that you had to kick a voter on his own shin before he would take an interest in conditions?

"What did you find, Michael?"

Serena Farr's breathless query brought the whirligig of his thoughts to a sudden stop. Bright pink spots burned in her cheeks, her eyes were as deep and blue as Burmah sapphires.

"Nothing but this. Ever seen it before?"

He held out his hand. His aunt stared down at it incredulously.

"Seen it! It is the second prize for the girls! I put it on the large table over there after the last couple left. I don't understand how a thief could have looted this house with Dicky's dog sleeping beside the child's bed. Shreddy barks at the slightest strange sound. Guy has fussed about it ever since he arrived."

Shreddy! Michael remembered that the dog had made no sound when he had flashed the light into the boy's room. Had he been there? He dropped handkerchief and clip into his pocket.

"I will keep this at present. I'll turn it over to the girl who won second prize later. It is queer about the dog. I'll run up and take a look. It's a mean shame that your grand party should blow up in a burglary, Serena."

"Who said it had blown up? There is still something to eat and—the prizes. I wonder—" She looked across the hall. "The other package is still on the table. That's a break. Curious that the thief took but one. More curious, when I come to think of it, how he knew that there were diamonds in the one he took."

"He, or they, must have used X-ray. They knew exactly where to look for valuables. The men will be down after they have been through the rooms. Better start supper, Serena. If this hubbub quiets down, we may be able to think. Get going."

"I'm glad to see you smile, Michael. You were ghastly a moment ago." Serena Farr approached the group of girls. "Come into the dining room, everybody. Supper is showing discouraging signs of lowered blood-pressure, and the servants are fairly jibbering with fear that they will be given the third-degree. They must be kept busy. Come as you are, girls. Those in house coats better not go up to change."

"Go up!" shrilled the champagne blonde. "I wouldn't mount those stairs till that thief is located if I had to go nudist for lack of clothes. It's a break for you, Michael. This robbery will serve to bring to the voters the hair-raising thought that what happened here tonight may happen to them tomorrow night. You ought to poll a big vote."

"Michael!" Phyllis D'Arcy caught his arm as he started for the stairs. "Bend your head." She put her lips close to his ear. "Remember I told you that the Nash couple would bear watching? He was here at the house all the time the rest of us were hunting."

Michael jerked away from her. For an instant, a split instant, a doubt of Tom Nash flashed through his mind. Angry that her absurd suspicion had registered, he commanded roughly:

"Talk sense or keep quiet, Phyl. Where is Sonia? Here she is with Guy! Find any clues, Guy?"

"Not a clue. I wasn't very thorough. Had one of my

passing-out streaks." He brushed his right hand across his eyes. "When one of those—"

"Where's your ring?"

Guy Farr looked at his hand as if he never had seen it before, then he laughed.

"For Pete's sake, m'lad, don't pounce like that. For an instant you had me dazed. I thought friend burglar had snitched my talisman while I slept. He didn't. Remember how loose it was? I sent it to my jeweler to have it made smaller. Superstitious as I am about being without it, thought it safer to spare it for a few days than perhaps lose it altogether. What the dickens have you there, Nash? Shreddy!"

With a tender croon of sympathy, Sonia patted the rough head of the dog in Tom Nash's arms. His short tail wagged feebly, his usually snapping eyes were dull.

"Where did you find him?" Michael demanded.

"On the ground among the shrubs. Evidently had been dropped from the balcony, bundled up in a bed puff. This was tied tight about his nose."

He held out a large handkerchief.

"See how fine it is. Look! The monogram has been cut out! I'll say our burglar has a nifty taste in *mouchoirs*. We don't need the police, Farr, all we need is that monogram— or one like it. Now who's here?"

A man in overalls shifted his feet awkwardly on the threshold of the dining room. Tools were tucked under his arms. Tools protruded from his pockets.

"Excuse me for butting in on the party, Mr. Farr, but Mr. Elkins told me to report to you."

"That's right, Burns. What put out the lights? Trouble at the power house?"

"Nope." The man's grin almost split his face. "Guess you've got the village cut-up here an' he was trying to be funny. The lights were switched off in the cellar."

For an instant Michael was conscious of Phyllis D'Arcy's triumphant eyes meeting his. Confound her infernal suspicion! He said quickly:

"Then we haven't far to look. We—Guy!" He caught his brother as he swayed.

Chapter XIX

Sonia waited only until Guy had pushed Michael aside and stood erect before she spoke in a low tone to Serena Farr.

"I have been hunting in these clothes for hours. I must

change. It won't take me but a few minutes. Go on with the supper. Don't wait for me. Who won the first prizes, Serena?"

She was ashamed of her fervent hope that the answer would not be, Phyllis D'Arcy and Donald Brandt.

"Jean Derby won first. I've forgotten which man hunted with her. Look at her in that backless green frock! Can you tell me why a girl with the shoulder blades of a lion-tamer bares her back to the waist?"

Laughing at Serena's comparison, Sonia sped up the stairs. At the top she looked down. Phyllis D'Arcy in a white Mandarin coat heavy with embroidery was tucking her hand under Michael's arm. They turned toward the dining room.

"He's wax where that woman is concerned! Just wax!" Sonia reflected bitterly, as she closed the door of the boudoir behind her.

She controlled a shivery impulse to keep her eyes over her shoulder as she passed through her lighted bedroom to Dicky's. It gave one an eerie feeling to know that someone had been rummaging through one's belongings. Now that the filthy fingers of crime had touched their possessions perhaps the girls downstairs would use their influence to push Michael's candidacy. Merely to vote for him was not enough. Women had demonstrated how powerfully they could influence public opinion. Why shouldn't they mobilize to enforce law and order?

She bent over the boy's bed. He was sleeping quietly. A breeze from an open window stirred a curl of his soft hair. A surge of thanksgiving brimmed over in tears. Sonia blinked the moisture from her lashes. Dicky was safe. For one horrible instant when the hue and cry had started in the hall she had thought of Guy Farr's threat to take him from her.

She broke her own speed record dressing. In a gold lamé frock before the mirror she adjusted her long jade earrings. They were real and choice, thanks to Jane and Tom. Curious that the thief had not taken them.

"Curious! It's more than curious, it means something," she told herself, as she frowned at the reflection of the satin covered bed, the orderly room. The girls had said that theirs looked as if a cyclone had swept through. Why had hers been left undisturbed?

Fool question. As if it were not common knowledge that she had no jewels. Hadn't she come to Kingscourt in the guise of a poor relation? Doubtless the thief had arrived with a card-index list of the loot to be lifted and to whom it belonged. She adored rings but not having them had saved her a lot of anxiety tonight. Michael had said that some day he would show her a ring which had been his mother's. Why should the memory of his voice set her heart thumping in her throat? Doubtless at this very moment his ex-fiancée was purring against his sleeve:

"I was afraid—afraid for you, Michael, darling!"

Sonia snatched up a jade colored bag. Switched off the mirror lights. Accused in her mind:

"You are as much of a philanderer as your brother, Michael Farr. Only you are more subtle and for that reason more dangerous, a lot more dangerous."

She would better keep that truth on the top of her mind. She hadn't forgotten the heart-stopping thrill the sight of his hands on the wheel had given her not so many hours ago.

She stopped in Dicky's room to pull up the covers he had kicked off. She set his disjointed and shabby Teddy bear against the pillow. He still clung to the furry pet as a bed fellow even though Shreddy—

Shreddy! How could the thief have taken the dog without waking the boy? Had it been someone the Sealyham knew? That was a thought. Perhaps one of the servants? What was glittering on his couch? She snatched up a ring from the cushion.

A gold ring with a diamond! A big diamond. Guy Farr's! He had said that he had sent it to the jeweler!

Her fingers trembled with excitement as she dropped it into her bag. She answered a knock at the door. Michael still in tweeds confronted her.

"I was afraid—you have been gone so long—I thought the thief might have hidden in your room."

"Nothing so thrilling." Sonia closed the door behind her. "He wasn't there but—"

Better steady her voice or he would suspect something. She must not tell him what she had found. There was no doubt that the ring in her bag was Guy Farr's. Was he the thief? Was that why he had collapsed in the hall when Tom had shown the handkerchief he had found about the dog's nose? What a crazy idea. Of course he had not stolen the jewels. Why should he? And yet—the dog hadn't roused the house—Guy's ring on the couch—his assurance that he had sent it away—the idea was fantastic, incredible. Was Michael wondering why she was staring off into space? She said hastily:

"Hear those girls laugh. In spite of the burglary the party seems to be on the crest of the wave."

He stopped her at the head of the stairs.

"Just a minute, light-of-my-eyes."

She drew back quickly. Had he been about to catch her in his arms?

"Don't call me that!" She must say something to combat the response of her pulses to the caressing tenderness of his voice. "You Farr brothers have the same line, haven't you? Only you don't do it as convincingly as Guy. There he is! I must speak to him."

She ran down the stairs, sure of herself again, sure that she was immune to Michael's attraction, sure that she had a weapon of defense against Guy. Let him threaten to take Dicky and she would produce his ring and tell where she had found it.

The rugs had been pushed back. Someone turned on the radio. A gay foxtrot, all saxophones and fiddles and drums, set the air vibrating, set feet tapping out the rhythm. Guy Farr spoke to her.

"I'm going up, Sonia. Sorry not to dance with you. I'm hard-boiled but having a thief on location has knocked me out. See you in the morning."

She watched him as he mounted the stairs as if too exhausted to pull himself up. Michael coming down stopped beside him.

"Need help?"

"For Pete's sake, don't make an invalid of me, Mike. That flop a few moments ago didn't mean anything. Have 'em all the time. When I can't get upstairs alone I hope someone will knock me on the head. Sent for the police?"

"No."

"Think you're making a mistake, m'lad, but it's your hunt."

That didn't sound as if he had anything to hide. Sonia's hand closed tightly on her green bag. She could feel the ring. Finding it had not been the figment of a dream. Guy Farr was an excellent actor. Hadn't he kept his marriage to Ruby secret for a month while all the time he had been coming to see her?

He was almost at the top of the stairs. Would he hunt for his ring? Should she tell Michael that she had found it? No. Tom Nash was the person to follow him.

"Guy can make the grade. Don't worry, Sonia."

She didn't care for the expression of Michael's eyes nor the tone of his voice as he stopped beside her.

"Of course he will make the grade. He always does, doesn't he? You'll have to give him that. Did you think I was registering worry? It was starvation, your Majesty."

He caught her wrist in a grip which hurt.

"I don't like the way you said, 'Majesty.'"

"Sorry. I strive to please."

She twisted free. Horns gleeful and windy and mocking, piccolos whimpering and whistling, oboes and clarinets brooding and wistful, accompanied her thoughts as she crossed the hall. Her conscience smarted. Why had she been so hateful? It wasn't what she had said but the way she had said it. What had come between Michael and herself? One moment she believed in him, the next she remembered Guy's treatment of Ruby and distrusted anyone of the name of Farr.

Tom Nash was in the midst of a group of excited girls in the dining room recounting again the story of his discovery of the dog. Sonia tried to wireless a message to him.

"Speed, Tommy! Speed!"

He understood. He raised his colorless brows in response. His eyes bulged more like a cod's than ever. "But he's a dear," Sonia told herself in quick apology for the uncomplimentary comparison.

Would he reach her before Donald Brandt who was hurrying toward her? Would she have time to tell him? Would he understand without a lot of explanation? Men could be so dense.

"What's on the little mind, Sonia?"

She caught the lapel of Nash's coat, drew him nearer. Said very low:

"Guy Farr has gone upstairs to rest, he says. Follow him. Don't let him see you. Watch where he goes. . . .

"Did you win the gold coin of the vintage of 1826, Mr. Brandt?" she asked almost in the same breath.

For a second he looked at Tom Nash. He returned a guarded nod before he strolled from the room. Brandt answered gloomily:

"No, worse luck. Had plenty to eat, Sonia? If so, how about a little stepping? Hear the Beautiful Blue Danube coming over the air? Come on!"

His loud, possessive voice sent prickles along Sonia's nerve centers. She had forgotten how many billions there were but every one of hers was twanging. How silly when he was merely asking her to dance. She parried:

"'Come on!' Just like that. I have had nothing to eat. I'm starving."

"It seems to be my job to feed you. Remember the garden party? Slip out to the terrace. I'll bring you something. I must talk to you."

Was she the only person who had not had supper?

The other guests were dancing in the hall, swaying to the full rich harmonies of the waltz. The maids were clearing the still laden table in the dining room. She stepped into the tropical atmosphere of the enclosed end of the terrace where she and Michael had dined the evening after the garden party. Now it was beautiful with palms and deep chairs with crimson cushions. Water dripped musically from a wall fountain. In the pool below goldfish flashed in crimson and gold streaks.

With elbows propped on a small table, she looked unseeingly at her face reflected in the black mirror top. What should she do about the ring? What could she do until she had talked with Tom?

"Set it here," Brandt spoke to the maid who had followed him with a tray. "Give that the once-over, Sonia. Have I forgotten anything?"

"*Hors d'oeuvres,* essence of tomato *gelé,* salad, rolls, sea-food Newburg—I could die eating that—a whole pot of coffee and a delectable ice. You have forgotten nothing but a bottle of bicarbonate of soda. When I said that I was starving I didn't mean literally."

Brandt drew up a chair. "I am leaving before breakfast in the morning."

His voice had a resounding quality even when lowered to what he fondly believed was a confidential tone.

"Can you?"

"What do you mean, 'can I'?"

"I should have said, ought you to go, with the burglary to be investigated?"

"You don't suspect me—"

"Sit down! Of course not. I merely thought that the police might need your testimony."

"Has Farr sent for the police?"

"Why so jumpy? You should cultivate repose of manner, Mr. Prospective Congressman. You will need it in your new position."

Why had she intimated that she believed that he would be elected? She didn't.

"To proceed from where I was so rudely interrupted, I don't know whether the police have been called in or not. I supposed that they would be."

"Farr said that he would wait for a few hours. He has some fool idea that he can handle the case himself, he and Nash. When you spoke so confidently, I thought he might have changed his mind. Speaking of Nash, he told me a few minutes ago that he was ready to sign on the dotted line for the new house. His wife has ordered the furnishings already."

"The house is sold! Marvelous! It will be a great ad for us. Jane has exquisite taste. Will we begin on another at once?"

"No. After the first of January I shall be in Washington."

Sonia regarded him curiously. His assurance was startling and almost convincing.

"You haven't the slightest doubt but that you will be elected, have you, Donald Brandt?"

"What can stop me?"

"I'm not politics-wise, but a majority of the voters casting their ballots for Michael Farr, I presume. The more I think of his platform—is that what you call it?—the more I think that every voter in the district should back it. Think of what happened in this house tonight. Is there anything this country needs more at present than a mighty crusade against crime? If I were a registered voter here I would organize the women to fight it."

"You are irresistible when your eyes blaze, Sonia. Lucky for me that you can't vote here."

His tone of amused indulgence infuriated Sonia. She opened her lips on a scathing retort, closed them. What was the use? His self-assurance was invulnerable. Instead she encouraged:

"How you will love Washington. Don't forget the humble architect you leave behind. You may be able to steer a few contracts her way. Thanking you in advance, etc. This ice is refreshing."

"But I don't intend to leave her behind—long. I want her in Washington with me."

"Planning to go into the building business there?"

"Is your surprise genuine, or are you deliberately misunderstanding me? I am asking you to marry me as soon as my divorce is granted. It is being put through with speed. I have influence."

He waved his hand in his grand manner at the moment Sonia raised a glass of fruit punch to her lips. Hand and glass collided. Sonia sprang to her feet and shook a little pool of liquid from her golden frock. On his knees Brandt dabbed at her skirt with his handkerchief.

"I'm sorry. Sonia—"

"Unfortunate time to butt in, but your campaign manager wants you on the phone, Brandt." Michael spoke from the embrasure of the long window.

"Wouldn't you know it," Sonia demanded of herself,

"wouldn't you know that he would appear at the wrong moment?"

As Brandt came not too easily to his feet, she snatched his handkerchief and mopped her frock. With an indistinct word to her he entered the dining room.

"Can I help?"

Sonia continued to mop without looking at Michael Farr as he approached.

"No, thank you. I spilled punch on my dress."

"So I see. Curious how the demon telephone chisels in at dramatic moments, isn't it? Brandt is wanted. I come after him and find him at your feet."

"Why dramatize the drying of my gown?"

"Was that all he was doing?"

Sonia raised disdainful eyes as high as Michael Farr's chin. Something about the set of it stopped them there.

"I really don't remember."

"You've got to remember. I thought that would make you look at me. I've never seen such lashes as yours. They are like fringes."

Sonia closed her eyes to shut out the ardent eyes burning into hers. The music coming over the air had changed to something poignant and tender. The throb of harps, the ecstatic singing of violins, the quaver of horns, the haunting thread of melody, swept over her spirit, engulfing it in a tide of romance. Michael's grip on her shoulders tightened.

"Don't you understand why I asked about Brandt? I am responsible for you—in a way. I almost forced you to come to Kingscourt with Dicky. What was he saying to you?"

"I wonder how I managed to get on in the business world for five years before I met you."

"That tone won't get you anywhere. What was Brandt saying to you? I have a reason for asking, Sonia."

"I have a reason for not telling, 'Michael darling'!"

"Did you mean that last?" She was in his arms, his cheek against her hair.

"S-sonia! S-sonia!"

The sibilant whisper came from behind them. Michael's arms loosened. The laughter in his eyes stopped Sonia's heart.

"Saved, this time! Don't say it again unless you are ready to take the consequences. Any news, Tom?"

Nash's eyes met Sonia's. Had he discovered something about Guy? She listened breathlessly to his answer.

"Nothing that counts—as yet, but enough to convince me that this is not a case for the police. What happened to your dress, gal?"

"An application of punch. Look at Don's handkerchief. Will the color ever come out?"

Nash caught the stained square of linen in his hand and turned it corner by corner.

"So this belongs to the wonder-boy?" He pulled a handkerchief from his pocket. "Look at this one. Alike as twins, aren't they? Except for—"

"Except for what?" Michael Farr prodded curtly.

"Except that the one Sonia had has a monogram. See how perfectly it fits into this cut-out corner?"

Chapter XX

"Of course I like you. What has become of your superiority complex that you ask such a question? But give me time."

"My offer has a time limit. Until after the rally tonight, Sonia."

The words came clearly to Michael Farr as he stopped abruptly on the threshold of the library. His brother and Sonia were standing by the fireplace, Guy had the girl's hands tight in his. She had asked for time. Time for what? As he approached she put her hands behind her back. Was Guy up to some of his deviltry? Michael said as lightly as he could with the question hammering at his mind:

"Serena wanted you to know that tea is being served, Sonia."

"I will join the hungry horde at once. Dicky, where did you come from?"

She dropped to her knees beside the boy who appeared in the doorway. His wavy red gold hair had been brushed until it shone, his eyes were as blue as his linen suit and socks. The Sealyham, on a leash made by the cord of the child's dressing gown, squatted beside him.

"Looking for me, Most Dear?"

"Aunt Sewena said I might have a little pink cake if you were willin'? May I, Sonia?"

His eyes were big and anxious.

"You may, Dicky. Why do you keep poor Shreddy on leash?"

The boy picked the dog up in his arms and hugged him. He tried unsuccessfully to dodge a rough tongue on his face.

" 'Fwaid I'd lose him. Nanette said someone stole him last night. I won't let him go again, ever. He's my vewy own dog. Why should they steal Shweddy, Sonia?"

"Put him down, Most Dear. He is heavy for you. Let's find those pink cakes of Aunt Serena's."

Hand in hand, they left the room with the Sealyham trotting beside the boy.

"Glamorous girl," Guy Farr said softly.

"And a grand boy," Michael supplemented.

"I don't like kids."

Michael regarded his brother's lips twisted into an unbecoming sneer. He wouldn't. He was too selfish.

"When will you acknowledge him as your son?"

"What's the rush?"

"Rush! The boy is over three years old. Three years is a long time for a child to be nameless. Get this. If you don't say that he is yours before tomorrow noon, I shall do it for you. I have waited to give you a chance to come across like a grown man. I won't wait much longer."

"Serena has beaten you to it. She has set the moment for the dramatic dénouement at tea this afternoon. I'll do it when I get good and ready and not before."

He was frowning as he perched on a corner of the large flat desk. What was he thinking, Michael wondered. Why had he delayed claiming his son? He hadn't attempted to deny his marriage to Ruby Carson. Unless he had changed mightily since his illness, he was planning something. Was it something to annoy Sonia? She had not appeared especially annoyed while standing with her hands in Guy's. Neither had she seemed annoyed when he had found Brandt at her feet. He had reminded her at that time that, in a way, he was responsible for what happened to her at Kingscourt, and then, maddened by her indifference, he had caught her in his arms.

"What's the latest from the crime belt? Put the police on the job yet?"

Guy's question broke the spell of memory. Michael crossed the room to the window, that log window beyond which lay the terrace, the gardens, the lake black now as a slab of obsidian. There was a streak of gold on the horizon, but the sky was dark. Was that patter rain?

"It's raining like a sieve. I can see where my constituents curl up in their armchairs before the fire tonight and let my opponents take care of the rally." He returned to the desk. "No, we haven't called in the police. Tom Nash—he's a good little sleuth—is sure that he is on the trail of the thief."

"What do you mean, trail? Got a clue? Oh, for Pete's sake! What's the matter with this lighter?"

"Nothing but your unsteady hand, I should say. Give it to me." Michael held the light to Guy's cigarette. "There you are. You have been doing too much since you came home. Better go slow."

"I'll say I'd better. My nerves are all shot to pieces and the last twenty-four hours haven't helped them settle down. I passed out completely last night when Burns reported that the electric switch had been pulled. I had thought the burglary something of a joke before. I'll drop in on old Doc. Bradley on the way to the rally and have him give me the once-over. Don't like the way I sleep. After the last couple started on the hunt yesterday, I dropped down on the couch in this room and slept like a log. Heavy. Almost as if I had been drugged. The old Doc. has known me since I was a kid, he won't try to scare me to death as the specialist did. So Nash-the-Canner is off on a little treasure hunt of his own? Thinks he can find the loot, does he? Sure that is the only reason he doesn't want the police called in, are you, m'lad?"

Phyl D'Arcy's warning jumped up in Michael's mind like a Jack-in-the-box. Had she made Guy suspicious too?

"What do you mean by that?"

"Nothing. Nothing. I was just wondering. So long as you are not calling in professionals—I think you're wrong—I'll try my hand at sleuthing. Too bad to keep it quiet though. The papers and police would have broadcast the news of the burglary, and every solid citizen who heard about it would back your candidacy, if he weren't crazy. Crazy or dumb."

"Why worry about lack of publicity? You don't think the girls who lost their jewelry will keep quiet about it, do you?"

"You're right. The tongue of the female of the species is more deadly than the male. What does Brandt say about it?"

"He agreed with the rest of us. Better to hold off the police as long as we could."

"He would agree to that, the Big Noise. Is he still here?"

"He left before breakfast. His campaign manager phoned him last night."

Guy Farr whistled, a long, low whistle.

"You don't suppose he swiped—"

"Certainly not." Better say nothing yet about the likeness of Brandt's handkerchief to the one found about the dog's nose, Michael decided. "That maroon convertible of his was just ahead of me all through the hunt. The burglars did their stuff while we were all away, didn't they?"

"Not quite all. Nash was here. I was here. It was only a thought about Brandt. I happen to know that he is up to his ears in debt. He has been pyramiding until his fortune is toppling. He is straining his credit for all it is worth until after election."

"How do you know so much about his affairs?"

"A little busy-bird in the city chirps in my ear occasionally. Let's join the tea drinkers, Mike."

"Don't wait for me. I want to run over my notes for the rally. In the recent hullabaloo I had forgotten, almost, that I had a speech to make."

"Expect any excitement?"

"If there isn't any it won't be my opponent's fault. We are speaking in a factory town from which Brandt buys building supplies."

"I get you. Dig into your notes, Mike. Tell the solid citizens what they're up against. I'd like to see you lick the pants off that white-haired *hombre*. I don't like him. I'll be cheering on the side lines for you tonight. Go to it!"

Michael's eyes followed his brother as he opened the long window which led to the terrace.

"Where are you going? Have you been so long abroad that you have forgotten that that wide door opens on the hall?"

"Don't go sarcastic, it doesn't suit you. Thought I'd get a breath of fresh air, even if it is damp, before I walked in on the tea fest. All right with you?"

Michael laughed and nodded. "My mistake. Big brother stuff. I know you hate it."

He waited until the window closed before he turned back to his desk. Even then his thoughts were busy with Guy. Why was he so bitter against Donald Brandt? He hardly knew the man—yet, he seemed posted as to his financial standing. Standing! According to Guy, he wasn't standing, he was toppling. Was it because he suspected that Brandt was interested in Sonia? Did he want her for himself? He wouldn't dare suggest it after his treatment of her sister. Wouldn't he? Guy would dare anything to get what he wanted. What had he meant by, "My offer has a time limit"? What offer?

Michael jerked his notes nearer. He would better get at his speech if he wanted to put himself across tonight. Why steam up over the apparent *rapprochement* between Sonia and his brother? She knew him for what he was. She was quite capable of looking after herself; hadn't she reminded him of that last night? Last night! He'd better forget that until after the rally. Why did the premonition that Guy was preparing to stir up trouble persist in his mind?

Stir it up! Trouble was already on the boil, wasn't it? Sonia couldn't honestly say now, as she had said a few moments before Guy had made his dramatic re-entrance into her life at the door of the sportshouse, that the atmosphere of Kingscourt was "heavenly," that she hadn't believed that daily living could be so smooth. Almost from that moment the place had simmered with conflict. Conflict deep under the surface, but it was there. Last night it had boiled up and over. Guy couldn't be blamed for that. Who was behind it? Phyl's suggestion that Tom Nash was responsible was too silly to think of. Why did it keep popping up in his mind?

The atmosphere seemed happy enough at the moment. One listening to the laughter and chatter and tinkle of silver on china in the hall would not suspect that a burglary had been staged at Kingscourt last night. The girls were good sports. They were singing lustily:

" 'Happy days are here again.' "

Michael impatiently pushed back his chair. How could he keep his mind on his speech while the mystery of the theft was yanking at it with hints for its solution? He would have to rely on his notes as they were for the basis of his appeal and take a chance that inspiration would provide a few extras when he faced the crowd tonight. An unfriendly crowd, intuition warned him.

He crossed to the window. It was black outside. Rain lashed at shrubs and trees, wind blustered about the house. Bad weather would be used as an excuse by his constituents to remain at home. How much interest had they in this election, anyway? Did they give a hang who represented them in Congress? Would the robbery at Kingscourt help his candidacy or would it crack up his chance of election?

Rap! Rap! Rap!

The staccato sounds against the window pane followed each other in quick succession. Michael listened. Had that been a dried vine tapping, or was someone on the terrace summoning him surreptitiously? It might be an attempt to find out if the room were occupied. Had the thief lost his nerve and come to restore the jewels?

He stood motionless waiting for the next move. His brain was radioing caution. Every nerve in his body tingled from the warning. The guarded tapping again! He waited. A face was pressed against the glass.

Michael choked from his convulsive effort to swallow a shout of laughter. It was Tom Nash. Nash with a slouch hat drawn low over his prominent white-lashed eyes in the best movie-bandit manner. He put his lips close to the glass.

"Let me in! Quick!"

Michael soundlessly opened the French window. Nash slid in.

"Fasten it! Draw the curtains!"

He shook rain drops from his hat before he tiptoed to the other window and cautiously pulled the hangings over it. He drew a long breath.

"Gosh sakes! That was an escape!"

"From what?"

"Someone hunting at the root of the vine where I found the dog."

Music difted in from the hall. A tango orchestra playing with irresistible tempo and fire was coming over the air. Michael's spirit responded to the stimulating syncopation. A stabbing gleam of conviction that he would win the election split his doubts.

"The election and Sonia," he said to himself. Aloud he questioned:

"Who was it?"

Nash paused in the process of lighting a cigarette.

"What's in my news to make you look as if you had had the world handed to you on a silver platter?"

"It's the music. Hear those up-and-at-'em trumpet calls? They give me a sort of Monte Cristo, the world-is-mine feeling."

"Oh yeah! Well, the world won't be yours unless you get busy on this robbery business. How do you know Brandt won't set a story going that you did it?"

"I! I steal! Have you lost your mind?"

Nash grinned. "I thought that would bring you to earth. Now listen. I was poking round near the vine down which we suspected our light-fingered gent had slid when I heard someone coming. I hid in the shadow of a shrub."

"Could you see who it was?"

"I could."

"Don't gulp! Talk! Who was it?"

"Keep your shirt on, Farr. It was—"

"Are you stopping for dramatic effect or because you don't know? Who was it?"

"Your brother."

"Guy! But he left here only a few moments ago to join the tea party in the hall." Even as he protested Michael remembered that Guy had left the library via the terrace window. He remembered something else, and drew a breath of relief.

"He told me that he was sleuthing on his own. What was he doing when you saw him?"

"Poking over the ground."

"Did he find anything?"

"Guess not for I had been over it first. Why was he there? That's what I want to know. Going to be a tough night if you ask me. Wind rising. What do you make of your brother prowling around in the wet?"

"After a clue, probably. Here come the girls. Drive me

to the rally. It will give us a chance to talk things over. Here's your man, Jane. Sure, we are coming out for tea."

The rain had developed into an able-bodied storm as Michael and Tom Nash drove away from Kingscourt. Michael was turning over and over in his mind the conversation he had interrupted between Sonia and Guy. Was he annoying her? He visualized her as she had appeared at the dinner table without a trace of anxiety on her charming face. If during the meal the chatter had strayed for a moment from what Jane Nash facetiously dubbed "our late unpleasantness," it veered back as sharply and continuously as a compass needle pointing north.

"Gosh, what a night! The wiper can't move fast enough to keep the windshield clear." Nash broke a long silence as they entered a town. "What a crowd! The electorate in this town isn't afraid of bad weather."

They made their way slowly through streets running with water, jammed with automobiles, cars of all types and makes. Against the misty skyline red and green lights scuttered about a frothing beer mug of heroic proportions; their reflections writhed like a red and green serpent on a window opposite. Steady lights glorified the names of movie stars above a doorway; white lights twinkling through a curtain of rain lured to a delicatessen where spits dripping meat juices turned slowly in a window.

The hall was crowded when they entered. From their vantage at a side door they could see the platform. The committee in charge and Donald Brandt were seated. Brandt wore the uniform of a major in the American Expeditionary Force. His Sam Browne belt, his puttees, his spurs gleamed.

Michael's brows met. A Veteran of the World War! Could a man in plain blue serge stand up against that uniform in this crowd and win? Nash pinched his arm with a force which made him flinch.

"Get on to Brandt in uniform! The fancy wrapper sells the goods! Gosh sakes, you'll have to do your darndest, Michael!"

Seated on the platform, Michael Farr heard the rain beat and clamor at the windows, heard the wind wrench at the roof until it groaned. What a night! There were more of his neighbors in the hall than he had expected to see. Had their interest been aroused by the news of the robbery? The house party from Kingscourt occupied seats in the middle of the front row of the gallery; they had come in the gayest of dinner costumes. A mistake; their clothes might turn the tide against him. Where was Guy? Was Sonia with them? Yes. Hatless but simply dressed in a green chiffon frock. She had a flair for appropriate clothes. He must keep his eyes away from her and his mind on the speakers.

A fanfare of trumpets. The rally was on. The chairman, with a sense of the fitting so often lacking in a chairman, introduced Brandt briefly. The uniformed man rose amid applause which shook the building, that part which was not already shaken by the storm. Michael conceded his impressiveness. His white hair shone like silver; his ruddy face was unlined; his eyes were brilliant; his voice boomed through the hall. Added to that, he promised voters and veterans—he pulled out the tremolo stop on veterans—everything they wanted or could possibly think of wanting. The audience surged to its feet and whooped for him till the roof trembled. He painted a glowing future beside which a ruddy rising sun was drab in comparison.

It seemed hours to Michael before the chairman could restore order and introduce him. As he walked to the front of the stage, the crowd began to boo. At first he laughed and waited, waited for passions and tempers to quiet down. A faint hiss like escaping steam spread through the hall; catcalls followed; jeers and hoots.

Michael felt his color recede. He kept his eyes on the clock. Two minutes! Three! Four! Five! He wondered if fury would have burned up his voice by the time his chance to speak came. They were letting up. No. The hissing had begun again. What should he do? Do! What had his ancestor done when he had been caught in a storm which threatened to destroy his ship and his life? Had he turned yellow? Not the Admiral. He had shaken his fist at the breakers, had yelled defiance. Had his descendant less nerve?

Michael brought his fist down on the speaker's desk with a force which shook it. He shouted above the babel:

"Damn you! You've got to listen to me!"

Chapter XXI

A catcall broke in the middle. A hiss sputtered out. Hundreds of pairs of eyes focussed in fascinated attention on the white-faced man on the platform.

Seated in the front row of the gallery, Sonia felt as if her breath were stopped forever by her excitement and apprehension. The hall was so still that she could hear the rain lashing at the windows. Would the tumult break out again? Couldn't those hooting, hissing creatures realize the sort of man Michael Farr was? His white, set face tore at her heart.

She loved him for his courage, for his strength, and above all for his smile. For he was smiling now as with easy assurance he faced what had been a yelling, bantering mob.

She sat forward on the seat her hands clenched in her lap. He had sworn at them—no whitewashing that fact—and told them that they would listen to him. Would they?

They did. Tensely. Sonia's taut muscles gradually relaxed as she realized that every face was turned toward Michael. Necks were craning. Heads were bobbing for a better view of the speaker as he told them that he would leave the questions of taxation, of bonus payments, and other legislation to more experienced fighters. He told them why he believed he could help in the drive against criminals, help prepare Federal laws to prohibit interstate transportation of stolen property, laws making bank robbery a Federal offense, laws to make punishment swifter and more certain; why he was convinced that it was worth his time and best effort to drive home to the tax payers of the country a knowledge of the boiling, seething volcano of vice on the thin crust over which they were so complacently sitting.

Without exaggeration, without tragic details, with telling force, he drove into their minds the knowledge and realization of crimes which had been committed almost at their very doors. He made them sense the terror of parents who had been threatened; the grief of parents who had lost; the anxiety of wives for their husbands; the despair of small business men held up for tribute.

For twenty minutes they listened. When he had finished, an ovation shook the roof. Sonia was limp with excitement. Phyllis D'Arcy bridled.

"Wasn't Michael marvelous? Don't wait for me, any of you. I have my own car. I'll drive him home."

Sonia's happiness bubble burst. Jane Nash slipped an arm within hers. Eyes on the slim white figure hurrying toward the exit, she sniffed.

"Says she! 'Wasn't Michael marvelous?' and she hasn't the faintest idea what it's all about. One might think to hear her that she was wholly responsible for our young orator's success. Snooty cat! Who is the man with Miss Serena who is looking at her as if he would eat her up?"

The expression in Serena Farr's eyes as she gazed up at the face bending over her brought a lump to Sonia's throat. Did love last through the years like that? She herself had talked glibly of love before she had known what it was. She knew now. She had known when Michael faced that hooting, yelling crowd.

Jane Nash squeezed her arm. "Don't go to sleep on us,

darling. Who is that distinguished looking man? One just knows that he is somebody."

"Doctor Jim Neville."

"Not the great Doctor Neville?"

"Yes. He is an old friend of Serena's."

"Nothing old about the way he's looking at her. It's still being done that way by the youngsters. Will he come back to Kingscourt for supper? I'm crazy to meet him. I want him to look Dicky over."

"What's the matter with Dicky?"

In spite of her effort to appear amused a trace of panic shook Sonia's voice. She didn't like the proprietory tone in Jane's.

"Nothing is the matter with Dicky. Don't be silly. Miss Serena is trying to say something to you, Sonia."

Serena was saying that she would drive to Kingscourt with Doctor Jim. Sonia nodded understanding.

Brandt was waiting in the foyer as Jane and Sonia came down the stairs from the gallery. He smiled patronizingly as he met them.

"Grand show, wasn't it?"

His voice boomed as if amplified. Passers-by turned to look at him.

"It goes that way, sometimes. Makes the fight more exciting. Just wait until election day though, and you will see the tide turn again." He bent his head to Sonia and reminded:

"Then I shall expect you to answer that question I asked you last night. Sorry to leave you but I am due at a conference."

Tom Nash heard the last words. He raised his white brows as he watched Brandt join a group of arguing, gesticulating men.

"What was that bozo saying to you, Sonia? Ever see anything neater than the way Michael clamped the brakes, four-wheel and emergency, on that gang of wild men? Brandt's natty uniform didn't sell him to that crowd, did it?"

On the steps Jane tucked her arm under his with the expression of a woman whose every wish was gratified.

"How come that you can devote yourself to us, Thomas? I thought you were driving our candidate?"

"He is going in my roadster—not with the widow D'Arcy, though she tried to get him—one of his advisers wanted to talk things over. Here's Dow with the limousine. The late house guests have gone home. The party's over. Quite a party, everything considered. Michael will be at the house in time for a snack with us. Hop in, girls. Quick! The rain is beating into the car."

Sonia drew her wrap close about her shoulders and curled up in a corner of the back seat. If only she had had a chance to ask Tom what he discovered when he had followed Guy last night. Once during the day she had cornered him, but he had whispered:

"Nothing to say—yet." Did that mean that he had found out something?

How the rain beat against the windows. It gave one a sense of security to be inside this powerful car, especially after hearing of the tragedies which Michael had dragged into the light tonight. Of all crimes kidnaping seemed the most cruel. The agony of not knowing what had become of a person one loved. She couldn't get the facts he had told out of her mind.

Better think of something else or she would be imagining horrors. Her own affairs needed some thought. Guy had insisted that she must tell him after the rally tonight if she would marry him. If! There was no if about it. She wouldn't. How could she refuse and still keep Dicky? Wasn't she bright enough to work out some sort of compromise? Thank heaven, her answer to Brandt did not require thought. A crisp, decisive "No" would be her response to his offer.

The wind flung itself against gaunt trees by the roadside until their long branches writhed and twisted as if in agony. Against the light the rain seemed like a swaying curtain of crystal beads. Dow stopped the car while he and Tom Nash cleared the road of a fallen branch. Lights like great misty jewels crept toward them and passed. Drivers were taking no chances this terrible night.

Sonia shivered and closed her eyes. Usually she loved a storm, but there was something menacing about this one. It seemed so—so relentless. Was that a tree crashing? Tom and Jane would think she was asleep. So much the better; she could give undisturbed thought to her recently realized love for Michael Farr—had she cared for him always without knowing? Had Guy been serious in his thinly veiled threat to take Dicky from her if she did not marry him? Would he be so cruel? Could Michael stop him? Would Michael stop him, or would he think that the child should be with his father?"

She settled deeper into the seat. The world was glorious even in a storm. Why did it have to be rent and crippled by conflict? Why did individuals tangle realities and great experiences? Mostly they did it themselves and then talked of their luck. Her years weren't so many, but enough for her to realize how lives could be twisted and distorted by foolish mistakes.

Her thoughts turned back to Ruby and the coming of the child. She remembered the night she had promised to keep Guy Farr in ignorance of the fact that he had a son. It had been a ghastly night, a night as black and turbulent as this, with storm and crashing trees without and her sister drifting into unconsciousness within. The memory of the following three years was like a stream of cool water flowing over her troubled reflections. She had had work, plenty of it, work that she loved. Then she had lost her job. Came her illness pressing down upon her unbearably, bringing a fevered, frenzied realization that she was criminally unjust to the child in keeping him out of his name and inheritance. She recalled the effort she had made to get to Michael Farr's office. She could see the paneled room as if it suddenly had been flashed on a screen; lived over the tense moment when his eyes had met hers. She could see him, keen, controlled, patrician, looking at her across the broad desk. He had been suspicious, had doubted her story.

She thought of her first visit to Kingscourt, and she thought of how she had watched Michael Farr's face as he had spoken to the child. He had not doubted then. She remembered the sharp ring of the telephone; clearer than all else she remembered his husky voice, his eyes, as he had turned and asked her to marry him.

She shivered from intensity of feeling. It had been a swift touch of madness, of course, he had acknowledged that later. Suppose she had married him? Would he have had the slightest respect for her? Foolish question. Of course not. He would have hated her when he found that Phyllis D'Arcy was free. How could a man who had faced an unfriendly crowd as he had tonight be deceived as to the real nature of the D'Arcy woman? Curious how it eased the ache in her heart to call Phyllis "the D'Arcy woman."

She shut her eyes and visualized Michael Farr as he had stood on the platform waiting—waiting for the crowd to quiet. They had quieted. And then he had talked. She had seen human passions gripped and held by human aspirations.

"Fare, lady!"

Tom Nash's voice crashed into Sonia's reflections. The limousine wheels crunched to a stop on gravel. Had they reached Kingscourt already?

"Here so soon?"

"Soon! We crawled. You snoozed all the way home. Hustle up the steps, girls. You'll get soaked if you don't."

The door opened as if by magic. Jane and Sonia ran

into the hall laughing and shaking drops of rain from their hair.

Sonia slipped out of her wrap. "Isn't it a marvelous feeling to get in from the storm, Jane? Two fires blazing— how the lamps glow! I wonder if we are grateful enough for the comfort."

"Oh, Miss Sonia! Miss Sonia!"

The sobbing cry was like a hand of steel gripping Sonia's heart. She stood as if petrified watching Nanette as she ran down the curved stairway. Nanette, no longer immobile, but crying, frightened. She tried to speak. She put her hand to her contracted throat.

"Oh, Miss Sonia! Dicky's gone!"

"Gone!"

Jane flung an arm about Sonia's waist. Nash caught the maid's wrist.

"Pull yourself together. Where's he gone?" he demanded. "What do you mean wagging your head like that? Speak!" His voice was harsh with fear.

"You are frightening her, Tom. Tell me, Nanette. What happened?"

"I will, Miss Sonia, I will. I tucked Dicky into bed as usual. He was good, but he didn't like the storm much— the trees were groaning something fierce. He—"

"Oh, for heavens sake, girl! Don't stop to gulp! Go on! Go on!" prodded Jane Nash in an agony of apprehension.

"I'm talking as fast as I can. Dicky asked, would bad men come for Shreddy again tonight—the kid has had that on his mind all day. I said, 'Sure they won't. I'll let him come up on the bed with you.'

"I knew you didn't like that, Miss Sonia, but he was so kind of upset—"

"For gosh sakes—don't stop for that! When did you miss him?"

"About an hour ago, Mr. Nash. I was putting my light out when I heard the long window in his room banging to beat the band—"

"The window! Tom!"

"Stop shivering, Sonia. Of course the boy is in the house somewhere. Go on, Nanette."

"I fastened the window and then I l-l-looked at the b-bed. D-Dicky wasn't there."

Sonia put her arm about the maid's shoulders and held her tight.

"Wait a minute till your teeth stop chattering, Nanette. Now tell us the rest as fast as you can."

"There isn't m-much more to t-tell. I looked everywhere. Th-then I told Mrs. Libby and Mr. Elkins, and they and the maids have been all over the house. S-Shreddy's g-gone too. You l-look terrible, Miss S-Sonia. It wasn't my f-fault. It wasn't! I'm c-crazy about that k-kid!"

Would shock turn a person to stone? Sonia's mind seemed to be floating in space. She was conscious of Jane's arm about her, of Tom's tortured eyes. Were they so sure that something tragic had happened? Did they think Dicky had been kidnaped like the children Michael had told of tonight? That was a fool idea. She had no money. No one knew yet that the child was a Farr. Perhaps some gang did know that, know that a fortune was behind the boy. With all her spirit she fought the tide of fear which dragged at her. She caught Nash's arm.

"Michael ought to know. He would think of something."

"I'll get him on the phone somewhere. I'll go over the grounds myself. Sit down, Sonia, and take it easy till—"

"Take it easy!" Sonia clamped her teeth shut. Almost she had screamed with laughter. "Take it easy with Dicky —I'm all right, Jane. Don't hold me. I'm going over every inch of this house."

She ran up the stairs with Jane Nash at her heels. Together they tiptoed into Dicky's room. The bed clothes had been thrown back. One of his little blue moccasins was near the window.

"His—his wrapper's gone!" Sonia whispered hoarsely. "Hear the wind! The rain! No one would take a child out on a night like this—no one but a fiend."

Through her bedroom, through the boudoir, opening closets, the two women sped on. They stopped to speak to white-faced maids, to trembling Libby. No one had seen a trace of the child.

They ran down the great stairway. Michael Farr was placing the phone on its stand. He caught Sonia's hands.

"I know, dear, I know. Steady!"

"How can I be steady? Jane and I have been over every inch of this house and—"

"Found anything, Dow?" Michael demanded of the man on the threshold of the dining room.

The chauffeur twisted his cap. "Mr. Nash said as I was to tell you, sir, that he's found out nothing. He thinks you'd better get the police to radioing."

"I will."

"Anything I can do to help, sir? Seeing as Mr. Guy isn't here—perhaps—"

"Not here! Isn't his roadster in the garage?"

"No, sir. Cummings, the man in charge tonight, said he

phoned at about seven-thirty for it to be brought around to the house."

About seven-thirty! Guy had not been at the rally. She had looked for him. A steel band clamped Sonia's heart. Squeezing it. Squeezing it. Silly! Silly! She scorned herself. Would the man kidnap his own child? Why should he? He had said he would wait until after the rally for her answer, hadn't he?

"Drink this coffee. It's black and strong. You're ghastly." Jane Nash held a cup to the girl's lips. Sonia pushed it away.

"I don't need it. Why stop for things like this, when—"

Michael Farr took the cup.

"Drink it, Sonia. Every drop."

She swallowed with difficulty. Jane's eyes were full of tears as she watched her.

"That-a-girl! That will set you up. I'm about wild myself. I want that boy more than I want anything on earth. Tom and I thought perhaps—" She snatched the cup from Michael's hand and dashed for the dining room.

Sonia paced the rug.

"What shall we do next? Hear the wind howl! Would they hurt—"

Michael caught her and held her close in his arms.

"Stop imagining. I want to help in the search, but I can't leave you like this."

"I won't think. I promise. Go! Please! You loved Dicky. You—"

The outer door banged.

Sonia stared at Guy Farr on the threshold. How she hated him! Hated that sardonic gleam in his eyes. His drooping lid made it more sinister. He looked guilty. He had Dicky! She knew it! Rage choked her. Not for years had she been so furiously angry. She clinched her hands behind her. He was coming close!

"Well, Sonia. Going to marry me? Michael says okay. What the dickens—more jewels snitched?"

"Haven't you heard? Your—"

Sonia interrupted Michael's hoarse voice.

"Trying to force me by kidnaping Dicky, are you, Guy Farr? Try to keep him, just try. I will have a few things to tell the Court. Michael approves of my marrying you, does he? I wouldn't marry you—I wouldn't marry a man named Farr if—" The sentence trailed off in a harsh sob.

Guy Farr caught her wrist. "Have you gone crazy? What do you mean? Why should I kidnap my own—"

"H'llo, Sonia!"

The light, childish call came from the curved stairway. Sonia stared incredulously. Was that Dicky? Dicky standing halfway down in his blue wrapper? Dicky with Shreddy tethered by the cord of his dressing gown squatting beside him?

"Dicky!"

Her choked cry brought maids hurrying to the gallery. She had a nightmarish awareness of eyes, millions of eyes, staring as she ran up the stairs and caught the child in her arms.

"You're real, Dicky! You're warm, Most Dear! Where, where have you been?"

"Hidin'. Somefin banged my window. Fought they'd come for Shweddy so I hided us bofe."

"Hided! Where? Where, Most Dear?"

"Under your bed, Sonia. An' I guess I went to sleep an' Shweddy—you cwyin'—"

Sonia flung him from her. She couldn't see! She was going down—down—she must not drag him—

Chapter XXII

Michael charged up the stairs. Sonia shook her head as she clung to the balustrade.

"I shan't faint. It was the relief—that's all—the relief—" She shivered.

"Don't think about it. Come down to the couch in the library."

"No. No. Please don't notice me."

Dicky laid his cheek against hers. The Sealyham squatted on the stair beside him, cocked his head and watched.

"You sick, Sonia?"

"No, Most Dear. I'm—I'm—sometimes I just love to sit on the stairs, that's all."

"I like you. I'm your vewy own boy, aren't I, Sonia?" His voice was troubled.

"Of course you are, Most Dear."

Libby appeared in the hall.

"What's happened, Mr. Michael? They told me that Miss Sonia—"

"Nothing happened. When she saw that the child was safe, she went dizzy with relief, that's all. Tuck Dicky in, will you, Lib? Mrs. Nash has gone to pieces and Nanette can't do anything but cry."

"Please don't make so much of it. I will put him to

bed," Sonia protested the while she still gripped the balustrade with white nailed fingers.

"Let me do it, Miss Sonia. He'll be good with me." Libby held out her hand. "Let's call on the old parrot before we go up, shall we, my lamb?"

Dicky's eyes sparkled as he ran down the stairs. He hopped and skipped beside her, dragging the reluctant Sealyham, who dragged back intrigued by a sound behind the paneling.

"May I give the pawwot a cwacker? Will he say 'Attaboy!', Libby?" His laugh was like the tinkle of silver bells.

Guy, standing by the fire, shrugged.

"There he goes, serene as a smiling morn after having turned the house upside down. If you ask me, I think he should be spanked good and plenty."

"But we haven't asked you." Sonia's voice was far from steady. "And we—"

"Go up yourself, will you, Sonia?" Michael interrupted. "If you don't feel able to walk, I will carry you."

"Don't be absurd. I'll go up under my own power, thank you. My mind was full of your speech; that is why I imagined the worst at once. Good-night." She looked steadily at Guy. "It is after the rally and my answer is, 'No.'"

Michael waited until she had reached the gallery before he crossed the hall to his brother.

"What were you saying to Sonia when I entered the library this afternoon?"

Guy stared at him in insolent amusement.

"How long has it been your business what I say to a girl?"

"It's my business now. You broke her sister's heart and now you have started on hers."

"You flatter me, m'lad. That girl hasn't a heart for anyone but the boy."

"Have you been trying to force her to marry you?"

"I wouldn't call it forcing. She's fond of the kid. I was mad about her before I married Ruby. I thought we'd settle down and take a crack at domesticity."

"Why did you tell her that I approved of her marrying you, you li—"

Michael's face was chalky, his voice rose in anger. Guy took a menacing step toward him.

"Don't you call me—"

"Boys! Boys!"

Serena Farr came into the hall like a whirlwind. She caught an arm of each. "Don't quarrel, don't. Don't spoil the happiest night of my life." Her voice broke in a sob. Michael lifted the velvet wrap from her shoulders and shot a warning look at his brother before he asked:

"Do you always cry when you are happy, Serena?"

She smiled through tears. "It is silly, isn't it? Jim's wife is dead, Michael."

"Well, I call that a mean break for friend wife."

"Guy!"

"Don't bite, m'lad. Only trying to give the occasion the light touch. Wasn't that your idea? Glad that like the Northwest Mounted you will get your man, Serena."

"Jim brought me home from the rally. He couldn't come in with me. He was on his way to a consultation. Someone's baby is frightfully ill and they had to have Jim. It—it doesn't seem possible that after all these years we are to be married. Where is Sonia? I want to tell her."

"She went to her room early; in fact everybody has gone up. The storm on top of the burglary rather shook their nerves." Michael walked to the foot of the stairs with his arm about his aunt's shoulders. "Good-night, and happy dreams, Serena." He returned to his brother. "Come into the library, Guy. I want to talk to you."

Elbows on the mantel beneath the portrait of the Admiral, they faced each other. Antagonism faded from Guy's eyes as they met his brother's.

"I'm on, Mike. You love Sonia, don't you?"

"Yes."

"Believe it or not, I didn't know. Guess I was so taken by my own feeling that I didn't think of anyone else. You heard her turn me down flat. Now it's up to you. Come in, Nash. You might as well hear what I have to tell Mike."

Michael remained by the mantel. Tom Nash straddled a chair. Guy perched on a corner of the flat desk. He raised a lighter to the cigarette between his lips. His eyes above the flame were at their most devil-may-care as he said lightly:

"I dropped in on old Doc. Bradley tonight—that's why I didn't get to the rally. He's given me my walking ticket. I'm to make a break for the south of France, pronto, or—well, I chose the south of France. Have a hunch that it will be more merry and bright than the other place. After I left him I beat it to a lawyer—no time to waste, the Doc. drove that into my mind—and made you the kid's guardian forever, Mike."

"I can't believe it, Guy. Are you sure Doc. Bradley knows?"

"He knows, all right. I've known, only I wouldn't face

it. A year perhaps in a warmer climate and then—" He shrugged. "I'm not crabbing. I've had my fun."

Tom Nash's eyes resembled nothing so much as shiny marbles as he stood up.

"I don't wish to appear hard-boiled but before you start on this journey perhaps you'll tell us where to find those jewels you snitched."

For an instant there was no sound in the room but the crackle of the fire and the lash of rain against the windows.

Michael started forward. Had Nash a brainstorm? Guy held up his hand.

"It's all right, m'lad." He drew a long package from his pocket and laid it on the desk.

"There they are. With the compliments of the season."

"Guy!"

Michael impatiently cleared his voice of hoarseness. His brother a thief! It was incredible. He was actually grinning complacently as he watched Tom Nash spread the jewelry on the desk.

"They are all there. I intended to produce them after the rally, with a grand ballyhoo, but after I had seen Doc. Bradley I couldn't get here fast enough. Kept thinking, 'Suppose I should pass out with the goods on me.' The Secret Service lost a great little sleuth, Nash, when you went in for canning. Check 'em up with the list in the envelope. All there except Serena's diamond clip which I took from the table to draw as a herring across the trail."

Michael shook off the spell of unbelief.

"Why, why did you do it? Money? I would have given you—"

"For the love of Pete, don't make a tragedy of my little joke, Mike. I did it to help you. Haven't I told you you are the only person on earth I care for?"

"Will you tell me how a robbery here at Kingscourt could help me? You must have been out of your mind."

"Perhaps I was, fella. All o.k., Nash? See that the owners get their property, will you? The names are there. I did a nice little bit of bookkeeping."

"All here. I'll give you a receipt for them."

"The perfect executive! I figured that a robbery in the neighborhood would make the voters in the district crime-conscious, Mike, and that election on your platform would go over big. I thought, also, that the excitement would pep up the house party. I started something when I shifted the cards for the treasure hunt. I didn't figure, though, that the exertion of stirring things up would knock me cold."

"I should have recognized your fine hand in the mix-up." With difficulty Michael kept his voice even. "Do you realize that your theft was behind Dicky's fear for his dog? Was responsible for Sonia's fright? When she started to pitch down those stairs—"

Guy laid his hand on his brother's shoulder. "Pull yourself together. She's all right. She'll tread on air when she knows that I am out of her life and the boy's—forever. Forever! Kind of gives one a chill, doesn't it?"

He cleared his voice. "How did you get on to the solution of the Perfect Crime, Nash?"

Tom pushed the paper he had signed across the desk. Something dropped on it with a little thud.

"That."

Guy snatched up his ring. Its diamond eye blinked as he held it under the desk lamp. He slipped it on his finger.

"Where did you find it?"

"I didn't find it."

"Who did?"

"Sonia."

"Sonia!"

The brothers echoed the name in unison.

"Yep. Must have dropped from your finger when you picked up the dog. It was on his couch."

"She has had it ever since?"

"No. I've had it. That's why I have stalled on calling in the police. I may be only Nash-the-Canner, but I didn't believe that you, playboy that you are, would steal."

"Thanks for them kind words. I guess that's about all."

"Just a minute! You might clear Brandt of a share in your side-splitting joke. Why use his handkerchief?" Michael demanded.

"That was a masterly touch, what? Needed something to tie round the dog's nose. Took it from Brandt's topcoat in the closet. Cut out the monogram to make it harder. I don't like that white-haired *hombre*. Don't glare, Mike. I think I rate a solid gold medal. Didn't I pull off the robbery to help you? When you're in Congress and I'm—Well, I'll be seeing you."

His laugh did not wholly conceal the break in his voice. Guy was frightened. A surge of affection, the old feeling that he must protect his brother brought hot tears to Michael's eyes.

"If I abhor the way you took to help me, I appreciate the spirit. Get that? Good-night."

He watched Guy cross the hall before he turned to

Tom Nash who was standing by the fire unashamedly wiping his eyes.

"Your voice when you said good-night turned on the water-works, Michael. Always thought I'd like a brother to pal with or—or a son. Sorry. I'll be all right in a minute."

"What started you on Guy's trail, Tom?"

"The ring. But, first, I was sure that someone in the house had turned the trick or the dog would have barked and raised the roof and wakened Dicky. I wish I could distribute that jewelry tonight, but I might get smashed up in the storm and then where would we be? I'll sleep with the stuff under my pillow. It's a—a break for Sonia that you are to be guardian of the boy."

He cleared his throat. "His father doesn't want him. If —if she were willing, would you let Jane and me have him for a time? It's this way. Jane is mad for a child. So am I. Looks like we'd never have one. That's all right with me. I have my wife. We've talked it over. We bought Brandt's house so the boy would be near Kingscourt—in case you let us have him—mind you, we don't mean to change his name or adopt him legally, but Sonia is set on going back to the city—"

"Who told you Sonia was going back to the city? Why should she?"

"Her job. She has a living to earn, she says."

"That's rank nonsense."

"That's her story. Hope she doesn't keep on working for Brandt. There is one point on which I agree with your brother. I don't like that *hombre*." He thrust his hands into his pockets and crossed to the door.

"Fierce night. I'll be going up. Jane's a good sport, but she hates the wail of the wind. Think over what I said about the boy, will you? We'd be mighty good to him. We wouldn't spoil him, I promise. We would remember too well what indulgence had done to his father, we would do our level best to make him a man like Michael Farr."

The emotion in Tom Nash's voice recurred to Michael a few days later as in the library he glanced from him to Jane, then at Jim Neville whom the husband and wife had called in to back up their plea that they might have Dicky. Doctor Neville believed in a settled home for a child.

"Here comes Sonia," Nash warned.

The girl paused on the threshold.

"Elkins said that I was wanted in the library. Sounded mysterious. Here I am. Why are you all here? Is this conference week?" A strain of panic drove the lightness from her voice. "You aren't here to tell me—has anything happened to Dicky?" Her frightened eyes appealed to Michael.

"No, no, Sonia. I heard Dicky shouting with laughter a few minutes ago. The Doctor has something to ask you."

Jim Neville's shaggy brows drew down over his keen eyes.

"I'm not the one who is asking, Miss Sonia, I am stating the case for Mr. and Mrs. Nash. They beg that you will let them have your sister's child to bring up as their own."

Sonia's eyes blazed as she turned to Michael.

"Do you approve of this? While you have made me believe that you wanted me to have Dicky, have you been planning to give him away? And I thought you sincere! As if anyone of your name—"

"Hey! Hold everything, gal! Listen to your old Tommy."

"I'll answer her, Nash." Michael felt as if his face had been drained of blood. "Stop and think, Sonia, how conditions have changed. The matter had to be settled today as I am sailing with Guy tomorrow. I couldn't let him start on this—this journey alone. Serena will leave Kingscourt in a few weeks and—"

"And, of course, I cannot stay here unchaperoned. I hadn't intended to stay here. I hate this place. I have a job in the city. Dicky and I—"

"Just a minute, Miss Sonia." Jim Neville's deep voice was like a steadying hand on a pulse which had been running wild. "A job in the city would mean that the child would be cooped up in a small apartment, wouldn't it? You care enough for him to do what is best for him, don't you?"

"Care! Care! I adore him! Don't you realize that Dicky is all I have left in the world of my own family?" Sonia's hands clenched till the knuckles showed white. "Of course when you put it on the ground of the child's health, Doctor Jim, I give in. Jane may have him. I realize now that she has been after him for years."

Michael caught her arm as she turned away. "There is an alternative. Marry me, Sonia, and we will keep the boy—"

She interrupted in a passion of fury.

"Always ready to sacrifice yourself for someone, aren't you, Michael Farr, or ready to sacrifice someone else? You approved of my marrying your brother, knowing what he is! I wouldn't marry either of you if I never saw Dicky again." Her eyes flashed from face to face. "You are all traitors! You have been planning this when you have been smooth and sweet to me. I hate you! I hate every one of you!"

Michael started after her as she dashed into the hall. Tom Nash caught his sleeve.

"Better let her cry it off, Michael. I've seen her blow up like this before."

Had Sonia's anger been the result of shock and affection pulled up by the roots, or had she meant that she would not marry him if she never saw Dicky again, Michael wondered for the hundredth time as he waited in his brother's stateroom on board ship as Guy signed some securities. He should not have allowed Tom to stop him when she had left the library. He should have gone after her, should have held her in his arms till he had made her understand his attitude, understand why he believed that Tom and Jane should have the child. He had tried to see her before he left Kingscourt, but she had gone to the city for a few days, Libby had told him. He wouldn't be away long. When he came back he would make her see him.

Michael watched his brother's thin transparent fingers. What was Guy thinking behind the pale mask of his face? Through the open porthole came the distant roars, the thin whispers of a great city, the strain of cables, the creak of chains, the rumble and bang of baggage trucks, excited voices, gruff voices; came also the odors of asphalt, old wharves and the sea.

Guy flung down the pen.

"There you are, m'lad. Turn them into cash when I cable. If it's got to be a short life, you bet it will be a merry one. There will be plenty left for the boy, too much, probably. When the story of his parentage broke, it got headlines in the papers, didn't it? Rather pushed the news of our election off the front page. What's to be done about him?"

"Tom Nash and his wife are to have him this winter at least."

"What does Sonia say about that?"

"The arrangement was made with her consent. She is planning to be in the city, working."

"Is that so? With Brandt?"

"I don't know."

"They tell me that he's got a second wind, has fixed up his credit, and is pyramiding again with the sky the limit. We'd better get on deck or you may be carried off. Wish you were going with me, fella. Never minded going alone before."

The hint of boyish wistfulness in his brother's voice was like a tight hand about Michael's throat. He resisted the impulse to put his arm about the thin shoulders. Guy would resent that. He said as lightly as he could with emotion tugging at his heart:

"But I am going with you. Linda Hale is waiting outside to take these papers. Didn't think I would let you go alone—this time, did you?"

"Going with me! For Pete's sake! Come out! I—I'll smother here."

Dusk was stealing forward when they reached the deck. Dusk opal and faint rose, dusk misty as a bridal veil backdrop against which the shadowy shapes of vessels swung with the tide, their top-masts burning like flames from the afterglow. Far off a sail flashed like mother-of-pearl. A single star shone shyly in the darkening sky. The water deepened, heaved as if sinister subterranean secrets were forcing their way up, a rising wind lashed it into foam.

"Looks like a rough night. Why don't they muzzle that buoy? It moans like a lost spirit. It—"

"Here I am!"

Michael looked down in amazement at the woman who had linked her arm in his, a woman in smart gray tweeds.

"Phyllis! What are you doing here?"

"Are you registering surprise or joy? I'm sailing on this ship, of course. Didn't Guy tell you? Hear that camera click?"

Michael looked at his brother whose face was blank with consternation.

"Come over here a minute, fella. We'll be back pronto, Phyl."

He drew Michael in the direction of the gangplank crowded with departing flower hawkers, messenger boys, friends of passengers. Lights were blossoming in the buildings along the skyline. A ship's officer hurrying by reminded curtly:

"This boat sails in five minutes."

Michael jerked his head in the direction of the woman they had left.

"What the dickens did Phyl mean?"

Guy groaned. "My Machiavellian touch. Thought it might help your love-life if the clinging Phyllis were out of the way. I dropped a hint that you might cross with me; she decided that she would go too. For the love of Pete, why didn't you tell me you were going? I tried to help you, honest."

Michael looked at him. "Running true to form, aren't you? Everlastingly setting trouble on the boil!"

Guy's mouth twisted in a sardonic grin. "You never can tell. The Captain expects a rough passage and the widow D'Arcy, I have been informed, is a poor sailor. Add that up."

Chapter XXIII

It was the last word in automobiles. It would be if Tom and Jane owned it, Sonia reflected, as she looked from the window at the roadside going by like a panorama. Curious that they should be satisfied with the comparatively small house she had planned and Donald Brandt had built. Where was he now? He had laughed at her refusal to marry him. It had taken more than one stormy interview to convince him that she meant what she said, that she did not intend to marry anyone.

Didn't she? The newspaper picture of a woman and two men on the deck of a ship flashed with cinematic clarity on the screen of her mind.

MRS. PHYLLIS D'ARCY AND
THE DISTINGUISHED FARR BROTHERS

the caption had informed. Why shouldn't Michael go back to his first love—had he ever left her? Phyllis might be catty, but she never would blaze at him as Sonia Carson had blazed that last day in the library at Kingscourt. She couldn't remember now what she had said but doubtless it had hurt. She was apt to be good when she got started. Her anger had smoldered for forty-eight hours, then had burned out, leaving her horribly ashamed of herself and fairly aching with love for Michael Farr. It would serve her right if she never saw him again, never heard the caressing tenderness of his voice.

She slammed the door or memory and forced her attention to the outside world. Gaunt trees flaunted a few leaves much as a beleaguered fortress might keep ragged flags flying. A light snow powdered the skeletons of shrubs which bordered the black shining road. How different from the countryside as she had seen it on her first visit to Kingscourt months ago. Not only the foliage had changed since then, the pattern of her life had changed as completely, almost as swiftly as the jeweled glass in a kaleidoscope shifts at the turn of a wrist.

Curious feeling to be returning for Serena Farr's wedding. It was three weeks since Jane and Tom had carried Dicky, Nanette, and Shreddy triumphantly to their new home. Her heart had ached intolerably as she had watched them go. The boy had turned on the steps of the limousine, had called:

"I'll be wight back, Sonia!"

He had not come back. Jane and Tom had been good sports. They had ignored her passionate outburst in the library, had shown her affectionate consideration. Jane had written and phoned that Dicky seemed perfectly happy. That had hurt a little. How wise Doctor Neville had been when he had advised a settled home for the boy. Her job in the city had proved a mirage. It had lasted two weeks. When she discovered that she had been given the chance ahead of a young married man with two children she had promptly resigned to give him the position. What would she do next?

Next seemed to be Kingscourt. Not to stay, of course, just for the wedding. Almost there. Going through the village at the crossroads now. The roofs of the houses sparkled with light snow. The world had donned bridal white for Serena's marriage. Exciting to be coming back. Jane had phoned that she was not to bring a gown for the wedding—just enough of her own things for the week-end—that she had one for her. A Christmas gift in advance. What would it be like? Perfect, of course.

Would Michael be at the ceremony? The possibility brought her heart to her throat. She must keep him out of her mind. Had he really cared for her he would have sent some sort of message.

There it was! Her house! The house she had planned with such thrilled conviction that it would be a gem. The windows seemed like friendly eyes beaming a welcome. The brick chimney fairly melted into the skeleton arms of the great maple. Had she dipped the red-brown shingles of the roof herself, she could not have secured a more perfect color. Tom already had the gardens staked out.

There was Dicky! Dicky and Shreddy! Dicky's hair was like red gold. What a darling blue suit. Jane would have everything perfect for him.

She didn't wait for the faultlessly trained chauffeur to open the limousine door. She was on the steps with her arms about the child before the man had left the wheel.

"Most Dear! Oh, Most Dear!"

The boy drew a chubby finger down her cheek.

"Cwyin', Sonia? Sowwy to come?"

"Sorry! I could eat you up, Sweetness. Oh, Jane! Here I am!"

"Sure, it's you!" Jane hugged her before she held her off at arms' length. "You've grown thin. Come in. I can't

178

wait for you to see the house. Haven't everything yet, but it isn't grubby."

With Dicky's hand tight in hers, Sonia entered the spacious living-room. The double window corner was a mass of bloom. Blazing logs in the capacious fireplace threw grotesque shadows on the walls of knotty pine.

"Did I really plan this house, Jane?"

"You and nobody else. Richard, Nanette is waiting for you in the nursery. Lunch. Ice cream!"

The authoritatively maternal voice sent a queer little shiver over Sonia. Dicky never would be all hers again.

"Ice cweam! You comin' up, Janey?"

Jane Nash preened just a bit.

"He loves having me sit with him while he eats," she explained. "Not today, darling."

The boy started for the stairs, stopped, ran to Sonia. He flung his arms about her knees.

"Aren't you comin'? You alwus used to come."

Sonia pressed her lips to his hair. "Perhaps I will read to you while you are having your supper. Won't that be grand?"

"She won't be back from Aunt Serena's wedding in time for that, Richard. Run along! Call your houn' dog, beloved."

"I didn't want him to count on it," Jane explained. "I never make promises to him I cannot keep."

The virtuous tone irritated Sonia. Was Jane telling her how to bring up a boy?

"I didn't promise, I said perhaps," she corrected curtly. She watched the plump little legs mounting the stairs she had designed. The Sealyham hopped up one step at a time. At the top Dicky looked down and waved:

"I'll be seein' you!"

Sonia forgave Jane as she noted the expression of her eyes as they rested on the boy. She adored him.

"Isn't he the cute trick? Come on. You and I will have luncheon and then I will show you the rest of the house."

For some inexplicable reason Sonia was too shaky inside to eat as she sat at the perfectly appointed table in the yellow walled dining-room. Was she reflecting Jane's mood. She appeared as if strung on wires. What had happened to her?

"Where is Tom?" she asked.

"Gone to the city for the happy groom. Serena begged him to go, said that if the doctor relied upon Bigges to bring him he was likely to be switched off to see a patient at the very hour set for the wedding. You know Serena and how she would say it."

"I do. Will Doctor Jim be able to get away from his office long enough for a trip?"

"Yes. Bermuda. When he and Serena were engaged years ago they planned a honeymoon in Bermuda. Serena has traveled over the world but she never would go there. Now they are going together. You haven't eaten anything, Sonia."

"I'm not hungry. For some reason I'm all excited. One would think it was my wedding in the offing."

"Darling—"

Sonia looked at her unbelievingly. Color had swept to Jane's hair, her eyes glittered with tears. What had she on her mind? Was Tom worrying her?

"I'm glad that you feel excited too, Sonia. I can hardly sit still I'm so—so thrilled. Come and see your gown for the wedding. It's perfect."

Jane was right, the frock was perfect, Sonia agreed, as later she passed a mirror in the hall at Kingscourt. Rich burgundy velvet, the last word in berets; the clasp of the matching bag was own twin to the exquisite clip at her throat, pink tourmaline set in brilliants. Perfect—but what an impractical costume for the wardrobe of a working girl. And how like Jane. Whether she were practical or not, she was a dear.

"Wait in the library. I promised I'd look Serena over before she came down. She's wearing amethyst velvet. It's a velvet year," Jane whispered.

Sonia laughed. "One might think you were the nervous bride, Jane, except that your black gown is too somber. Pull yourself together, you are shaking with excitement."

"I am, and I don't care who knows it. Wait in the library. Ceremony is to be there. No one but the family and us."

The "family" wouldn't make much of a crowd. Who was there left but Michael? Sonia had started twice to ask if he were back from Europe, but Jane had broken into the question with an irrelevant observation.

Logs blazing in the great fireplace in the library. Blue brocade hangings drawn across the long windows. Pale yellow roses and heliotrope banked high at one end of the room on a console, floor cushions before it. Tall lighted candles.

Sonia looked up at the portrait of the Admiral. His nose, his mouth were like the present Michael's. Had his gray eyes once pulled a girl's heart from her breast? Had his voice been rough and husky as he had asked:

"Will you marry me?"

Why, why was she spending a moment on the past? She needed all her thoughts for the future. Where was her living coming from? She hadn't much money left from the commission she had earned.

The sun going down behind purple hills was sending one golden ray through the glass of the conservatory upon masses of regale lilies and palms and ferns. The fountain trickled musically. Sonia drew forward a luxurious chair and watched red-gold streaks darting about the mossy pool. There was adventure. Round and round in a pool.

She visualized Dicky as he had come to Kingscourt the first time. Then she had been his world, now she was nothing to him. The emotion she had been holding back since she had seen the boy so happy with Jane, so forgetful of what she had been to him, submerged her in an overwhelming tide. Elbows on her knees, she rested her face in the palms of her hands and drew a long sobbing breath.

"I can't expect to rival a goldfish in sartorial effect," a voice behind her observed, "but you might notice that I'm correctly turned out for the wedding."

She looked up. Michael! Michael! He wasn't abroad with Phyllis! He was here! With an inarticulate cry she ran to him, pressed her face against his shoulder.

"Dicky-y doesn't c-care for me any—more," she whispered brokenly. "I—I don't count with anyone."

His arms tightened about her; she felt his cheek against hers.

"All right, you don't count with anyone. We will take that up later. You want Dicky to be happy, don't you?"

The laughing tenderness of his voice warmed her cheeks till her rising color dried the tears. How could she have flung herself at him like that? She slipped from his arms and said as composedly as she could with her heart running its engine like mad:

"I am on my knees in apology for turning sob-sister. Of course I am glad that D-Dicky is so happy with J-Jane. I was sitting here just l-letting myself go—having a beautiful time being miserable, and then you appear suddenly and —and get the benefit of my reaction. I—I'm sorry."

Was he listening? He hadn't moved. He seemed almost dangerously cool, but his eyes, his low laugh set her pulses quick-stepping.

"I got the benefit, all right. After that welcome, do you think you'll ever get away from me again, light-of-my-eyes? It wiped out all the misunderstandings of these last weeks."

He caught her in his arms, kissed her fervently, kissed her lingeringly, released her abruptly.

"You know now, don't you, that I never would have allowed you to marry Guy? When he said that I approved, he was—We won't go into that. I had to go with him—he never will come home—and all the time I have been mad to get back to you. Didn't know that, did you? I am sailing for England tomorrow."

"Tomorrow!"

"And you are going with me?"

"I! Just like that! Taking an architect along, perhaps?"

"Shouldn't let your voice shake when you mean to be flippant, Beautiful. I—I am taking my wife along."

"Your wife!"

"Careful! You will back into the pool. Come here." He drew her toward him. "I've got to talk fast. I want you to marry me here, now."

"Michael!"

"If you look at me like that I shall have to stop and kiss you and I haven't time. This isn't the first time I have asked you to marry me, so you can't accuse me of taking you by surprise. There is a noted criminologist going over to study police schools. He has offered to take me with him. By sailing tomorrow I can put in some time with him and get back before Congress convenes. Jane and Tom have helped me plan. I have the license here." He tapped his breast pocket.

"Were you so sure of me?"

"Sure! After what you said to me that day in the library? I've been riding the gale in a storm of doubt. Marry me, Sonia?"

"Yes, Michael."

"You would say it like that, you beautiful—"

"Here comes the bride!" someone whispered behind them.

Sonia felt as if she had been caught up in a cloud, as if she were seeing and hearing through a fog. Serena Farr, the black-gowned clergyman, to whom she had listened every Sunday in the little stone church at the crossroads, seemed like shadows. Only Doctor Jim's face stood out like a clear cut cameo. She must pay attention. She must listen to Serena's responses. It would be her turn next. Her turn. This was a dream.

After that nothing seemed real to her, nothing but Michael's firm clasp of her hand, his voice saying, "I do," the feel of a ring on her finger, a sonorously rich voice intoning solemnly:

"Those whom God hath joined together let no man put asunder."

The feeling of unreality persisted as she poured tea for the wedding party in the library. The sharp ring of the telephone cut through the haze. Michael answered.

"You are wanted, Doctor Jim."

"For me? Sure? No one but Bigges knows where I am."

Serena stood beside him as in a chair at the desk he answered the call.

"Doctor Neville speaking—You know I won't go, Bigges —Get Shaw on long distance at once. Tell him there are other baby men in the country—Can't help it if the parents are wild with anxiety—"

"Wait a minute, Jim." Serena laid her hand on his shoulder. "What is it? Who needs you?"

He patted her fingers with his free hand. "Shaw, the stomach man in Denver, wants me to fly there—consultation—sick baby—only child. Parents never will have another. He can get someone else. I'm going to Bermuda."

"Could you save the baby, Jim?"

"Let them get someone else. I'm going to—"

Serena's eyes were starry behind tears but her voice rippled with laughter as she confided:

"It has been one of the dreams of my life to go to Bermuda via Denver, Jim."

Neville dropped the phone and encircled her waist with his arms.

"Won't you mind, Serena? I'd like to help those parents. My dear. My dear, you're wonderful. When I think of the years we've missed I—"

He turned his face against her breast. She smoothed his gray hair with unsteady fingers.

"I'm thinking of the years we have ahead, Jim, God— and Bigges willing."

Chapter XXIV

"Happy days, Sonia. These are for you. I want you to have them now so that I may have the fun of seeing you wear them, you lovely girl."

Sonia's fingers closed over the velvet case Serena thrust into her hand. It felt real. From the top of the steps she waved to the groom and radiant bride. The tears in Jane's eyes, Tom's gruff voice were real.

"Be a good girl. Have a large time. I've tucked my wedding present into your bag."

The cars drove away. Michael put his arm about her shoulders as they entered the house.

"All right with you if we stay here tonight, Beautiful? Elkins and Lib have planned a wedding feast. It would be a pity to disappoint them. Come into the library and we'll open Serena's gift."

Sonia nodded. Her voice still seemed to be swallowed in a fog.

Under the light of the lamp on the desk he took the case from her hand and snapped it open. On the white satin lining glowed and sparkled a necklace, bracelets and earrings of emeralds and diamonds. Sonia's eyes were wide with incredulity as she looked at them.

"Are they real? Is anything real?" she whispered.

"Real! Of course they are real. How Serena must love you to give you her precious emeralds. I don't wonder that you feel as if you had been caught in a cyclone. Why not go up to your rooms till things stop whirling? Libby is there. I must phone about some final arrangements. That is a stunning frock you are wearing, but won't it rest you and bring you down to earth to change for Elkins' party?"

Sonia crashed through the fog.

"Change! I—I haven't any other clothes here, Michael."

"Trust the efficient Jane to provide for that. No, I won't tell you."

With that possessive arm again about her shoulders they crossed the hall. At the foot of the stairs he caught her hands tight in his.

"Just a minute! You know, don't you, that I would not have sailed tomorrow without you? You knew that I would have camped on your trail until you promised to marry me, don't you—Mrs. Farr?"

"S-something tells me that you would have," Sonia conceded breathlessly.

She knew that he watched her as she ran up the stairs. She didn't look back. Over and over in her mind whirled his last words.

Mrs. Farr! Only this noon Sonia Carson had been wondering what she would do next; and now she was Sonia Farr. It was unbelievable! It was fantastic! It was—it was breath taking!

Libby, in a crisp gray gown, was bustling about her bedroom. Her cheeks were beautifully pink, her eyes sparkled. She said in a matter-of-fact voice, quite as if she attended a bride every day:

"I laid out the white velvet frock, madam. Mrs. Nash said you'd probably wear that for dinner. It is to be packed for the steamer. And Mr. Michael wants you to wear these. They were his mother's."

Sonia looked through a haze at the lustrous pearls lying on the satin bed of the case Libby had snapped open. For her? And Serena's emeralds! So much for her who had had nothing of value before? A little prayer rose in her heart, a prayer that she might never forget what it meant to be in need; that she might grow in wisdom, in sweetness and beauty of spirit so that Michael would love her more and more as the years went on.

From the pearls her eyes traveled about the room. Were those labeled trunks really for her? She read the name on one of them. <u>Mrs. Michael Farr</u>. The last wisp of fog vanished in a blaze of happiness. It was true! She was sailing tomorrow with Michael! She pressed her wedding ring hard against her lips. That was real.

"Mrs. Nash left this note for you, Miss Son—Mrs. Farr."

"You aren't any more used to that name than I am, are you, Libby. I—I—hope you are pleased?"

"Pleased! Elkins and I never were so happy about anything in our lives." She stopped a tear which was riveleting down her cheek. "There, child, read your note, while I'm drawing your bath."

Sonia ripped open the envelope.

"The trousseau is a wedding present from me and your 'vewy own boy.' Tom has tucked something into your bag for his offering. Thought you'd rather have cash than jewels. You said I acted as if strung on wires! The nervous strain has been terrific. I've nearly lost my mind since Michael and I planned this coup. 'Suppose she won't?' I kept asking myself and kept answering, 'She loves him! I know she loves him!'

Happy days, darling! Happy days!
Jane."

Sonia's emotion bubbled over. "Libby, Libby, did you know about these clothes?"

The pink cheeked woman paused in the process of laying out stockings fine as cobwebs.

"Certain I did, Miss—madam. Such goings on as there's been here, what with Miss Serena getting ready and Mrs. Nash planning all this for you. Wait, let me take off your frock so as not to muss your hair."

"Mrs. Nash is wonderful. I'm glad that she has Dicky. She wants children so much and none seem to come."

Libby's chuckle was comfortable, plump, and knowing.

"She'll have 'em now that she's adopted one. I never knew it to fail. Put out your foot, child, while I unfasten your shoe."

Later, in the white velvet frock, the pearls gleaming softly on her neck, Sonia looked from the window at the sky. Its sweep, its calm, its majesty were like a quieting hand laid on her racing pulses. What a night! The half moon hung in the sky like a broken silver plaque against an indigo velvet canopy sprinkled with gilt stars above shadowy ridges of hills. The earth was lightly clothed in bridal white. Across the black mirror of the lake lights in distant windows glimmered like brilliant topaz eyes.

A knock! At the door of the room which had been Dicky's! Sonia's heart mounted to her throat.

"Come in."

Michael opened the door. He looked tremendously tall without his coat. His black tie was knotted to perfection, but the cuff of his white shirt sleeve dangled unfastened. There was laughter in his voice and eyes as he reminded:

"Didn't you say that life was much more of an adventure if a man dashed into his wife's room for her to slip in his cuff links?" He held out his arm. "Fasten it, will you? I left Johnny with Guy."

Sonia felt the color burn to her ears, felt his eyes on her as she fumbled at his cuff.

"You have the most outrageous memory of any man I ever met."

"It's a gift." He pressed his lips to her bent head. "Like me, Sonia?"

She kept her eyes on a button of his black silk waistcoat.

"Some. There! It's fastened."

He held her by the shoulders.

"Trust me?"

The low husky question did something to Sonia's voice. She whispered:

"I'm here."

With an unsteady laugh Michael caught her in his arms and kissed her tenderly.

"Sure, you are here, light-of-my-eyes. There go the chimes. Wait until I slip into my coat and I'll be with you, Mrs. Farr. We will make a grand entrance into the dining room and thrill old Elkins."

With radiant eyes Sonia watched him as he crossed the threshold to his room leaving the door wide open behind him.

THE END